MW01287145

A Debt So Ruthless

A Dark Mafia Romance

Titans and Tyrants
Book 1

Vero Heath

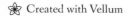 Created with Vellum

Content Notes

This is a dark age-gap mafia romance with themes that may disturb some readers. The hero, Elio Titone, is not a good man. Nor is he a particularly reasonable man, especially when it comes to getting what he wants – namely the heroine Deirdre. If you would like content warnings, please visit my website.

Chapter 1

Elio

"What about collateral? There's the house."

"I don't care about your fucking house."

I don't care about this deal at all really. O'Malley's in deep with one of the three most powerful Camorra clans in Toronto and he needs money, fast. Clearly, he thinks he can try to play one Italian crime organization against another, begging on his knees to La Cosa Nostra to bail him out when Severu Serpico's soldiers come knocking, which they will.

But the Titones aren't in the business of bailing people out. We're in the business of making money. By any means necessary. And even this sprawling gingerbread house of a Thornhill mansion behind us now isn't enough temptation. Everyone knows the Irish bastard is sinking fast.

A bead of sweat rolls down from O'Malley's temple, dampening his thinning hair. His hair still has the slightest sheen of rust, a memory of red beneath the grey. Another bead of sweat follows the first, and he swallows noticeably, his ruddy throat bobbing.

Despite the August sun beating down, I know the heat isn't why he's sweating.

He's sweating because he's come to me – the last and most ruthless resort.

And I've turned him down.

No more options, O'Malley.

I stand, doing up the button of my suit jacket. The sun drenches my black-clad shoulders and the leather of my gloves, heating my skin beneath the fabric.

Fuck. I can't wait for winter.

"Sell the house if you need money," I say. "You're not that old yet. Sell a kidney. I know someone who'll pay."

O'Malley jumps to his feet, his cushioned monstrosity of a patio chair clattering over backwards to the perfectly landscaped stone.

He starts blabbering, half angry, half desperate. Telling me about how he's good for the money. How this is just a temporary blip. How we could...

I lose track of it all. All the words. All the bullshit flying like spittle from his mouth.

That isn't like me. To lose track of anything. I haven't gotten to where I am today, helping my uncle Vincenzo turn the Titones into one of the richest and most feared crime families in the country, by tuning out the details.

I got here by paying attention. Relentlessly.

That, and a whole lot of blood.

But something else has cut into the conversation. A scattered drift of notes.

Music. Violin?

The notes grow louder. Become almost solid. Like if I squint hard enough, I can see them catching the summer light.

Ignoring O'Malley completely now, I start walking,

leaving the stone patio area. My black shoes crush the springy, well-watered blades of grass as I stalk over the lawn.

I scan the broad back of the brick house, searching for the source. I can't say exactly why I need to find it. I just do. The music is somehow both sharp and sweet. It pricks at my skin. Hooks into my ribs and makes my teeth grind.

Near the top of the back wall, I find the second-floor balcony. And on that balcony...

An angel.

I blink stinging sweat from my eyes, dragging my hand through my hair and slicking it back. I don't believe in angels. Never have.

A glossy mane of red hair tumbles down a slender back, the curling ends brushing the slightly flared skirt of a yellow sundress. Two pale arms float in the air, one still, the other sawing back and forth over what has to be a violin I can't see from down here. Every time she moves, the sunlight catches on her hair, setting it ablaze, a glittering inferno. My scars burn under my gloves, the ruined skin on my neck tingling. The scent of smoke from nineteen years ago fills my nose while screams echo in my head, and I'm reminded why I can't fucking stand red hair.

But the music distracts me from the past, from pain. It's deafening, yet somehow not loud enough. So soft it makes my throat go dry. So powerful it slugs me in the temple. Leaves me reeling.

Elio Titone. Fucking *reeling*.

Instincts jerk to life inside me. Instincts that have never once led me astray. Instincts telling me to cut and run. To leave, right fucking now, and never look back.

I ignore them.

3

I start walking again, circling around towards the left side of the house so that I can see her face.

From below on the lawn like this, I can only just see her profile. Thank fuck that's the only glimpse I get. Because even that one sliver of her face *ruins* me.

It isn't just her physical beauty. The high, round cheekbones or the shadows cast by thick, long lashes – I've seen it all before. I've been with women more alluring, more sensually appealing than her.

It's the expression shaping those features that does me in.

An expression of pure, deeply human joy. Something I wasn't entirely sure actually existed until now.

Her soft lips are drawn into a sublime half-smile. Her eyes are closed, her chin balanced delicately on the violin as her long, deft fingers spirit over the strings. Her other arm pushes the bow through the air with surprising force.

"What's that song?" I mutter. I almost don't want to speak. Don't want to make a single noise. But I have to know. Her song is strangling me.

O'Malley comes to a stop beside me, huffing and puffing, having followed me across the lawn. I shoot him a brutal glance, wanting to wring his neck for breathing so fucking loudly.

He pants, bending to place his hands on his knees before straightening.

"It's Irish. *An Eala Bhàn.* Was one of her mother's favourites."

My eyes crawl up the brick to the balcony once more. The girl's smile has contracted. Her brows furrow slightly. Tension creeps into her jaw and neck as her fingers fly faster, grinding the notes out harder.

The joy in the song, in *her*, darkens. Becomes edged

with pain. But even in that pain, there's beauty. Beauty I want to peel back, layer by layer. To understand.

To own.

My fingers twitch at my sides, wanting to clench into fists around something. The bow. The violin's neck. Hair the colour of fire I'd rather forget.

My next words come without thought and without hesitation.

"That's it," I say to O'Malley, my eyes glued to his daughter. "The collateral."

"What?" O'Malley asks. "The violin? It was her mother's. It's worth a fair bit now, but it's nothing like-"

"Not the violin."

If not for the music, there would be a long beat of silence before he explodes. His Irish accent, dulled by years in Canada, grows suddenly sharper.

"You want my daughter?" he sputters. "What, that the only way ye can get a woman, ye ugly piece of shit?"

My pistol finds his forehead before he can even blink. His cheeks, so red with rage a moment before, drain of all colour, turning ashen.

"Watch yourself, O'Malley," I murmur softly, already imagining the spray of blood and brains on the manicured lawn. I've killed men for less insult than this.

The music stops.

The softest tremor of sound, the call of, "Dad? Are you down there?" on the summer air has me hunching into myself, slipping the gun under my jacket. My breath shudders out of me. My guts burn with something I haven't let myself feel in years.

Shame.

There's something terrible about being a monster in front of a pure little songbird like that.

It almost makes me hate her.

"That's the deal," I hiss savagely, too quiet to be heard from the balcony above.

O'Malley scowls at me. But I can already see him cracking. Even his earlier rage didn't come from the place of a protective father but was the irritation of a man who didn't want to give up a prized possession.

"Fine," he grunts. "But it won't come to that," he adds quickly. He turns away from me, running a hand down the back of his neck. His next words are so quiet I almost miss them. But that torturous music has stopped, so I catch them despite the whisper.

"God help me."

My eyes dart up to the balcony.

But no one's there.

There's relief in that. No wide eyes watching me. No music clawing at the scar of something that might have once been called a soul.

"God can't help you now, O'Malley," I say, keeping my voice cold and steady. I mask the disgust I feel for him, so greedy and pathetic he'd offer up his daughter, a lamb to slaughter, to save his own skin. There's repulsion, too, for my own unexpected weakness. For my wanting.

But stronger than any of that – the disgust, the loathing – is the beat of that fucking music in my blood.

And I already know without a shadow of a doubt that even if I slit my own throat and bleed to death right here on the grass...

I'll never get it out.

Chapter 2

Deirdre

New Year's Eve 1.5 years later

"You're so lucky your birthday is on New Year's. Always guaranteed an awesome party," Willow says, grabbing a flute of champagne from the table beside us. "Welcome to your twenties, Dee!"

"It's not midnight yet. Technically my birthday is tomorrow," I remind her. "And I'm not sure I would call my dad's usual New Year's Eve bash an awesome party," I add with a snort, grabbing my own glass of champagne and taking a fizzy sip.

"Bitch, how would you even know what a good party is? You never want to go out with me. I told you I'd take you clubbing for your birthday and you said no!"

I smirk and roll my eyes at her. For my best friend, "bitch" is a term of endearment. Her name may be Willow, but there's nothing willowy about her. The only things sharper than her tongue are her cheekbones and the piercing crystal green of her eyes. Tonight, her jet-black hair is tied in a high ponytail, accentuating her bare neck and the plunging neckline of her curve-hugging black dress. She's actually a year younger than me, only just turned nineteen, but no one would ever guess that I was the older one between us.

She takes another sip of champagne and then tosses her ponytail over her shoulder.

"Fine. I'll grant you that this isn't the coolest New Year's party I've ever been to. It isn't even one of your dad's best, to be honest. Weren't there a lot more people last year?"

She's right. The crowd is thin this year, mostly comprised of my dad's clients and their wives milling around our large living room, picking away at the fancy cheese and pastries the catering company brought. Willow's dad, Paddy Callahan, is among them. He runs an Irish pub, *Briar and Boar*, in downtown Toronto. My dad is his business accountant.

"For a room full of mobsters it's actually kind of boring, to be honest. And they're all at least thirty years older than us. Which wouldn't normally be a problem, except none of them are hot."

My gaze cuts back to Willow, my lips pursing. I ignore her comment about older men – that's pretty much par for the course with my best friend – instead snagging on the other thing. The thing about the mobsters.

She raises her brows questioningly at me over the rim of her champagne flute, and I blow out a sigh. I can't even argue with her because it's true. My dad's an accountant. It's easy to pretend that he runs a normal firm and that his clients are all upstanding citizens. But the reality is that he helps clean money for businesses that funnel funds to the Irish mob.

It's something I don't like to think about and that I've

largely been protected from. Willow, on the other hand, doesn't give a shit. She embraces the life Paddy's a part of, taking everything in high-heeled stride. But even so, neither of us have any real standing. We aren't part of the ruling Gowan family. Our dads are at the bottom of the mafia ladder, and so are the other guests here. No one truly important to Toronto's crime scene has come tonight, and that's just fine with me. Willow's right – I don't care about parties, and I care even less about having some of the city's most lethal men in my living room.

"Sorry to disappoint you," I say with a laugh. "You can still hit up the club after this and get laid."

"Oh, you know I will, Dee. But I was more thinking about *you*."

"Me?"

"Yes! How am I supposed to act as a wing woman and get my best friend's sweet little cherry licked, sucked, and popped if there's no one here good-looking enough to qualify?"

Mr. Byrne, who runs *Byrne's Butcher Shop*, nearly chokes on a macaron beside us. Mrs. Byrne pats his back then glares at us while Willow smiles innocently back.

"Jesus, Willow," I mutter before taking a huge swig of my drink. Willow is my ride-or-die, but sometimes being around her requires vast amounts of alcohol.

"What? Someone's gotta do it properly now that Brian turned out to be a giant asshole."

I cringe at his name. The name of my very recently *ex*-boyfriend.

"Ugh, don't remind me. At least he's been gone all Christmas break. He's back in Ottawa with his family."

"Good," Willow says, nodding with satisfaction, eyes

crackling. "Because if he keeps up this stalker boy routine, I'm going to have to sic Ronan on his ass."

Ronan *looks* like a dishwasher at the pub, but he's actually there as security, one of Darragh Gowan's enforcers. He's a brooding, tattooed mountain of a man, and I can't help but picture him punching Brian in the face with his meaty hammer of a fist.

I dated Brian for the first half of this school year, from September until right before December exams. He's a law student at the University of Toronto where I study music. I thought he might actually be the one I'd lose my virginity to.

Until he tried to take it before I was ready.

I clench my teeth, my stomach twisting when I remember that night in his apartment. The beer on his breath as he caged me in with his body and told me he'd waited long enough. The hunted, animal fear that made me freeze, that left me unable to move, unable to fight back, unable to say a single fucking word. It was only when he clumsily undid his belt and knocked a glass from his bedside table to the floor, stepping on the broken pieces and stumbling, that I could move again. I bolted from his apartment and completely ghosted him after that.

Only problem is that he's developed an infuriating habit of turning up everywhere I go, begging for forgiveness and promising to be better. I've found him lingering outside classrooms and exam halls and even, once, outside the small music school where I teach violin to kids. In all honesty, I'm kind of surprised he went back home for Christmas at all. I thought he'd stick around just to keep following and pressuring me, and I'm beyond grateful for the distance his absence has created.

Willow must be sensing my mood, because her expression softens.

"Hey, I'm sorry, Dee." She draws me into a perfumed hug. "I'm not trying to be insensitive. What happened with Brian was fucking shit, and if he ever crosses my path, he better fucking watch himself. I just want your first time to be good. To be on your terms." She pulls back, staring at me steadily with serious green eyes. "If you give something away, no one can take it from you."

"Something can always be taken from you," I whisper bitterly. It's a lesson I've burned into my brain for ten years, starting the day my mother died.

Willow looks like she's about to say something else, but as her mouth opens, the resounding shout of "Ten!" makes us both jump.

"Already?" I ask, looking around in shock.

"Guess so! Happy birthday, babe!" Willow clinks her glass against mine and then drains it. I do the same, losing myself in the rosy feeling of champagne's warmth spreading through my body. I need the drink – I know what comes next. It happens every New Year's Eve. A requirement of my father's. I can already see him beckoning to me from across the room, ready for me to dazzle his friends and clients by playing *Auld Lang Syne*.

I love playing, but absolutely hate performing. My father likes it, though. Likes having the talented daughter he can put on display since he no longer has the talented wife. Mom was always the performer, the star. Not me.

Willow already has another drink in her hand when I set down my glass. As the people all around us chant together, "Five, four, three!" I grab my violin and head for the centre of the room.

I'm just setting my bow to the strings when bitterly cold air hits my skin, making goosebumps prickle. Somewhere in the house, a door is open, or a window. Which doesn't make any sense, because this is January in Ontario.

The sound of fireworks split the air, but even though it's New Year's that doesn't make sense, either, because it sounds like it's coming from inside this very room. It's only when screaming breaks out, and the sound repeats and intensifies, that I realize it's gunfire.

Chapter 3

Deirdre

I crouch to the floor, hugging my violin underneath myself, the most precious thing I have. Which is probably stupid. Really, really stupid. I should drop it, protect my head, and crawl to safety. But this violin was my mother's, and I can't let it go. Swearing, my heart slamming, I keep it tucked underneath my body, the bow in my hand like a blade, and army crawl under the nearest table of abandoned food. I tuck the violin and bow against the wall, then spin on my hands and knees, trying to make sense of the scene before me.

Only there's barely a scene left. Almost everybody is gone. Relief pours through me when I see Paddy dragging Willow out of the room towards the front door. She's fighting him, though, and through the ringing in my ears I distantly hear her screaming my name. Suddenly, her eyes find mine, our gazes locking, and she fights her father harder, but he loops his thick arms around her waist and hauls her out into the winter night.

Tears stream down my face, my throat contracting. I'm so happy she's gone, that she'll be safe.

But now I'm alone.

Where's Dad?

New terror grips me. If someone came into this house to attack, who else would they be looking for but the owner of that house?

No! My dad's just an accountant. He's not an enforcer, a soldier, an assassin. He's not a boss someone would have any reason to take out. So why the hell is this happening?

And where the hell did he go?

I'm not the only one with that question. I realize I'm not truly alone. Mr. Byrne is slumped over on the hardwood floor, clutching at a profusely bleeding shoulder, while a pair of black shoes approaches him. One of the black shoes presses against Mr. Byrne's crotch, *hard.*

"Where's O'Malley?"

I can't see the man's face, only hear his voice. My blood turns to ice in my veins. So, they are looking for my father.

And what will they do when they find his daughter instead?

I can't stay here.

My pulse races so hard in my throat that I can't breathe. Lungs on fire, I glance around the room to see if there's any easy way out. So far, I only see one guy with a gun. Whoever else was firing seems to have left the room. Unless it was Mr. Byrne who was the other person shooting. I notice with a swallowed gasp he's trying to reach for a gun that's slid away on the floor.

There's no way he'll reach it like this, with that other guy's foot bearing down on him. From this angle, I can see that man's black pistol shining, perfectly aimed, in the pretty golden lights of our living room.

No, the gun is too far from Mr. Byrne.

But it's close to me. Really fucking close.

"Where's O'Malley?" repeats the voice. "Mr. Serpico wants his money."

"Serpico... Severu Serpico?" Mr. Byrne pants.

Severu Serpico... I may be shielded from most of mob life, but I know who the major players are, and Severu is the leader of one of the most violent Camorra clans in the country.

The shoe presses harder, and Mr. Byrne howls, the muscles of his legs jumping beneath his dress pants.

"No questions. Only answers. Where is he?"

"I... I don't know! Fucking hell, man! I don't know!"

"You Irish really don't know much, do you? Did you know O'Malley's been siphoning money away from Mad Darragh's businesses? That he got cornered and then came begging on his knees to us for funds to cover it all up? The time on his loan is up, and unless you can tell me where he is you're going to pay the interest in blood."

"Fuck. Outside! He went outside!"

Oh my God.

My world tilts, everything I thought I knew about my father, my family, my *life*, evaporating in an instant. Dad was stealing? Lying? Betraying his own clients, his own boss?

This can't be real. This has to be a mistake.

But mistake or not, there's a man with a gun hellbent on finding my father. Without another word, he leaves the room, heading for the glass French doors that lead to our backyard and stepping through them.

He's going to kill my dad.

That thought gives me enough strength to get up and get out. To fight through the fear that's frozen my limbs. Without thinking, I grab the gun and sprint across the living room, tripping over broken glass and smooshed food that's scattered all over the floor. Thank God I'm wearing shoes. For a second, I wonder if I should stop and check on Mr. Byrne, but I know I don't have time. I'm not going to watch my father die on my birthday, and if I'm going to do something, it has to be now.

What I'm going to do, I have no idea. I've never even touched a gun in my life, let alone fired one at someone. Panic rises when I see my father running across the snow, the man heading straight for him, gun raised.

"Stop! I'm armed!"

The scream rips from my throat, splitting the air. The man stops and swivels. He sees me. Sees the gun I hold in my shaking hands. And starts to fucking *laugh*.

"Drop it, *bella*," he says, advancing towards me, his own gun raised to meet mine.

My toes are numb, snow seeping through the silk of my flats. Bitter wind buffets my hair. My teeth chatter, but I don't think it's from the cold.

My fingers cramp as my brain screams at me to pull the trigger.

Now. Now! Fucking now!

But I don't. I can't. I'm too weak, too afraid. I should have tried to shoot him when his back was turned before I saw his eyes. His eyes aren't laughing now. They're lethal. And I realize that everything I've heard about the Italian mafia not killing women and children is dead fucking wrong.

"Stop," I say, but this time it's a whisper. Not a command, but a prayer. I'm begging the man, the universe, maybe even God, to make this all stop. To go back to how things were fifteen minutes ago, when my life still made sense and I knew who I was, who my father was.

But he doesn't stop. And the fear has me again, tightening its jaws around me until I can't speak or think or breathe. I am completely immobile as he bears down on me.

But... I'm *not* immobile. Suddenly, I'm grabbed from behind and spun with such dizzying, catastrophic force that my feet leave the ground, my shoes flying off and my gun dropping down to the snow. Two shots ring out, one chasing the other. Whoever's holding me grunts and grasps me tighter against his broad chest with one arm. For a split second, I wonder if it's my father, somehow come back to save me. But no, this man is huge, far taller than my father. And there's no way Dad could have made it all the way back across the lawn by now.

I don't have time to figure it out, because before I know it, I'm slung over the man's shoulder and carried back into the house. I wriggle and kick, not knowing what else to do, but it's useless. The hand on my hip is like iron, holding me in place. I plant my hands on the man's back and crane my neck to see the other man, the one who was advancing on me, crumpled on the snow, the moonlight shining on a river of blood that streams from his head.

Did I get shot, too? I wonder in a daze, noticing that moisture is soaking the front of my dress, sticky and warm liquid coating my breasts.

The man carries me through the living room, something I only see in bits and pieces through the curtain of my hair hanging down and obscuring my vision. I don't see Mr. Byrne anymore. I wonder where he's ended up. And where my father is now.

The man takes me into the kitchen. It's bright in here, but a moment later we're plunged into darkness as he flicks his hand over the light switch on the wall. He doesn't stop walking until we're swathed in the shadows of the pantry built into the wall. Finally, he puts me down, and I can try to get my bearings on who he is and what the fuck is happening.

I've dimly pieced together that it's probably one of Darragh's men who's saved me. Word must have gotten out about the Camorra being here and the reinforcements have come. But I don't recognize the man before me, and when he tells me not to scream it's not with the kind of accent I'd expect. It's a mostly Ontario accent, but there's something else edging it. Something vaguely Italian.

Oh, God. He's one of them. One of Severu's men. Camorra.

"Don't scream," he says again just as I open my mouth to do it. He obviously senses I have no plans to obey, so he claps a huge, leather-gloved hand over my mouth, guiding me backwards until my spine hits the pantry's shelves.

"There might be more of them."

More of them? More of Severu's men?

So... he's not one of them? He did shoot that other guy, after all.

His eyes are so black they obliterate me. It's a gaze that feels like abyss. My own gaze tracks over his face, my nostrils filled with the scent of leather, blood, and the clean, luxurious spice of cologne. Dark, thick hair is slicked back from his broad forehead. One rebellious piece flops forward, curling, seeming almost boyish in stark contrast to the grim darkness of his face. There's nothing else boyish about him. About the hard, muscled frame of his body, the commanding grip of his hand on my mouth, the drowning black of those eyes. He has to be at least thirty-four or thirty-five, maybe even older, his bulk packed into a perfectly tailored suit.

As I look at him, my eyes snag on an area of skin at his

jaw and neck that looks wrong. Mottled and scarred. Like he's been burned.

And with sudden, breathless fear, I know *exactly* who he is. I've heard the stories – the stories of the man with the scars who never takes off his leather gloves.

He's not one of Severu Serpico's men.

He's not Camorra at all, but Cosa Nostra. And he's not a simple henchman, but the underboss of the most ruthless Sicilian family in the country.

Holding me tightly in my own kitchen, blocking me in with his massive body and watching me with an intensity that makes me shiver, is the tyrant of Toronto. A titan of bloodshed and king of crime. Vincenzo Titone's oldest nephew and heir.

Elio Titone.

The man who rules most of Toronto, of Montreal, and everything in between. The man who almost died in a fire as a boy back in Sicily, but who instead walked right through it, defying nature and death, defying God himself even as the good Lord tried to send him straight back down to hell.

His eyes roam downwards, and his nostrils flare when they get to my chest. I follow his gaze, gasping against his glove at the sight of all the slick red marring the white satin. I felt that blood, knew it was there, but the sight of it is still shocking smeared against the fabric of the dress and my pale skin.

Elio doesn't move his hand from my mouth. Instead, he shoves his gun lengthwise between his teeth, biting down on it the way an office worker might hold a mundane object like a pen when his hands are full. With his free hand, he pulls the front of my dress so hard it rips. The satin falls downward, the dress's straps ruined, until my entire front is bared to him.

Humiliation, rage, and fear all churn together, heating my skin and making my stomach clench. His gloved hand skims over my skin, poking, prodding. Pushing on the hand across my mouth, he forces my head back so he can inspect my throat before moving lower. He slides his hand over one breast, then the other, lifting each one and examining my abdomen. When my nipples harden under the hateful, arousing pressure of the leather, I start to squirm. With a grunt, he shoves his thick thigh between my legs, halting my movements. He takes the gun from his mouth and lays it on a shelf above my head.

"Stop moving," he growls.

His movements are quick but methodical, and I soon understand what he's doing.

So, he has the same question I did, then. Wondering if I had somehow been shot. But I know by now I haven't been. His thumb glides across my navel, indicating his inspection might move even lower.

I shake my head rapidly. His gaze narrows. Then he rolls his left shoulder experimentally. His expression tightens.

It's him. He's bleeding. The other gunshot...

I don't see any blood on his front, or a hole in his suit jacket indicating an exit wound, so the bullet must still be in there somewhere. His jaw works, and he looks pissed, but not overwhelmingly so. The guy looks like he just hit a patch of bad traffic on his way to work, like this is an annoying but daily occurrence for him.

Hissing out a sigh, he taps his ear, activating an earbud I hadn't seen before.

"Update, Curse?"

I can't hear whoever replies.

"Alright. Any sign of O'Malley?"

My mouth opens under his glove at the sound of my last name. He has to be talking about my dad.

But Elio completely ignores me, listening intently to whoever's speaking to him. Infuriated at the dismissal, I open my mouth even further, then snap my jaws shut, catching the pad of his middle finger between my teeth. I know the glove must dull the impact, but I bite down hard, and even so the bastard doesn't even flinch. Just raises a dark brow at me as he replies to the other person, telling them to take the bodies and move out.

Bodies? Plural?

Elio lowers his hand, yanking his finger from between my teeth, and I know this must mean there's no one left to hear me scream.

"What bodies? Where's my dad?" I ask, my words breathy and broken. I swallow hard, then cross my arms over my chest.

"Three Camorra goons. Dead now."

"And my father? Where is he?"

"If he's got any brains he's on his way out of the country."

What?

"No. No way. He wouldn't leave me here. And Darragh Gowan's men will be here soon to help. In fact, they'll be here any second. You should go before you get another bullet in your back."

I'm rambling. I know I am. And I'm probably being stupid as hell to threaten Elio fucking Titone with bullets. But he doesn't seem to particularly care about my words. He makes an odd expression. I can't tell if it's a smirk or a grimace. The scarring along his neck and jaw makes one side of his mouth pull lower than the other.

"Mad Darragh won't be sending anyone to help your father now. Or you, for that matter. Word's started getting out about O'Malley's penchant for skimming off the top. Your father may have paid back the money he took from the Irish, but Darragh's not going to forgive a betrayal like that. And judging by Sev's men here tonight, he still owes money to the Camorra." He leans closer, his breath tingling along my ear and neck as he whispers, "He owes money to me, too."

"But... you saved me!" I stammer. Why would he let my father or me live if we really owed so much? Mercy is not something Elio Titone is known for. "You got shot protecting me!"

"I didn't save you," he mutters darkly, so close that his lips brush the shell of my ear. He pulls back so I can see the ruthless darkness of his gaze. I'm horrendously aware of the hard length of his thigh pressing against my pussy and the scant protection my arms provide over my bare, bloodied breasts.

"I'm not your hero, Deirdre O'Malley. I'm your debt collector." He gives me a wolfish, crooked smile, and it's the most terrifying thing I've ever seen. "And tonight I've come to claim what's mine."

Chapter 4

Elio

This is the closest I've ever been to Deirdre O'Malley and I'm hard as a fucking rock. Heat seeps from her cunt, warming my thigh as she pants.

"I'm not yours," she whispers raggedly.

"You are now."

Her mouth tightens, and she shakes her head over and over again, as if she can shake herself right out of this reality. I take hold of her jaw, forcing her head into stillness. Her large eyes grow even wider. There's fear there. But defiance too.

"Let me make your situation perfectly clear," I say. My pulse throbs in my bleeding shoulder and my dick. "Your father owes me a great deal of money. He had until the end of the year, *last* year now, and he hasn't fucking paid. Now, that debt is transferred to you."

She swallows, delicate throat bobbing.

"We can pay it. Sell the house-"

"Not enough," I growl.

"Not enough?" she breathes. "How is that even possible? How much does he owe you?"

"Five point two million. With interest."

Her already pale face grows whiter in the gloom. I almost want her to fight me on this. Want her to command me to go track down her piece of shit of a papà instead of trapping her when she's completely innocent in all of this.

But she doesn't. She's too fucking good. Trying to protect the man who should have protected her. *Sweet little Songbird. I am going to cage you.*

"What are you going to do to me? How... how are you going to make me pay?"

She's trembling, and the defiance in her gaze wanes, replaced with terror. Her knuckles are white as bone as she clutches her own chest, hiding herself.

I let go of her jaw and ease my thigh out from between her legs. She gasps and nearly collapses with the lack of support. When her knees buckle, I grasp her waist, pulling her upright against my body.

"I may be an ugly bastard, but believe it or not, I don't need a whore." I inhale against her hair, smelling sweet vanilla. "Besides, I don't fuck redheads."

She's quiet for a moment before she whispers, "Then what do you want from me?"

What the fuck do I want from her? It's not like I haven't imagined turning her into my whore. Imagined what her pussy tastes like, what she'd feel like wrapped around my cock, my rule about redheads be damned.

I'm not sure I can even put it into words. The ache I have for her. Something far more than physical need.

"There's something inside you I need to understand," I murmur.

Something I saw on that balcony a year and a half ago.

Something I've witnessed at every single one of her violin performances since then as I sat watching alone in the very back row. "You're going to play for me until I can figure it out."

"Play for you?"

I release her waist, and she remains standing this time.

"Violin, Songbird."

Confusion, then understanding, crystallize in her gaze.

"You want me to... to be your own personal musician?"

"*Live-in* musician," I correct her. "Let's go."

"No. No way! I'll play for you, but I'm not living with you!"

"This is not a fucking negotiation," I grunt. *Merda*, my shoulder is really starting to throb. At least it's finally distracting me from my hard-on.

"I can't. I-"

"You're not staying here," I cut in sharply. "You will live under my roof until your debt is paid in full. That is the deal I struck with your father. If he doesn't pay, I take you. He didn't pay. Now I'm taking you."

"No," she says hoarsely. "He wouldn't-"

"He did," I inform her flatly.

For the first time, I see her large eyes fill with tears. She's actually held it together pretty well so far considering everything that's happened. But cracks are starting to show. A single tear rolls from one eye, and I halt its progress with my thumb. Before it can absorb into the leather, I raise it to my mouth and taste its sweet salt.

She watches me with horrified fascination, her shock at my action stopping her crying.

"Time to go," I tell her. It's not a good idea to stay here after Curse and I have killed three of Sev's men. There's a chance Mad Darragh will send soldiers, too, and when they don't find O'Malley they'll want Deirdre. Just like I do. Those are problems I'm going to have to deal with later. I take my gun from the top shelf, and when Deirdre sees me do it, she purses her lips and takes a shaky breath.

I don't hold the gun to her head. I don't have to. She knows she has no choice but to follow me as I lead her out of the kitchen. If she doesn't walk, I'll just carry her.

I do end up carrying her though, cradling her against my chest this time, when we reach the disaster of the living room.

"Put me down! I'll walk," she says, fighting against my hold.

"Glass," is all I say. She's got no shoes, and the floor of this room is a sharply glittering mess.

"I don't care. I'd rather slice my feet open," she hisses. I feel myself smile at that. My little Irish Songbird has a spine, that's for sure.

I clutch her closer as I stride through the room and out the front door.

"You're mine now, Songbird. And I won't let anyone damage what's mine. Not even you."

Chapter 5

Elio

Outside, I see my younger brother Accursio. Though no one calls him his full name except our aunt and uncle. To everyone else, he's Curse, the Titone family's most feared assassin, deadly as a plague. As I approach with Deirdre, he shoves the corpse of the man I shot along with two others into his black Escalade's trunk and slams it shut before turning towards us.

He knows what we've come for tonight. He knows Deirdre is mine. But when his dark eyes dip, ever so briefly, to her bare upper body in my arms, jealousy tightens in my gut.

It's an absurd feeling. Curse is my most trusted man. My only brother. He'll be my *consigliere* when I fully take over this family. I've literally walked through fire for him, and money can't buy loyalty that an act like that earns. And besides that, he's only ever wanted one girl, even though he hasn't seen her since we were kids in Sicily. But even so, even knowing all this and seeing that there's not a hint of lust in his gaze, I want to slug him just for looking at her.

I walk past him to my own black SUV, unlocking it and opening the door with Deirdre in my arms. My shoulder screams as I place her in the passenger seat. I don't miss the way she shakes, and I shrug out of my suit jacket, holding it out to her. She glares at it as if it's a venomous snake. I remember her comment about how she'd rather slice her feet open than be carried by me, and I know she's too proud, or too angry, to take anything from me now.

But it's too late for that. I already paid for the satin that sags, ruined, around her waist. Paid for the shoes lost somewhere in the snow. Paid for her whole fucking life the past year and a half, through the millions I loaned her father.

I stare down at her while she stares at the jacket, both of us unmoving, locked in a standoff.

I want to say, *fine*, and drop it. Let her be cold. Let her be proud and refuse me, even while she's naked and trembling, even while she has absolutely nothing left in this world without me. Who cares if she takes the jacket? Who cares if she's warm enough?

Apparently, I do.

Dio fucking help me. Even if you've never once helped me before.

I bend down to her, and she recoils, hunching against the leather seat. I wrap my hand around the back of her neck, forcing her forward enough so that I can slide the jacket between her spine and the seat. She's tense under my hand, already straining backwards and away from me. I let go. My sudden lack of restraint on her makes her cry out with surprise, and the back of her head bounces off the cushioned headrest. I do up the jacket's button at the front, my eyes catching on the blood smeared across her perfect pale skin. *My* blood.

Grim satisfaction is sick and hot inside me when I see

the way I've marked her. The way I've stained her. Bled for her and bled on her.

I'm about to close the door on her when she reaches for me, her hand slipping between the flaps of my jacket, fingers wrapping around my wrist.

"Wait!" she cries. "My violin!"

"I'll buy you a new one."

I'll buy her a whole symphony's worth of shit if it means I can figure her out. Understand her hold on me.

But she shakes her head and looks so suddenly sad that it makes my jaw tick.

"I can't leave it. It won't take long. I know exactly where it is – under a table in the living room. *Please*," she whispers.

And then I remember, casting my mind back to that stinking hot summer day and to what O'Malley said.

It was her mother's, he told me.

And as if I've been called to battle, I straighten and turn back towards the house.

The violin belonged to her mother.

And now that I remember that fact, I can't leave it behind either. I may be a scarred piece of shit, a monster, a murderer willing to take Deirdre's very freedom away from her.

But I'm not willing to do this.

I'm too sentimental about mamma shit. My one fucking weakness.

But with Deirdre in my car, her gaze like fire on my back, I start to wonder if that's not my only weakness.

"Watch her," I grunt at Curse. I toss him my keys. "Turn on the passenger seat heater."

My brother catches my keys out of the air with a nod as I stride back towards the house to retrieve the violin. With every step, I fight to keep myself here, in the present, in the depths of Canadian winter instead of Sicilian summer. But I can't help but feel as if I'm walking back into my past. Trying to get to my own mamma this time, instead of an instrument belonging to someone else's.

But I don't find my own long-dead mamma or the violin. I find a fourth Camorra soldier creeping through the living room. I'm faster than he is, gun in my hand, and I take him out by the kneecap. He howls and collapses, blood spurting between the fingers of his left hand as he shakily raises the gun in his right.

Not interested in taking another bullet tonight, I shoot the gun right out of his hand. The gun, along with three fingers, fall to the floor.

"Motherfucker... Fucking... Fuck!" he gasps, writhing and trying to clutch at both his hand and knee at the same time.

"Tell me why you're here," I say, crouching beside him.

"Holy shit." His gaze, hazed with pain, focuses on my face. "Elio Titone? What the fuck are you doing here?"

I don't know this soldier, but he knows me. Anyone in this city with half a brain in their head knows who I am.

"Getting what I'm owed. Now answer my question."

I think he's going to lose his shit on me. Maybe even lose consciousness. The metal press of my pistol against his forehead helps bring him back.

"Fuck! Here for O'Malley. Owes Mr. Serpico big time."

"How much?"

He scrunches up his face as I push the gun more firmly against his skin.

"Don't shoot! Eight hundred G's."

I don't even blink. I'm already in this for 5.2 million, what's another eight hundred grand?

"I'm going to let you live so that you can give Sev a

30

message." I press the gun even harder for a second, then pull it away, leaving a white circle on his forehead that quickly turns red. "Tell your boss he'll get his money. Courtesy of La Cosa Nostra."

"You... you'll pay O'Malley's debt?" he wheezes.

"It's not his debt anymore. It's hers."

I don't elaborate further. I stand and leave him bleeding on the floor. As I do so, I spot the violin and bow under a table, just where she said they would be. As I pick the items up, I make a mental note to let Deirdre know that the sum she owes has now reached a cool six million.

Chapter 6

Deirdre

The man Elio called Curse watches me with silent intensity from the driver's seat, a gun in his lap. There's something familiar in his gaze. I know Elio Titone has a younger brother, and I wonder if this is him. They have the same thick black hair, too, but otherwise they don't look much alike. If Curse weren't covered in tattoos, he'd look like a Renaissance sculpture come to life, his face chiselled like an angel's.

A fallen angel, no doubt.

When I can no longer stand staring back at him, I turn my head to the passenger window, looking at the house's front door, waiting for Elio to come through it. Heat from the seat warmer blooms along my quivering legs and my stiff back, echoing the body heat on Elio's jacket when he'd forced it around me. I should have ripped it off the second he was out of my sight. Should have let it fall to the snow, ruined it even more than the bullet and blood already did.

But some strange part of me had liked the way the jacket felt, so warm against my goosebumpy skin. And if I hadn't taken it, I'd be naked from the waist up now, with nothing but my arms to cover me. I pull the jacket a little tighter, shivering again, but this time with odd, hateful pleasure at the kiss of the jacket's silk lining sliding against my skin. Elio's scent surrounds me, the same scent from the pantry – exquisite and probably astronomically expensive cologne mixed with blood, leather, and a slightly deeper masculine musk.

Wrapped in his jacket and his scent, I see him coming through the front door. I should feel dread, but I can't help the flood of relief when I see he's found my mom's violin. He holds it by the neck in one hand, the bow in the other. They look small in the grip of his black leather gloves, almost like toys.

I've already noticed how tinted these windows are from the outside. There's no way he can see me in here, but even so, his gaze pierces right through the glass. It's like he can see right inside me, like even my deepest inner thoughts belong to him now.

As the bright moonlight cascades down his form, I observe him, trying to memorize and understand every detail, to know exactly who I'm dealing with. He's so tall – he's got to be at least 6'4 – and built like a fucking tank. His black dress shirt moulds to the hard planes and curves of his muscles. I drag my gaze up to his face and I'm certain that these two are brothers now. It's not just the hair and the eyes, but also something about the way they both carry themselves, the power that pours off of them in poisonous waves.

Elio comes around to the driver's side and Curse slides out to make room for him, the younger brother trading places with the older. Curse is a big guy too, but when Elio settles himself into the seat, the space in the SUV feels suddenly smaller. Elio takes everything – even all the air in here.

He says a few things to Curse, and, heart thundering, I watch him. It's the left side of his neck and jaw that are scarred, so I can't see the marred skin from here. I watch him closely while he tells his younger brother to "make sure Morelli's at the house."

I let my gaze track over his hard jaw, the rugged slashes of his cheekbones, the bold nose. He doesn't have Curse's classic good looks. I remember what he said to me in the shadows, calling himself an ugly bastard, but I don't see it. He's striking. He's not handsome in a refined way, but his features are so brutal and unapologetic that I can't stop staring at his profile.

Curse heads off to his own vehicle – a vehicle with a trunk full of dead men. My stomach lurches as Elio hands me the violin and bow. I try to block everything out and take comfort in the familiar feel of the wood, the strings.

But there's no blocking Elio Titone out. Especially when he turns towards me in the car's dark interior. I tense, remembering the way he touched me in the pantry. His hands on my throat, my breasts.

But he doesn't touch. He doesn't say a single word. He just grasps the seatbelt from beside my head, then tugs it downward, fastening it across my chest and lap.

He just kidnapped me in a chaotic storm of gunfire and blood and now he's worried about making sure I'm strapped in?

He's still silent as he shifts the car out of park and starts driving. Suddenly, the seatbelt thing makes a little more sense, because Elio drives fucking *fast*. Absurdly, I wonder if he has good snow tires on as he explodes out of our driveway and down the road.

Although maybe it's not that absurd, considering what happened to Mom and me. But we weren't the ones driving fast that winter day. Not like this, not like Elio.

I decide he must have snow tires on, considering how well the vehicle is handling on the slick roads.

It's crazy just how mundane that thought is. I wonder if that's a protection mechanism. If by focusing on things like seatbelts and snow tires, I can make it all a little less real.

But it is real.

This is happening.

I'm really being abducted by one of the most brutal men in this city, this country. The life I thought I had is gone, maybe forever.

No. Not forever. Dad will find me.

He wasn't among the bodies in Curse's trunk. Hopefully I've bought him enough time to figure out a way to fix this. I still can't believe what Elio has said – that my own father sold me out. I also can't believe that he would steal from Darragh.

But if he hadn't stolen from Darragh, why didn't any of Darragh's men come to help us?

It's all too much to think about. Instead, I focus on watching the landscape so I know where Elio's taking me. A chill runs through me when I picture where I may end up. A warehouse? A prison cell? Somewhere no one can hear me scream.

But he said live-in musician...

His house.

I don't fool myself. I could still end up in a warehouse, or worse, in a heartbeat if Elio decides he's done with me.

We're heading south, into Toronto proper, leaving my Thornhill neighbourhood behind. I wonder if we're going downtown. I allow myself small glances at Elio, and I see how wet his shirt is with blood at the back.

"Your shoulder," I whisper.

He keeps his eyes on the road, though he's only driving with one leather-gloved hand on the wheel. His left hand rests limply on his thigh.

"Worried about me?"

"I'm worried you'll kill us both when you lose consciousness from blood loss," I snap before I can stop myself. I clamp my mouth shut, internally berating myself. Talking back to a Titone is not smart, and I prepare myself for the blowback.

But it doesn't come. Instead, Elio laughs, a dark, gruff chuckle.

"Too many men want me dead as it is. Don't plan on making things easier for them by doing it myself."

I stare at him in disbelief. He's been shot. He's bleeding badly from the shoulder and obviously isn't using his left hand at all right now. And yet, he seems completely unperturbed. His grip on the steering wheel is relaxed and he commands the road with ease even while driving twice the speed limit.

I lurch in my seat as he takes a sharp corner.

"You're driving too fast!" I cry, unable to hold it in.

"This is slow for me, Songbird. Consider it a courtesy since I know you're not used to this yet. Soon, you will be."

Those last words are ominous, and I try not to think too deeply about what they mean.

"Aren't you at least worried about being pulled over?" I ask.

He laughs again, a disbelieving bark of sound. It's like I just asked him if he ever worries about Santa putting him on the naughty list. Like it's something nonsensical.

I lapse into silence, unsure why I've even engaged him in conversation in the first place. I return my attention to the outside world. We pass Edward Gardens and turn onto Brindle Path, one of the most expensive streets in one of the country's most expensive cities.

I've never been in this neighbourhood, but I know exactly where we are. *Millionaire's Row.* A lush, secluded neighbourhood of sprawling mansions on gigantic lots. It doesn't even feel like we're in Toronto as we pass castle-like houses on entire acreages of their own. My house is large, but it's nothing like these ones.

We continue along the street before turning onto a long and winding driveway. Gigantic trees arch on both sides, casting shadows on the glistening drive that's like an entire road unto itself. Despite the drifts of snow on either side, the driveway is immaculately snow-free and salted, its smooth black surface reflecting moonlight like still water.

We travel so far into the trees that the main road disappears. I worry at my lower lip, feeling like I'm falling further and further into a trap. Like I'm headed for the underworld and I'll never claw my way back out.

A huge gate looms ahead, manned by a tattooed guy in a booth. Elio doesn't stop, doesn't even slow down, and I gasp, thinking we'll crash right into the wrought iron, but we don't. The gate slides sideways, the man in the booth giving a deferential nod as we drive through.

I wrench around in my seat, staring backwards as the gate closes behind us. Black bars slicing through the night and cutting me off from where I came from.

From everything I've ever known.

I turn around to face my new future as Elio stops the car and darkly mutters, "Welcome home."

Chapter 7

Deirdre

Home.

This building isn't like any home I've ever seen. Maybe on TV, or in an architecture magazine, but not in real life. It's gigantic, a massive geometric structure of glass and metal. Rectangles on top of rectangles glittering in the dense woods of the property. Dimly, I wonder how close the nearest neighbouring property is. As if he can read my very thoughts, Elio tells me that the closest house to this one belongs to his Uncle Vincenzo, head of the *famiglia*, where he lives with his wife Carlotta and daughter Valentina.

The fact he guessed what I was thinking makes me feel like I'm not even safe in my own head, and suddenly I can't stand being this close to him. I unbuckle my seatbelt and force the car door open, holding my violin and bow awkwardly in my arms, wishing I had the case. My feet hit the freezing pavement, and I'm reminded of my lack of shoes. But I refuse to be carried this time.

Elio doesn't try it. He just gets out of the car and watches me from in front of the vehicle.

He's not the only one watching me. Two mafia soldiers stand at the house's massive, metal front door.

"Going to run?" Elio asks. He perches his hip against the SUV's hood and leans sideways in a pose of easy languor, like he doesn't really care if I do. But his eyes give him away. They're intense. Ravenous. Showing me the truth of the hunter ready to strike beneath the relaxed exterior.

"No," I tell him. Where would I even run to? Into the woods without shoes where his men would track me down in no time flat? No, I have to be smarter than that. Keep myself safe, alive, until I can figure out another plan. I raise my chin and hold his stare, fighting the urge to dance back and forth from one foot to the other. My feet are so cold it hurts, but I focus on the pain. It gives me something to anchor myself.

Elio looks satisfied with my answer and straightens up. He raises his right arm in an *after you* sort of gesture. I swallow hard and walk towards the door.

The soldiers at the door aren't looking at me now but at Elio. Waiting for the slightest signal from their boss, ready for the subtlest and most silent of instructions. One of the men punches in a code and then opens the door. I kick myself for not taking note of what the numbers are.

I hesitate in the large doorway, panic inside me telling me that maybe I really should run. If I go through that door, there's no coming back, and I know it.

But Elio is at my back, his heat penetrating the jacket and oozing down my spine. I hate the way it contrasts so sharply with the pain of the cold. It turns his body into a vicious sort of comfort, something a terrible part of me wants to sink into. I take a swift step forward through the door just to get away from him.

But of course, he follows. The door closes with a quiet boom, and I jump, nearly dropping my violin. Part of me is still confused about why Elio went back to get it in the first place, and I hug it to my chest, seeking comfort in my new prison.

If this is a prison, it's a beautiful one. The entryway is massive, with natural grey stone cut in big slabs for the floor. To the left, I can see an expansive dining room with a long, live-edge wood table. To the right is a huge open-concept living and kitchen area. Straight ahead is a set of iron steps leading ominously upwards.

Elio grasps my arm and heads for the stairs.

"Where are we going?" I ask, stumbling along with him. His legs are so much longer than mine and our strides are mismatched. I wouldn't be surprised if he normally takes the stairs two at a time.

"Upstairs," he grunts, and I shoot him a sharp look from the side. No fucking shit we're going upstairs. It's what we're going to find upstairs that I want a warning about.

But there's a new tightness in Elio's jaw, his brows pinching. When I fall just a little behind, I step in wetness on the stair below him before he hauls me up to his level, and I see how much he's still bleeding. The injury is finally getting to him. It makes him seem just a little more human.

And makes me feel a twinge of guilt.

I try to beat that down. If he hadn't been at my house to *kidnap me*, he wouldn't have gotten shot.

But if he hadn't been there...

I'd probably be dead right now.

"Why did you take a bullet for me?" I ask quietly. I don't really expect him to answer, but I watch him anyway. His jaw tightens further before he schools his expression into something more neutral.

"I already told you that you're mine now, Songbird. Everything about you. That includes your life."

"Does that mean you'll eventually take it from me?" I stop walking, and Elio stops too, looking down at me from one step above, making him tower even more than he usually does. His hard gaze tracks over me in my entirety – my face and dishevelled hair, his jacket sagging at my shoulders, my bloodstained dress that now is nothing more than a skirt, my bare feet sticky with his blood.

"I may be a monster, but I don't kill pretty little songbirds like you."

"You keep calling me that. Why?" I've never even met the man before tonight and yet he wants me as his own personal violinist. He knows I play, but how? I'm good, but I'm not a professional filling concert halls. I have no reputation as a musician in this city. Even if I was a professional, it would take me a lifetime – *more* than a lifetime – to earn back 5.2 million plus interest. It makes no sense.

"You ask a lot of questions," he mutters. He's still holding me by the elbow, and he tugs. I take a wobbly step up to his level. I want to tell him that this is nothing. That I've got about a million more questions swirling inside me, banging on the inside of my skull to be let out. But I sense that now is not the time to ask, and I try to just be grateful that I'm still alive and unharmed.

We're so close like this that my jacket-clad chest brushes his on every ragged inhale.

"You should go to the hospital," I say. There's the fucking guilt again. Always the guilt. Guilt that's been with me since Mom's death, intensifying, getting thick and ugly, as I watch Elio bleed. I shouldn't care about what happens to him, but I do. And I hate myself for it.

He gives a soft, dark laugh. It's a quieter version of his

laugh in the car, when I'd mentioned that the police might pull him over for speeding. Apparently, going to the hospital is just as outlandish as dealing with the cops in his world.

Noted.

"No need. Morelli's here. But good try."

As we continue ascending the stairs, I try to figure out what he means.

But I can't. My brain feels like sludge.

"What do you mean?" I ask, giving up on trying to guess as we reach the top of the stairs and start walking down a long hallway with hardwood floors.

"Good job trying to get me out of my own house while you're in it."

I blink. I hadn't even thought of that. That if he went to the hospital and got put under for surgery he wouldn't be with me.

"Yeah, right. You'd probably just drag me there with you," I say with a bitter sigh. My head hurts.

I keep my eyes ahead but hear the slight grin in his reply when he says, "Smart little Songbird. Smart to try to get away from me. Even smarter to know that it will never happen."

"But it will, won't it? If I pay off the debt?"

My words freeze him, and his hold on my arm halts my forward progress. He pulls me around to face him. Any trace of a grin is gone, his gaze cold and narrowed as it swallows mine.

"You got six million lying around?"

"Six?" I cry, stunned. "That's not what you told me earlier!"

"That was before I took over your father's eight

hundred-thousand-dollar debt to Severu Serpico. In fact," he adds, his hold tightening on my arm, "I'll probably have to throw the Camorra an extra couple hundred grand for killing three of their men tonight so we don't start a fucking war. So, add that to your mental tally."

I swallow hard, refusing to let tears fill my eyes. I can't even sell the house on my own – it's in my father's name, and at this point I wouldn't be surprised if it's mortgaged like crazy. I could sell everything I own but it wouldn't even be a fraction of the sum. I don't even have any of my stuff with me anyway. I've got nothing but this violin and the ruined clothes on my back. No money, no phone.

Holy shit.

I shift my weight slightly to see if it's there, and it is. In the dress's pocket, a small rectangle bumping my thigh.

Dresses with pockets are freaking miracles.

It's something, at least. A connection to the outside world. But it won't solve the problem of that debt hanging over my head.

A dark thought makes my stomach turn, and I don't even want to say it, but I do anyway.

"There are ways for young women like me to make good money fast."

His nostrils flare.

"I told you I don't need a whore."

I bristle. "Who said that you would be the client?"

Somehow his gaze turns blacker and burns brighter at the same time. I give a small, startled cry as he forces me backwards until I'm against the wall. His hard thigh is once again between mine, forcing my legs apart. The smooth leather of his gloves finds my jaw, trapping my face so there's nowhere to look but at him.

"What part of *your life is mine* did you not understand before?" he growls. "Everything you have belongs to me now. The clothes on your back, which I've already paid for. The phone in your pocket, which won't do you any good here, by the way." His voice grows gruffer, more raw. "Every flaming hair on your pretty little head, every breath you dare to breathe, every song in your fucking soul. *All. Fucking. Mine.*"

He nudges his thigh harder against me. Heat explodes along my spine as he bends to whisper against my ear, "And that includes what's between your legs."

A hot, hateful throb goes through me. My nipples prick against his jacket while I shove against his chest with my elbows, trying to protect the violin and bow.

"I thought you said you don't fuck redheads," I hiss. It had seemed such a bizarre thing for him to have mentioned before, but I latch onto it now like it's a lifeboat.

"I don't," he grits out. "Doesn't mean I won't kill any man who tries to touch what's mine."

Another treacherous pulse between my legs makes my insides squeeze. My heart beats so fast it feels like a buzz. My breath is shallow as I wriggle in his hold, but every move I make just puts more friction between my clit and his thigh until I'm aching. Aching and ashamed and *needy*, needing *something* but I don't fucking know what.

More pressure. Maybe even pain.

Some kind of release from all of this.

And I get it – a literal release. Elio lets me go and straightens when a voice calls his name from down the hall. The man who called to him is tall and thin, with grey hair and round spectacles perched on his nose. His sleeves are rolled up, and he's drying his hands on a pristine white towel as if he's just washed them.

"Come on," Elio says. He doesn't grab my arm this time, but places a firm hand against my lower back. "Time for your first performance."

Chapter 8

Elio

"Elio," Morelli says with a nod as Deirdre and I walk into my bedroom.

"Doc," I grunt in reply. Doctor Tommaso Morelli is one of the few people who calls me by my first name instead of *boss* or *Mr. Titone*. He's earned the right. He's been sewing up my scrapes since before I got my first pube. When I was fourteen, he was the one who bandaged my burns, pumped me full of antibiotics, and got me in good enough shape to leave our home in Taormina for Canada. In the end, he came with us. It wasn't safe for any of us in Sicily anymore, and as my Uncle Vincenzo's best friend, he was tainted by his link to our family, so it wasn't safe for him, either.

Didn't work out too badly for him, though. Working for our family he earns twice what the most sought-after plastic surgeons in this city make and all he has to do is be on-call to pull out the occasional bullet or sew up a knife wound now and then. He met his wife here, too, and now they have adult twin daughters, Lucia and Giulia.

"The girl?" he asks in Italian as I settle myself on a stretcher that's been brought up from the main med room downstairs. He and I both look at her, and I see what he sees. A young woman with a ruined dress soaked in blood.

"She's fine. It's all my blood," I reply, also in Italian. It's Morelli's preferred language of conversation. He was almost forty when he left Taormina and learning English was harder for him than it was for Curse and me.

"You know the drill," he says, snapping on a pair of latex gloves. "Shirt off."

I unbutton the garment with my right hand, trying to keep my left arm still. As I do it, I keep my eyes on Deirdre. She watches me silently from a corner of the room. There's wariness in her eyes, amplified by that little stunt I pulled in the hallway, shoving my thigh between her legs and telling her that her pussy was mine.

Must be the blood loss. I'm losing all sense of sanity, of control. But I hadn't expected her to challenge me like that. To imply she'd start whoring herself out just to be free of me.

Even now, the idea makes my teeth grind and my fists clench.

Morelli frowns at me, noticing I've stopped.

"Do you need me to cut off the shirt with the scissors?"

"No," I reply, forcing my hands to relax and undoing the last few buttons. Mostly using my right hand, I peel the destroyed garment from my body.

I don't miss the sharp inhale from across the room as I toss my shirt aside. I smirk mirthlessly at her and raise my eyebrows, daring her not to look away.

And to her credit, she doesn't. Her eyes track from my neck down the long, angry line of ropy scar tissue that mars my left shoulder and upper arm. Those burns weren't even the worst – the worst are my hands. Even I can't stand looking at my own hands. Not because of what they've done, or who they've killed. But because of who they couldn't save.

Deirdre's eyes are still moving, drifting away from the marks the fire left to newer scars. Knife wounds and bullet holes that Morelli has dutifully sutured during the past twenty years in Canada. Years spent fighting tooth and fucking nail alongside my uncle to turn the Titones into something. A *famiglia* to be feared instead of one that has to flee their homeland in the dead of night.

Morelli works quickly at my back, cleaning blood from my skin, disinfecting, and taking stock of the injury. He knows better than to offer me morphine – I never take it. I don't hide from pain. I breathe it in. Consume it, let it fill me like rage, until it's a part of me. Until it forms yet another scar. It's a penance of sorts. For being alive when she isn't.

I bite back a hiss when Morelli stars digging for the bullet in the back of my shoulder. Deirdre presses her lips into a thin, bloodless line. Her face is pale, but she doesn't turn away.

Morelli's an observant son of a bitch. Always has been. I don't know exactly what it is he sees in my gaze as I stare at Deirdre, but just as he yanks out the bullet and drops it onto a small metal tray, he flicks the back of my head and sternly tells me, "No fucking tonight. You've lost too much blood."

I snort and want to tell him I've never lost too much blood for that, but it's a moot point. I didn't bring Deirdre here to fuck her, no matter what my wayward dick thinks.

I brought her here to play for me.

"I told you it's time for your first performance," I say in

English, grimacing when Morelli starts the sutures. "So start playing."

Deirdre jumps, as if she was lost in a daydream and isn't expecting to be spoken to. Morelli joins in with thickly accented English, nodding as he works, "Ah, *sì*. Beautiful music. Good for healing. Soothing."

Deirdre's music has never been soothing. Not to me. It's electrifying. When she plays it makes me feel like my heart has crawled outside my fucking body and I need to understand why.

"Play," I repeat. Shakily, she rolls up the jacket sleeves that are gaping around her arms and raises her violin, placing the bow to the strings. My fingers curl around the edge of the stretcher I'm seated on and I lean forward until the sutures tug which makes Morelli scold me.

This is the first time I've been so close to her when she plays. Thirty-four years old and I'm practically holding my breath like an excited little kid.

That held breath comes out in a sigh when she stiffly grinds out the notes of *Twinkle Twinkle Little Star*.

"Not like that," I chide her.

She narrows her gaze at me, frowning.

"It's the first song that came into my mind."

Morelli finishes up at my back, bandaging the wound with a thick roll that goes under my arm and around my shoulder. I slide off the stretcher. He mutters that I should be wearing a sling, but he knows I won't do it. He cleans up, puts his tools on top of the stretcher, then wheels it out of my room. He reminds me in Italian not to forget what he said about no fucking tonight as he goes.

I start walking and then stop in front of Deirdre, keeping some space between us.

"Play something else."

Her eyes dart around the room. She licks her lips, and that pink tongue draws my eyes like metal to a magnet.

"*Play for me.*"

"I just... I just don't like performing!" she stammers.

"I know for a fact that that's not true," I say.

Confusion wracks her features. She doesn't know that I've attended every single one of her violin performances over the past year and a half. I don't offer her an explanation. Don't bother to explain I've seen her play more than a dozen times by now. That I know she's always stiff and nervous when she first hits the stage, but then she closes her eyes and lets the music take over. When that happens, its like the entire audience disappears, and it's only her and me in the room.

Just like now.

Play that song your mamma loved, I want to tell her. That ballad I heard on her balcony and haven't experienced again since then. Oh, I've listened to the song – some nights I play it on a goddamn loop until it becomes a part of my heartbeat. But I haven't heard her play it since that summer day. *An Eala Bhàn*. I don't even attempt the Irish pronunciation.

I can already tell I won't get what I'm looking for tonight. Deirdre's face is pale under her smattering of freckles, and she's trembling. I see what this night has done to her, what I've done to her, and I force myself to let things lie for now.

"I'll be right back," I tell her. "Stay here. When I get back, I'll take you to your room." Just before I head for my bedroom's adjoining bathroom, I close the last bit of distance between us and drag my leather-bound fingertips along her jaw until her blue eyes meet mine. "Don't even think of trying to run, Songbird. I've got soldiers stationed all over this house."

Her eyes flash, but she nods against my fingers all the same.

Chapter 9

Deirdre

Elio disappears into a massive adjoining bathroom. He leaves the door open, and I hear the sound of water running. While he's gone, I take quick stock of what's around me. We're in a gigantic bedroom – probably his. Like the rest of the house, the room is done in natural wood and grey stone, with accents of dark iron. The bed is huge – bigger than any King I've ever seen – its frame rectangular and metal. The space is cool and clean, and would almost feel industrial if not for the warm colour of the wood and the weirdly homey touches. Homey touches like bookshelves by the bed, lined with tomes on politics and history and art and...

Music.

There's an entire shelf devoted to books on music, musicians, and theory. Some of them appear to be Italian books on opera and other traditional music, but my stomach drops when I see that most of the music shelf is taken up by books about violin. Violin masters, violin makers, books about how to play violin, from beginner to advanced.

What the actual hell is going on here?

Maybe Elio has some kind of music obsession, specifically violin, and that's why he wants me. But there are far more accomplished players in Toronto he could have chosen, pro violinists he could have simply hired instead of kidnapping an amateur one at the stroke of midnight on her twentieth birthday.

Near the bookshelves the theme of music continues to dominate the space. There's a massive sound system built into the wall, and I quickly realize that there are surround sound speakers along the ceiling and in the corners of the room. There's a record player, too, and a small shelf of CDs. The CDs seem out of place to me. Elio doesn't seem like the type to engage in just slightly out-of-date technology. I feel like he'd either be playing the oldest, most expensive vintage records in existence, or else listening to music digitally. I don't get close enough to look at what albums he, for some reason, has collected in CD format. Instead, I force myself to keep looking around the room to see exactly what I'm dealing with.

There are four doors leading out of this room. One is the door we came through from the hallway. Directly across from that door is the bathroom door, which still stands open. A quick glance tells me that Elio remains out of sight, and I still hear running water. I wonder if he's taken off his gloves to do whatever he's doing, then remind myself to focus.

The other two doors, one on my right and one on my left, are closed. I assume one is a closet. Maybe the room has two closets? That seems like it would be a thing for an excessively wealthy mafia titan.

So, right now, the only sure way out is the door we came through.

But he has men everywhere. He told me that himself. I lean my head out of the room to see a man dressed in all black stationed at the top of the stairs Elio and I came up before.

Shit.

As I straighten up and turn to face the bedroom again, my phone bumps my thigh. He told me it wouldn't be of any use in here – does that mean there's no service?

I keep my eyes on the open bathroom door as I gently place down my violin and bow and slide my phone out of my pocket.

I want to weep with relief when I see that I have full bars. Along with about twenty-five unread text messages from Willow. A quick look at the last few texts confirms that at least some of what Elio told me about my father was true.

12:48am: *what the hell did your dad do???? hes on the outs with fucking everyone!!! no wonder half the usual crowd didn't show up tonight. apparently darragh is tearing toronto apart right now looking for him AND YOU!!!! WHERE THE FUCK ARE YOU???*

12:49am: *my dad is freaking out that we were at your place tonight. if he finds out im texting you i can say goodbye to my phone. if that happens ill find another way to contact you.*

12:51am: *please, please tell me youre ok*

It's 1:38am now, and there's nothing else from her, which makes me think Paddy probably did take her phone. Willow is a fighter, and there's no way she would have stopped texting me in a situation like this.

I take a shaky breath and remind myself there isn't anything she can do for me right now, anyway. It's safer for her if she stays away. Clearly, my family is now completely blacklisted by the leader of the Irish mob. Darragh Gowan doesn't forget and he definitely doesn't forgive. There's a reason he's called Mad Darragh, and it's not because he's some mad lad, life of the party sort of guy.

Dad, where the hell are you?

The idea that he can fix this, that he's even still alive, feels dimmer and dimmer. I want to weep again, but this time it isn't with relief. I swipe viciously at my eyes and then, before I can talk myself out of it, I dial 9-1-1.

I hold the phone so hard against my ear it hurts. When the operator answers, "9-1-1 emergency services, do you require ambulance, police, or fire?" her voice seems way too loud in the space. Cringing, I notice the water has stopped running in the bathroom. I turn my back, hunching forward, trying to be as quiet as possible.

"Police," I whisper, heart in my throat.

A moment later, another voice is on the line, this time a man.

"Toronto police service. What is your location?"

"I... I don't know. Brindle Path. I don't know the address."

"Ma'am, I'm going to need you to speak up, please."

He sounds bored, almost irritated with me for being too quiet.

Damn it! How am I supposed to speak up when the man who abducted me is right in the next room? *Maybe you should just listen fucking harder!*

Despite my desperate frustration, I try to make my whisper less muffled. It comes out in a shaky, shouty hiss.

"I've been abducted. I'm at a house on Brindle Path. Please, I need help!"

"Are you alone? Is anyone with you?"

My insides turn to ice when a huge gloved hand closes over mine. Elio lifts my hand, and the phone, away from my ear and holds it in front of his face, stretching my arm upward. His expression is unreadable, his voice smooth, deep, and undeniably authoritative as he says, "She's not alone. She's under the care of Elio Titone."

There's a pause on the other end. My chest hurts with the force of my heartbeat. It's so loud I almost don't hear the officer's reply.

"Mr. Titone! Honour to speak with you, Sir. There's no problem here. No problem at all. I'll disconnect the call now and I hope you have a pleasant evening."

Elio doesn't say anything else, and my throat constricts when the unmistakable sound of the dial tone punctuates the air. Disbelief mingles with fury. I can't believe I've been abandoned by the very people who are supposed to protect me. The police.

My father.

No. I refuse to believe my father's given up on me. He may have done something incredibly fucking stupid, but he's clever by nature. I have to have faith that he'll get me out of this. That he's still the man I always thought he was. *I have to.*

"I told you this wouldn't do you any good in here," Elio says. For a second, I wonder if he's going to smash my phone. Or maybe me. But instead, he just holds it out to me. I'm shocked by the lack of violence in the gesture but I understand instantly it isn't one of generosity. He's not giving me my phone back as a gift or an olive branch. He's giving it back because he's so fucking powerful it doesn't matter who I contact, who I call, who I beg for help. I'm in his world now. His domain, under his rule.

She's under the care of Elio Titone.

That's what he said. *Care*. What a crock of shit.

I stare at the screen in a daze, afraid to take it and afraid not to. I don't know what he's thinking, what he wants right now, and I'm too exhausted to try to figure it out. When I don't move, Elio leans forward and slides it into my pocket for me. His hand at my hip, so close to my groin, makes adrenaline jolt through me. His thick black hair is wet and messy, and the slick, curling tendrils brush my cheek. I shiver as a single drop of water rolls down to my jaw, then down my neck, making goosebumps rise. His breath is a heated fan over my skin as he draws away. He straightens and stares at me, his expression still unreadable. Bits of hair made rebellious by moisture curl over eyes like smouldering coal. He's basically dressed the same as before just without the ear piece and shirt – wearing black dress pants and shoes and leather gloves. The leather doesn't look wet. *So he does take them off sometimes.*

Once again, just like when he first took off his shirt for the doctor, I'm overwhelmed by the hard, masculine bulk of him. At first glance, the scars are what draw my eye. The slashes and deep marks, so many I can't even count them all. Then there's the vicious, roiling red of healed burns on his shoulder, neck, and jaw. But even with those scars, there's a brutal, unrelenting allure in his form. The flexing of hard muscle dusted with dark hair that makes my stomach tighten involuntarily.

God, I hope the next time I see him he's got a shirt on.

And that I have one on, too.

When his eyes dip downward, I'm reminded of just how exposed I am. His jacket is huge on me, and its done-up front button sags somewhere in the vicinity of my navel, leaving a plunging view of cleavage. Drawing the sides of the jacket together sharply, I turn and grab my violin and bow.

"You said something about a room?" I ask tersely. I don't particularly want to see what cold, dark corner Elio plans to put me in, but at this point anything is better than being in a room with him.

His gaze shifts to the door near the bed. The one I assumed led into a closet.

"In there."

I start to panic at the thought that I'm going to be imprisoned in a small space. A tiny, lightless closet right beside his bed. I shake my head rapidly, stumbling backwards. Elio ignores me, striding to the door and opening it.

It's not a closet. It's not a prison cell.

It's *beautiful*.

I can't see much from here, looking through the doorway. But what I do see takes my breath away. It's a totally different vibe from the clean, almost minimalist feel of Elio's room. The hardwood floor shines, polished to a rich gleam. The large bed I see from here doesn't have a metal frame, but is one of those wooden four-poster beds I always associate with princesses in movies, piled high with heavy crimson bedding and about a dozen luxurious matching pillows with golden threads at the seams. Floor lamps on either side of the bed cast a softly shimmering glow. Elio stands beside the open door, watching me, waiting for me to go in.

There's no way to avoid it, so I walk past him into the bedroom. The rest of it is just as lovely and sumptuous as the bed. Another door stands open, giving me a view into a glittering bathroom. I turn to look at the rest...

And freeze.

Elio stands in the doorway, and flanking him all along

the walls are shelf after shelf of slim books I recognize instantly as sheet music. And not just sheet music. There's a sheet music stand, extra strings, duster cloths, and box upon box upon box of rosin for my bow. It's like somebody searched the internet for *what do violinists need?* and then bought the entire list ten times over. I place down my violin and bow on a small, pretty desk and try to take it all in.

Did Elio do this?

I can't imagine him doing anything even remotely like buying these things. He probably has people to do that stuff for him. But he would have had to have given the command in the first place...

"Like it?"

His question startles me. He's leaning against the door frame, arms crossed.

"Would it even matter if I didn't?" I sigh, because I do like it, and I don't want to like anything he offers me.

Elio doesn't answer, and I raise my chin.

"It doesn't matter if I like it. I don't plan on staying here long."

His dark brows rise in mocking challenge. "Oh?"

I force my voice to remain steady, force myself to fully believe the words as I say, "My dad will find a way to get me out of this. He may owe you money, but there's no way he'd leave me here."

Elio breathes out harshly, his expression darkening.

"Stay here," he mutters as he turns and heads back into the other bedroom. As he goes, my eyes land on the bandaging at his back, covering the wound he got standing between me and the gun that would have killed me. I hold tightly to all the reasons I should hate him so that I don't start sliding into guilt again, into caring that he's hurt.

When he returns, stalking into the room like an agitated

wolf, he thrusts paper at me. Confused, I take it, letting my tired eyes run over the words.

No.

It can't be.

It's a contract. A contract dictating the terms of the loan Elio gave my father. And in the space beside the question of collateral, in my father's handwriting, is my own fucking name. *Deirdre Elizabeth O'Malley.* My father's signature is there, too, at the bottom of the document, as is a savage slash of ink that must be Elio's. Between the signatures, binding the agreement, is a red wax seal.

"Still think he's coming for you?" Elio asks. There's cruelty in his question, a dark taunting that I'm ashamed to admit actually hurts me.

"You're a monster," I whisper.

Elio just takes the paper back from me and rolls it up, aloof and business-like.

"Never said I wasn't. In fact, I'm pretty sure I already told you that I am."

I stare down at my feet through a haze of heated tears. The roll of paper prods beneath my chin until my face is tipped up to Elio's.

"Your father is the sort of bastard I am intimately familiar with," he says quietly, his eyes twin black holes. "I knew he'd never pay me back when I gave him that money. From the very beginning, I didn't consider it a loan, but an *investment.*"

"Why?" I croak. I don't understand any of this. A multi-million-dollar investment into *what*?

He doesn't answer me. He just leans even closer, tucking my hair behind my ear and whispering, "Happy birthday, Songbird."

Before I can even try to figure out what sort of game he's

playing with me, he's gone. The door closes softly behind him, and I can instantly see there's no way to lock it from this side.

There are locks in this house. Locks and walls and bars.

But none of them are to protect me. They're here to cage me.

And Elio is the only one with the key.

Chapter 10

Elio

There's a lock on Deirdre's door, but I don't use it for two reasons.

One: she won't get far even if she opens the door and tries to escape this house.

And two: locking her in there when there's no other way out of her room is piss-poor fire safety.

Her only exit is through my bedroom. Exactly how I wanted it. I'm in my bedroom now, stalking back and forth, shoulder pinging with pain and the back of my neck prickling with awareness that Deirdre's in the very next room. The girl I've watched for the past year and a half, whose music gets into my bloodstream like a drug, is finally here. I've planned for this evening for months.

And despite all that, it actually hasn't gone much to plan at all. There weren't supposed to be other soldiers there tonight.

Fucking O'Malley. He was supposed to fully pay off his debt to the Camorra with my money, not leave another eight hundred grand hanging like that. For an accountant, he has the worst money management skills I've ever fucking seen.

And to top it all off, the original hole he needed to fill – the one that he created by stealing from Darragh's businesses, the reason he's in debt to Sev in the first place – has now been discovered. Mad Darragh's after him. And probably after Deirdre. Not that he'll fucking get her now.

Sev should be easier to deal with than Darragh. Pay O'Malley's debts and then add a little extra for the men I've killed. Should be enough to avoid a war. And if Sev decides he doesn't like that, I can always try to broker a deal with one of the other Camorra clans. Unlike La Cosa Nostra, with a strict hierarchy, the Camorra is much more decentralized, with multiple powerful groups all vying for power. While the Titones are the ruling Cosa Nostra family in Toronto, there are three more or less equal Camorra clans active in Ontario. If I need to, I can pit one or both of the others against Sev.

Darragh's going to be more of a challenge. The man holds grudges like a Sicilian. I won't be able to hand him a cheque to make him go away.

Severu and Darragh. Two very rich and bloodthirsty men. Two complications I don't need right now.

I don't like complications. Typically, I just shoot them in the head. Probably not the best course of action in this case.

But despite it all, despite the problems and the obstacles and the way this night has kind of gone to shit, I have her.

And ultimately, that is all that fucking matters.

My mind is on her again, wondering what she's doing on the other side of that door. Wondering if she's still wearing my jacket. Instantly, I'm overcome with the vicious need to get that jacket back when she's done with it. I don't care that it's crusty with my drying blood. I don't care that there's a hole blown open in the back of it. That jacket touched her bare skin and I am fucking keeping it. I pull out my phone and use voice-to-text to send a message to Rosa, our head housekeeper, instructing her not to throw it out.

Or wash it. Ever again.

I'm distracted from thoughts of dry cleaning – *Cristo santo*, fucking dry cleaning, never thought I'd see the day – by Curse's voice.

"Uncle Vinny's here."

I turn to my brother who is standing in the open doorway of my bedroom. We're alike in some ways. Both over six feet tall – though he's a little leaner – and same dark hair and eyes. But he got all of our mamma Florencia's beauty. Now that he's twenty-eight, the cherubic look his face used to have is gone, replaced with high, hard angles. He's scarred now, too, just like me. But at least he never burned. I made sure of that.

My fingers stretch and curl inside my gloves as I walk to my closet and grab a black dress shirt. Uncle Vinny may be largely a figurehead these days, with most of the real power resting in my hands, but even so, I know he won't tolerate me walking into a family meeting half-dressed. He's probably already going to be up my ass about Sev's men, and I don't need the added headache of him harping on about my lack of dress and decorum.

"Where is he?"

"In your office. Aunt Carlotta and Valentina, too."

"He had to bring the women?" Do Zizi and Valentina, my aunt and cousin, really need to be there while I update Uncle Vinny on how many men we shot tonight?

Curse shrugs.

"You know how Valentina is. Now that she's eighteen she insists on being part of the family business. And Zizi insists on chaperoning even though she hates this shit."

That's an understatement. Zizi tends to wrinkle her nose and ignore the gory details of the family business. Doesn't have any problem spending the millions of dollars that very same business dumps into her bank account, though.

I start doing up the buttons and swear at the shooting pain down my left arm, the weakness in my fingers. I let my arm fall useless to my side, remembering Morelli's comment about the sling. I start doing the buttons up with only my right hand, but that shit's a lot harder one-handed than undoing them.

In an instant, Curse is in the room. For a guy almost as big as me, he doesn't make a sound. Part of what makes him such a good killer. He moves like a ghost.

He doesn't say anything, and neither do I, as he starts deftly doing up the buttons. I watch his fingers as they move quickly and precisely up the length of my shirt. Even when I don't have a bullet wound in my back, his fingers move more easily than mine. The scar tissue on my hands makes some small, repetitive movements, like writing with a pen, a pain in the ass. Luckily, I don't have any problems firing a gun.

As he does up the last button at the top, my eyes catch on the name tattooed across both sets of his knuckles, one letter per finger and thumb. F L O R E N C I A, followed by a bloom of frangipani, Sicily's flower, on his pinkie. He pats my cheek firmly as he finishes and nods, and when he turns from me I wonder what he would have been like, what *we* would have been like, if the beginning of our lives had been different. If we hadn't lost what we'd lost.

If our piece of shit papà had died that night instead of our mamma.

But they're both dead now, and there's nowhere to go

but forward. Unless you want the past to rise up and drown you, you have to keep putting one foot in front of the other, over and over again, until you reach the future you want, the future you've created with sweat and gunpowder and blood.

That, or you're in the fucking ground.

I follow Curse out of the room. As I pass the door that leads to Deirdre's quarters, my inhale is a little too hard, my heartbeat just a little too quick. I shake it off and head for the stairs.

Curse and I reach the ground floor, passing several guards who nod and mutter deferential greetings as we head for my office at the back of the house. My office door is open, and I can already see Uncle Vinny, Zizi, and Valentina inside. Zizi and Uncle Vinny are seated in the large leather armchairs in front of my desk, while Valentina wanders the room, inspecting the bookcases lining the walls.

Valentina sees me first, her blonde head turning just as I enter the room.

"Elio!" she says warmly, coming around the desk to greet me. Though she's my cousin, she's more like a younger sister. Her parents raised Curse and me as their own, even going so far as to give us their last name. Or maybe they didn't really give us the name Titone. We just took back Mamma's name from before she married the man who'd be the death of her.

Valentina stops short, letting her father greet me first. Uncle Vinny rises from the chair and clasps his hands to either side of my face. I lean down to kiss him on each cheek before turning and doing the same to Zizi, then Valentina. Even though it's past two in the morning, and I don't know if they've come from a New Year's Eve party or they've just rolled out of bed for this, both Valentina and Aunt Carlotta are coiffed and poised. Their hair is perfectly in place – Valentina's natural dark blonde brightened by bleach, Zizi's dyed a deep burgundy colour. Their faces are streaked with all kinds of powdery stuff in shades of pink and bronze and black.

They both love that shit. I wouldn't be surprised if my cousin and aunt are single-handedly keeping Canada's cosmetics industry alive. I asked Valentina to help prepare Deirdre's quarters – she's the one who chose all the décor – and she filled the bathroom with about eight thousand dollar's worth of lotions and potions. It baffles me that soaps and shampoos could possibly cost that much, but I know they do, because it was all charged to my credit card.

Idly, I wonder if Deirdre is using any of the stuff in the bathroom yet. If she's naked and scrubbing herself or if she'll sit in my blood just a little bit longer.

I'm not sure which idea appeals to me more.

I don't get to dwell on it long. Now that the kissing and greetings are out of the way, my uncle gets right down to business.

"So, what the fuck happened tonight?"

Unlike Morelli, Uncle Vinny speaks English and French fluently, though with a much stronger accent than me. When we first settled in Canada, we lived in Montreal, and my uncle pushed himself to learn the languages as swiftly as possible. Zizi did the same – she watched English and French soap operas all day long for years to learn. I'm pretty sure she still watches them, actually. Just doesn't need the subtitles now.

I walk over to my desk and seat myself at the high-backed leather chair there. Zizi sits back down, as does Uncle Vinny. He's much shorter than Curse and me – we got our height from Papà, and Vincenzo is our mamma's brother.

Was our mamma's brother. Twenty years later and it still sometimes feels wrong to say *was*.

But even so, even a head shorter and sitting down in a chair, Vincenzo Titone fills the space. At fifty-five years old, he's only just started going grey at the temples, the rest of his hair coal-black like Curse's and mine. And like Mamma's. His eyes are sharp, and he's built like a bull, broad-shouldered and bulky, wearing a perfectly tailored Brunello Cucinelli suit.

"Had to go get something of mine," I reply coolly.

Uncle Vinny's forehead wrinkles.

"The money you lent that Irish accountant? What the hell's his name again?"

"Jack O'Malley."

"Well, did you get it?"

Valentina's honey-brown eyes flash to mine. She knows what I know. That I never had any real intention of recouping that money. That I went for something, *someone*, else.

"Nope," I say. My shoulder throbs. As does my head. So, like any reasonable man, I take out a bottle of whiskey from the shelf beside my desk. I almost grab Scottish whiskey, but at the last moment go for Irish in honour of my songbird. I grab two scotch glasses, fill them, and raise a brow at my uncle, but he shakes his head and grunts. Valentina reaches for one of the glasses.

"That's not an appropriate drink for a young lady," Uncle Vinny says, pinning her with a hard stare. Valentina smiles, and I want to say it's sweet, but it's not. Not really.

She grabs the drink and holds it aloft in a cheery sort of

salute. "If I'm old enough to get engaged, I'm old enough to drink whiskey."

"Engaged?" I ask. It's the first I'm hearing about this. But as Valentina takes a swig from the glass, I notice the monstrosity of a ring on her finger. I'd have to be blind to miss it – that thing could be seen from outer fucking space. There's a giant pink diamond in the centre surrounded by two circles of smaller pink diamonds, all perched on a rose gold band inlaid with yet more pink diamonds. It looks less like a ring and more like a fucking cupcake to me, but what the hell do I know? Valentina loves pink, and diamonds, so maybe she likes it.

"Now that she's eighteen it's time she does her duty to *la famiglia*," Uncle Vinny says. "Marry well and help grow the Titone empire."

I watch Valentina's face carefully as Uncle Vinny speaks, trying to gauge her reactions. She looks vaguely annoyed, but not overly upset. It's not like she hasn't been groomed for this by her parents since birth, but still, I want to make sure she isn't too unhappy about her husband-to-be.

I still remember the day she was born. I was sixteen and she was a wrinkled little thing who could scream the goddamn house down. I was the third person to hold her, and as my lanky teenage arms tried to awkwardly get her into a comfortable position, she promptly shit on my chest. Staking her claim and telling subtlety to go fuck itself. I smirk at the memory.

Valentina's a force to be reckoned with, but my protective instinct towards her runs deep, and I ask, "Who's the lucky guy?"

"Dario Fabbri," Zizi says, beaming nervously, her eyes flicking back and forth between Valentina and Vinny. She's always been the peace-keeper, trying to smooth over disagreements between her powerful husband and head-strong daughter. "We'll announce it after Valentina's nineteenth birthday in the summer."

Now I know why Valentina only looks mildly annoyed by all of this. Even though she's only eighteen, she could crush a guy like Fabbri under her heel any day of the week. The guy is slimy and skinny with thinning hair and a nasal voice that drives me up the wall every time I hear it on the TV or radio. But his father owns one of the largest real estate development firms in the country, and he's been newly elected a Toronto city councillor, so from a purely business point of view, I can understand the logic of the match.

My head gives a throb of complaint at the idea of having Dario fucking Fabbri yammering on at future family events. I take a sip of my drink, and Valentina follows suit, as if to say, *you and me both.*

"*Basta!* Enough about the engagement. I want to know what happened tonight." Uncle Vinny's eyes are on me. "You didn't get the money, and now we've got three dead Camorra soldiers on our hands."

"I got what I went there for," I say with a shrug that I immediately regret as my sutures pull.

"Got what you went there for? What, a fucking bullet in your back?" Uncle Vinny presses.

"O'Malley's daughter," I say. There's no way to get around it. He'll find out sooner or later.

My uncle's dark eyebrows rise in astonishment.

"You're telling me you're on the verge of starting a war with the Camorra over some freckled fucking *puttana?*" He twists to look at Curse. "This the same girl Darragh wants?"

Curse nods from his place at the door. Red-faced, my uncle turns back to me.

"So, we're going to have Severu Serpico and the Mad fucking Irishman breathing down our necks just because you wanted some tight Irish pussy?"

I stare my uncle down, my grip hard on my drink. Too hard. I owe Uncle Vinny and Zizi everything. They could have left Curse and me to die in Sicily after my father's betrayal if they'd wanted to. But they didn't. They took us with them to Montreal, raised us as their own. Gave us a new chance in a new country, a country that we are slowly but surely bending to our will. I respect my uncle more than most men probably respect their fathers. And for the first time in my life, I want to strangle him.

I don't. Instead, I put down my drink, stand, and keep my tone smooth and deadly as I say, "Deirdre O'Malley is now mine. I will keep her here and do with her as I see fit. This is non-negotiable. If there are consequences, I will deal with them." I slow my speech so that there's no mistaking my next words. "But the one thing I will not do is let *anyone* take her from this house."

My uncle's nostrils flare, and his jaw works. He's pissed – no, *enraged* – by what I've done and the fact I'm standing against him now. But he understands that arguing with me is useless. He knows me too well, knows what kind of will I possess when I get close to what I want, and what I want is Deirdre. Besides, I'm his heir. His underboss. I'm the closest thing he has to an eldest son and Aunt Carlotta can't have any more children. He's handed over more and more power to me over the years and he knows that if I wanted to, I could upend this entire operation, start a war within our own ranks. A war that I would win.

A feminine voice breaks the tense silence that follows my words.

"She's here now?" It's Valentina asking. I nod without

looking at her. From the corner of my eye, I see her leave the room. Zizi clicks her tongue anxiously, swivelling in her chair and calling Valentina back to no avail.

I turn to my desk and open one of the drawers.

"Now, if you'll excuse me," I say taking one last sip of my drink before grabbing a pen, "I have a rather large cheque to write to Severu Serpico."

"Fine," my uncle says tightly, rising to go. "You can give it to him at the gala tomorrow night. No doubt he'll show his pretty face. Let's hope he doesn't turn it into a fucking bloodbath."

I forgot about the goddamn gala. There's always something on our social calendar and it usually involves a bunch of rich bastards toasting our latest charitable donation. Events like that are a way to remind this city that the Titones can give as much as they take. I don't even know what tomorrow's gala is celebrating. Zizi and Valentina always plan these things. I just write the cheques.

"It's at the Art Gallery of Ontario. The new wing we paid for," Zizi reminds me. I decide not to comment on the fact that planning a gala for the evening of January 1st is stupid and that everyone's going to be hungover. It was probably Valentina's idea. She hates when parties or holidays end and always wants to drag things out as long as possible. New Year's Eve 2.0.

The goodbye kisses are short and perfunctory. I know these two well enough to be able to tell from their body language that Zizi's anxious as hell and Uncle Vinny is still furious. But ultimately, my uncle trusts me. He knows I take care of shit when it counts.

When they're gone, Curse approaches my desk. I sit down, grab my chequebook, and start scrawling a whole lot of zeroes after the number one.

"Didn't get a chance to tell you before. But I've got a line on O'Malley."

My pen halts. I look up at Curse.

"And?"

"And it looks like he's ditched his credit cards and his phone. But one of my contacts at Pearson Airport reported that he just used cash to buy a last-minute ticket to Bermuda. Flight leaves in," he checks his watch, "eighteen minutes." My brother looks at me. "Do you want me to get him off that plane? I can make a call."

Bermuda. Nice little island. Also a tax haven. I wonder how much money O'Malley has stashed there. Money he's using to save his own skin instead of his fucking daughter's.

I'm furious on Deirdre's behalf, livid that he could leave her here. But even though I'm angry, I'm not surprised. This story has played out in my own life, and it's one I know all too well. The image of my father running from the flames, running from his own fucking family, is so seared into my brain that I can conjure it up perfectly.

He only turned back to look at me once. Turned back to see his eldest son in the flames. He watched me punching through an eight-year-old Curse's burning door, melting my own fucking skin to save his younger son the way he should have.

He fucking *saw me*. Saw me burning and fighting for our family. Heard Mamma screaming and Curse crying. He stood in the carnage his own betrayal had created, whispered, *Dio me pardoni*, then turned and fled.

It wasn't God he should have been begging for forgiveness, but me.

He did beg me, in the end.

Not that it did him any good.

I finish writing the cheque, hating my dead father as I

73

do it. I hate O'Malley, too, for what he's done to Deirdre. And maybe that's hypocritical, because I'm far worse a man than the greedy Irish fool. He sold Deirdre, but I'm the monster who bought her.

"Let him go," I tell Curse. I got what I wanted out of O'Malley. I have no use for any of the money he has left, and honestly? I want him as far from Deirdre as possible.

Normally, I'd just kill him. Both for trying to screw me over and for the crime of what he's done to Deirdre. I have a real fucking thing about fathers failing their families, something my papà learned the hard, bloody way. But even after showing her the contract, I get the impression that Deirdre is still holding out hope her father will come back for her. That she still loves him even though he sure as hell doesn't deserve it. If I kill him, she will grieve him, and I don't want her wasting a single second of attention or emotion on her piece of shit progenitor.

The only man who will matter in her life from this day forward is me. I will be the only one she feels anything for.

Even if that feeling is hate.

Chapter 11

Deirdre

After Elio leaves, I stand silently in the room for a long time. I'm exhausted but too tired even to move or to sit down. I stare at all the music stuff, a shrine to violin, barely seeing it.

He really does want me to play for him.

I don't understand it, but it seems to be true. He brought me here for my music. The only question now is why?

Something he said to me earlier in the night comes back to me. When we were alone in the darkness. *There's something inside of you I need to understand.* I close my eyes, trying to remember what else he's said, but this entire night is like a broken mirror in my head. Some bits and pieces are clear before cracking and leading into darkness. I can't put it all back together right now.

I sway on my feet, then force myself into movement, heading for the bathroom. It's just as gorgeous as the bedroom. It has the same natural grey stone I've seen elsewhere in the house for the floor, along with the biggest bathtub I've ever seen and a giant shower in the corner, enclosed by glass. There are a few switches on the wall, and I learn quickly that one of them is for a floor heater as warmth flows into the soles of my feet.

I catch sight of myself in the mirror and gawk.

I look like a fucking mess. Mascara rings my eyes and is smudged along my freckled cheeks. My hair is a tangled disaster, and my outfit is even worse. The top half of my dress is basically destroyed, hanging down in front of my hips and legs like an apron. My upper body is swimming in Elio's jacket, far too large for me.

For some reason, I don't rip the jacket off my body. Not at first, anyway. I let my fingers drift over the beautiful black fabric, tracing the perfect stitching. Every time I move, the silk lining drags over my nipples creating a resounding twinge between my legs.

What the fuck am I doing?

I cry out with confusion and disgust at myself, tearing the jacket down over my shoulders and letting it fall to the warm stone floor. I kick it as far away from myself as I can.

But now my reflection looks even worse. My front is streaked with dark blood. Elio's blood.

He bled for me.

Then trapped me here.

I go to the bathroom door and close it. Once again, there's no lock, and I purse my lips, weighing my options. I can stay bloody and sweaty and try to tie my dress up like a halter around my neck.

Or I can risk Elio walking in on me in the shower.

I can't get that image out of my mind. The huge man with the leather gloves striding in here like he owns the place because he *does*. His dark eyes tracking over my wet, naked body.

At least there are towels in here. If I have to, I can cover myself with something quickly. And it's not just towels in here. A quick look in the cupboards under the marble countertop tells me the room is better-stocked than a spa. Bottle upon bottle of shampoo, conditioner, moisturizing lotion, perfume. Serums and sunscreens and exfoliating acids. There's makeup, too. Face masks. Even a waxing kit.

One thing I don't see, though, is a razor.

I guess they don't want me to have anything sharp.

I survey the expansive, *expensive* array of bath products, noticing yet more bottles in the shower, and wonder if all of this was already here or if it was brought here just for me. I can't imagine that all the violin stuff was just hanging around this room – who else but me would use it? It had to have been purchased for my arrival.

I hurry over to the bathroom door, opening it and peeking out to make sure Elio hasn't returned to the room, then close it again. I put my phone on the counter, then I hurry out of my dress, leaving it in a wrinkled heap along with my panties and then hustle over to the shower.

At the last second, I change course for the bathtub. The adrenaline of the night is starting to dump out of my system, leaving my legs weak and wobbly. The last thing I need is to fall over in the shower, hit my head, and be naked and unconscious in this house.

I start running the bath, marvelling at just how huge it is. It has jets, too. I grab some body wash and shampoo and conditioner from the shower and get into the tub.

I breathe out slowly as the hot water fills the tub, running over my legs, soothing my shaking muscles. The body wash smells incredible, and I hate it. I try not to breathe in the tempting luxury of the scent as I use the suds to scrub every inch of my body until my skin is pink and sensitive. I do the same to my hair, scraping my scalp with soapy fingernails. As I work the shampoo violently against my scalp, flashes of the night go through my head. Gunfire ripping through my memories. My father running. That man with the gun getting shot in the head and stuffed into Curse's trunk.

I realize I'm gripping my hair so hard it hurts, making fists around the sudsy strands. I let go, then plunge backwards until my head is submerged in the water. And I stay there. It's a game I've played with myself ever since Mom died. Tipping back into the hot water and holding my breath for as long as I possibly can. Letting the ominous rush of the water block out everything else. Waiting, lungs burning, until the last possible moment before resurfacing. The euphoria that spikes through my body when I breathe again is like nothing else I've experienced. I feel that high everywhere – my chest, my head. Even between my legs.

The longest I ever lasted was a minute and forty-two seconds. Eyes scrunched shut, the tap still thundering fresh water into the bath, I start counting.

I only get to thirty-eight when a hand reaches into the bath, touching my shoulder.

The shock of the contact makes me inhale water. I sit up, coughing violently, eyes streaming.

"Holy hell, sorry! Sorry! Jesus, you looked fucking dead in there!"

I slap one hand across my chest and scrape soaking hair away from my face with the other. Right away, just from the voice, I know it's not Elio. I would have known even before hearing the voice. He wouldn't have grasped my shoulder that gently. He would have ripped me right out of the water.

A beautiful young woman is crouching beside the bathtub. She's my age, or maybe a little younger, her loose, dark blonde curls with ombre highlights framing her heart-shaped face. Her eyes are narrowed as they take me in – warm, golden-brown irises framed by very long, spiky black eyelashes. Her shiny pink lips are puckered in a concerned sort of frown.

"Nope," I say raggedly, my throat feeling water-logged. "Not dead."

Her face relaxes a little, a smile tugging at her lips.

"Well, good. Who's gonna use all this shit I bought if you don't?" She gestures at the shampoo and body wash at the side of the tub.

"You bought all this stuff?" As I ask the question, I scoot over to the other side of the bath, turning off the water. Then I swivel back to look at the girl who's appeared in this bathroom like some kind of fairy.

"Yup. Elio asked me to get the room ready for you. He paid for it all, of course. What do you think of this one?" She raised up the body wash that had smelled so heavenly. "It's one of my favourites."

There's something disarming about her. I have no idea who she is, and I'm naked, but she's chatting to me like we've known each other forever.

But I can't afford to be disarmed. Not here. Not now.

"Elio paid for all this? What, is it all getting added onto my debt?" I ask, voice flinty. I cross both my arms over my chest and hunch down into the water.

"Oof. Yeah. Heard about that. What is it, five mil?"

"Make that six," I grind out.

She sighs and puts her elbows on the edge of the tub, placing her delicate chin onto her interlocked fingers.

"We've all got debts," she says softly. "Prices we have to pay just to occupy our rightful place. Some of us are saddled with that shit the second we are born." Her gaze drifts down to a ring on her left hand – an engagement ring. She grimaces as she inspects it closer before flipping her hand to show me. "Ugly, isn't it?"

It's... something. I'm not sure anything with that many diamonds could be called *ugly*, but it's certainly not something I would call tasteful.

"You're engaged?"

"Yup," she says flippantly, rolling her eyes. "To the human equivalent of a skid mark."

Once again, I find myself totally disarmed by her. Beneath the perfectly applied makeup is a very young face. She looks like she could be in high school and she's *engaged*.

Despite the walls I've tried to put up, I can't help but feel a sense of kinship towards her. We're both caught in situations we clearly don't want to be in. For a split second, I honestly wonder if hers is worse. I may be subject to Elio's whims, but at least I'm not engaged to the guy.

I roll my lower lip between my teeth, deciding if I should shut down, shut her out, or if I should give into the instinct that she may be a kind of ally for me here. She clearly has free reign of this house, which means she's got at least some sort of power. Plus, as much as I don't want to admit it, I like her. Her forthright, almost blasé nature reminds me a little bit of Willow. Maybe it's stupid to trust her, but I could really use a friend in here.

"I'm Deirdre. Deirdre O'Malley," I say, giving her a tentative smile. I want to offer her my hand to shake, but its soaking wet, and I'm naked, and it just seems weird.

She clearly doesn't feel the weirdness, though. She grins at me and holds out her own hand to shake. With a wobbly laugh, I take it.

"Oh, trust me, you don't need to tell me your name. I know it. I've been working my ass off the past month getting the room perfect for you under Elio's supervision. What do you think of the bedspread? Beautiful, right?"

"Yes, it is," I say weakly. I am getting whiplash. First, I'm abducted out of my own house and told I'm massively in debt to the mafia, and now I'm finding out the luxury of that room was completely prepared just for me?

"Did you choose all the violin stuff, too?" I ask.

She shakes her head as she lets go of my hand.

"Nope. That was all Elio. He's fucking obsessed. Never seen him spend so much time researching mundane shit like what kind of cloths are best to clean a violin. God, he spent like a week on that! And don't get me started on those little boxes of waxy shit for the bow strings. Picking the brand was like choosing a name for his firstborn child."

I literally can't picture a single thing she's telling me. Whether she's telling the truth or not, she clearly knows Elio well. She spends a lot of time with him and doesn't seem afraid of him. And she obviously just walked through his bedroom unaccompanied.

I wonder what her relationship to him is. A funny, ugly sort of knot forms low in my belly.

"Is he... is he your fiancé?"

Her glossy mouth falls open, and then she gives a hoot of laughter.

"Hell, no! Miss me with that incest shit!" She gives a dramatic, exaggerated sort of shiver. "Got the fucking heebie jeebies now."

"Sorry," I stammer. "I'm just trying to figure out what's going on."

"No, no. It's OK. I probably should have introduced myself first before droning on and on about Elio's newfound horniness for all things violin." She tosses her long curls behind her shoulder. "I'm Valentina Titone. Elio's cousin."

Elio's cousin...

Vincenzo Titone's daughter.

I don't know what I was expecting, but I wasn't expecting this. That the Don's only child would be crouching beside my bathtub and talking to me so casually.

So, it looks like I'm gal pals with a mafia princess now.

But despite the shock of it, I'm glad she came in here.

"Hi Valentina. I'd say it's nice to meet you, but..."

"But circumstances prevent it?" she raises a flawlessly groomed brow and smirks.

Yeah, I really do like her. Can't help it. She's cute and clever and in a way is even more trapped than I am. She makes me feel a little less alone.

She rises and turns to look out the bathroom door she left open.

"Mamma and Papà are going to be looking for me. I'd better head back down." Her brows take on a pinched look. "Are you going to be OK in here?"

I can't hold back the bitter snort at that question.

"Tell your cousin to let me go and I might be OK."

The pinched look deepens.

"Hon, if what I hear is true and both Sev and Darragh are looking for you and your father, then there's nowhere safer in this city for you than here."

I seriously doubt that, but I don't get a chance to respond. A sound outside, beyond the bedrooms in the hallway, has distracted her.

"Could you close the door?" I cry after her as she turns and hurries away, high heels clacking on the stone.

I draw my knees up to my chest and wonder if I maybe shouldn't trust Valentina too much after all. I'm *sure* she hears me as she goes.

But she leaves the door open anyway.

Chapter 12

Elio

Valentina nearly collides with me in the hallway on her way out of my bedroom. I'm not sure I like how comfortable she's gotten going into my room whenever she pleases, but it was necessary for her to be able to get Deirdre's room ready when I wasn't around.

"Wondered where you'd gotten to," I mutter. I go to move past her into my bedroom, but she plants her hands on her hips and stares at me.

"What?" I grunt.

"I met Deirdre."

"And?"

"And she's sweet."

"Hmm. Haven't experienced that side of her myself," I reply as I step past her and into my room. I'm sure Deirdre can be sweet to other people. To me she's been a bit of a viper. I've got the teeth marks in my scarred finger to prove it.

"I'm serious, Elio."

Something in Valentina's tone makes me stop and turn. My cousin is smart as hell, but she hides it well when she wants to, behind loud laughter and inane conversation. But she's not laughing now. She suddenly looks about ten years older than she really is, her face sober.

"You're serious about the fact that she's sweet? Fine, I believe you," I snap. But something prickles along the back of my neck. Dread.

"She's not cut out for this. She's not from our world."

Fucking hell, I need another drink.

"Her father's an accountant for the Irish mob. Not exactly a white picket fence family," I remind her.

I can tell by the mulish fucking set to her mouth that she's not done with this conversation.

"You know what I mean! You need to be careful with her! I just went in there and she looked fucking shell-shocked! She's gonna have PTSD or some shit."

"She'll get over it."

Valentina gives a short, brittle laugh.

"Oh, like you and Curse did? You gonna tell me your brother doesn't torture men before he kills them just to keep his demons quiet?" Her voice lowers, but doesn't soften. If anything, it sharpens, like a knife. "You gonna look me in the eye and tell me you don't still have nightmares?"

Valentina's the only woman in my family I'll let talk to me like this, but even she can tell she's gone too far. She snaps her mouth shut at my expression and crosses her arms. I take a moment to compose myself before I explode. When I speak, my voice is icy with control.

"I asked for your help with soap and girl clothes and fucking bedsheets. That's it. I don't need your advice beyond that, and if I want to hear another word out of your mouth, I will fucking ask for it."

She hesitates, but because it's Valentina who couldn't

keep her trap shut even if she tried, she has to get in the last word.

"All I'm saying is, if you're not careful, you're going to have agonized over music books and strings and stands for nothing. There will be no one to use them because she'll be dead. You wanted no sharp things in the bathroom? Fine. No razors, no nail clippers, there's not even a pair of goddamn tweezers. But there are other ways to hurt yourself if you really want to do it. Other ways to make it end."

In a second, I've got her, my hands wrapping around her upper arms and squeezing.

"What the fuck are you talking about?" I've never laid a hand on Valentina like this. But what she just said about Deirdre dying has snapped something inside me. Some vital thread of control.

She glares at me for a long moment, as if considering if she should answer me.

"Valentina," I growl, her name a warning. I don't like to be kept waiting. And she knows this.

My cousin lets out a short breath then says, "When I went in there, she was in the bath. Under the water. Not moving."

My feet take steps before my brain can even tell them to. As I slam towards Deirdre's bathroom, my mind runs over and over the calculations of how long she's been alone. How long did I stand there arguing with my cousin? Two minutes? Five? Somewhere in the house I hear my uncle calling for his daughter, and Valentina leaves.

I don't stop until I reach the bathroom and I find Deirdre, not in the bath, but standing with a fluffy white towel wrapped around herself. She jumps and swears, then grabs her towel so it doesn't fall down, hugging it to herself. I stare at her long and hard, as if to make sure she's really still breathing, and she stares right back, eyes wide but defiant.

Fuck. Now that I know she's OK, I realize just how close I am to her in the room. Nothing but a couple of steps and that towel between us. Her hair is soaked, the gingery red turned to the colour of old blood by the water.

I've lost blood. My shoulder and head are aching.

And my dick doesn't care. It's already responding to her, thickening in the crotch of my pants. I had her dress half-torn off while holding her against me earlier, but somehow this is even more erotic. She's stripped of everything. Clothing, makeup, blood. All that's left is her, moisture on her clean skin, running in shimmering little rivers down her chest and legs. I lick my lips, suddenly aware of how fucking thirsty I am. How much I want to put my mouth on her skin and suck.

I don't. I turn from the room, heading back to my bedroom. I go into the closet, rummaging at the back. There's a toolkit back there somewhere, and I find it, taking out a hammer. I should probably use a drill to reduce the damage, but I'm too pissed off for precision. When Deirdre sees me with the hammer in my hand, she stumbles backward to the other end of the bathroom and away from me.

But the hammer's not for her. Turning, I aim a heavy blow at the top hinge of the door. I strike it over and over again until the metal warps and the screws sag out of the wall. Then I crouch, doing the same to the bottom hinge, until the whole door is hanging on by a thread, wobbly as a baby tooth. I toss the hammer down and seize it. I can feel my muscles straining, sutures pulling, but I don't stop until the door has come loose and I toss it, useless, to the floor.

"What are you doing?" Deirdre whispers, fear and anger warring on her face.

"Taking off this door."

"I can see that! But *why* are you doing it?"

I don't answer her. Don't tell her that the thought of her dying in my house makes me feel like there's smoke in my eyes and in my lungs. Like there's fire all around me, like I'm fourteen again and I can't fucking breathe. Instead, I just point to a small dot in the corner of the ceiling. Deirdre's gaze follows my finger and she gasps.

"Is that a camera?"

"There are cameras in every room of this house," I tell her. There are even cameras in my rooms. But the feeds to the cameras in her rooms and mine are the only ones that don't go to the main security hub of the house. They're private feeds that go directly to an app on my phone and laptop. No one else has access to them, not even Curse or Enzo, my head of security.

But she doesn't need to know that. The more eyes she thinks are on her at all times, the less stupid shit she's likely to pull.

"This is insane," she says, shaking her head. "You are insane."

I don't reply to that. I just grab my hammer and head out of the bathroom. She follows me, fury rising in her voice.

"I am absolutely not using that bathroom if there's no door! I'll just use your bathroom."

"Be my guest," I tell her, hefting the hammer when I reach the bathroom in question. "Because I'm taking that door off, too."

I end up taking down three doors and tossing them out into the hallway. Both bathroom doors and the door that separates our bedrooms from each other. Deirdre watches me the entire time, clutching her towel like it's armour.

When I'm done, I take the hammer back to my closet. At the last moment, I decide to toss it, along with the other tools, into the safe. Some of those tools could do some real damage to a person, and if Deirdre doesn't hurt herself, she may decide to smash my head in with a hammer in my sleep. Since I'd prefer to keep my brains inside my skull, I lock the safe.

I stand and turn, catching sight of my Songbird in her room, no door between us. This night may not have gone completely to plan, but something about this feels right. Deirdre here now, in a room that may as well be my own without a door for separation. I turn off the light in my room which makes hers glow all the brighter. I see her standing there through the open doorway like an angel illuminated. Watching me in the darkness from her place in the light.

With her eyes on me, I start to undress. I shed my dress shirt and then move to my belt. I don't miss Deirdre's sharp intake of breath and the way her eyes dip to my fingers as they undo the buckle and peel down the zipper. I let my pants fall, fully aware of how my thickened cock has created a bulge in my underwear. Deirdre's grip tightens on her towel, her knuckles bone-white.

But she doesn't look away. She's transfixed. Like she's fucking entranced. I wonder if there's something a little bit sordid inside my Songbird, because she's staring at my crotch like it's hypnotized her, and I don't think it's entirely due to fear.

I may as well finish this. I sleep naked, and I don't plan on changing that just because she's in the other room. I kick off shoes, socks, pants, then lose my underwear, letting my shaft bob free. Colour rises in Deirdre's cheeks, and fuck, I'm about to get all the way hard at this rate, just from her staring. Her gaze on my dick is like a physical touch, a shivering caress of contact. *All that violin playing probably gives her strong fingers. A tight fucking grip.*

That thought makes my dick twitch, a noticeable throb of movement. It breaks whatever spell has held her in place, and she scurries away to the light switch in her own room, turning off the overhead lights before switching off her bedside lamps. I stay where I am, listening for her, catching the sounds of her rustling through the closet that Valentina's stocked for her. When I catch a shadowy glimpse of her again, it looks like she's wearing some sort of pyjama set. Shorts and a silky top with skinny straps, her wet hair in a clump, twisting like a snake down her back.

I expect her to get into bed, but she doesn't. She retreats into the doorless bathroom, keeping the lights off, and stays there. Silence tells me she's not running water or doing much of anything else in there, and I realize she's waiting for me to move away. She's hiding from me with nothing but shadows as her shield.

It's pointless, really. You can't use darkness to hide from a monster. It's like using water to hide from a shark. While bleeding. *Profusely.*

I chuckle, my breath stirring the air. I wonder if she hears it. If the sound makes her tense up. Frightens her or infuriates her.

I move away from the door, grabbing my gun out of the pile of clothes on the floor. I shove it under my pillow, then lay my head down on top so there's no way for her to get to it without waking me. I'm a light sleeper. Have been since fourteen.

I stay awake, listening until I hear the quiet but unmistakable slip of Deirdre's body between bedsheets. She's exactly where I want her. Where I've wanted her since she was eighteen years old and I saw her making music in that sundress on a hot summer's day.

She's finally here. Snug as a bug in the bed I paid for. In the house I own. In the city I rule.

Even though my dick is aching and my shoulder's pounding, there's a satisfied smirk on my lips as I finally close my eyes.

Chapter 13

Deirdre

I wake up slowly, not wanting to become fully conscious. The blankets are so heavy and warm, cocooning me, and I snuggle down. The mattress is different. Newer and better. The pillow is different, too. So plush it's like I'm in a cloud rather than a bed.

It feels amazing.

And it feels wrong.

This isn't my bed.

My eyes fly open, and I sit up like I've been electrocuted. I hold the blankets around myself, looking at the room, remembering everything that happened last night. I swallow, my throat tight and dry, as I stare ahead through the open doorway that leads into Elio's room.

I don't see him, but it almost doesn't matter. The sight of him standing there, a shadowy figure illuminated only by the glow of light spilling from my room, is burned into my brain from last night.

My whole body flushes hot with shame. I stared at him. Like, *really* stared at him. He undressed, and I couldn't take my eyes off of him, off of the thick bulge beneath the smooth black fabric of his underwear. And then, when he took those off...

I groan, burying my head in my hands. What the fuck is wrong with me? When his cock was out, huge and long, my heart was going absolutely ballistic. Part of it was fear, but a larger part, a part I want to run away from and deny, was wondering how hot and smooth his skin there would feel under my fingertips.

It's a completely different reaction from when I was with Brian. When I was in Brian's bedroom that night, I'd been completely repulsed by him and the situation. It was like my entire body shut down with the fear. Everything turning to ice.

Elio is a thousand times more dangerous than a guy like Brian. There's no denying the huge, masculine threat of him – the power in that muscled, scarred body. So my response to him doesn't make sense. I shouldn't have been staring at his half-hard dick, wondering what it would look like fully erect. I should have been terrified out of my wits. But I wasn't frozen, my blood cold in my veins. I felt like I was on fire.

I'm not as scared of Elio as I should be. And that is fucking dangerous.

I press the heels of my hands against my eyes and rub. My eyes feel dry and grainy, and I'm dying for something to drink.

The sound of a door opening, then a clattering, rolling sound, makes my head jerk up. I relax slightly when I see that it's not Elio, but rather a short, round woman with greying hair tied in a bun at the back of her head. She's pushing a cart on wheels, and I gawk at the feast laid out on the tray on top.

"Breakfast, breakfast!" she says in a thick Italian accent. "Food. *Caffè*."

"Hello," I say tentatively as the woman brings the cart to a stop beside the bed. There are pastries, warm slices of buttered toast, a cup of yogurt drizzled with honey, and what looks like espresso in a small cup. I could definitely go for some caffeine right now, but I've never been much of a coffee drinker.

"Do you have tea, by any chance? Irish breakfast?"

The woman looks at me like I just spat on her mother's grave.

Coffee it is. It was probably stupid for me to ask for something else, anyway. I'm not a guest here. I'm a prisoner.

I pick up the small cup and take a tentative sip, wincing at the bitterly strong flavour that coats my tongue. The woman is watching me and mutters something in Italian that sounds kind of judgmental. She sighs and plants her hands on her hips then says, "Tomorrow, *caffè macchiato?* Some milk?"

I nod and smile weakly. "Maybe with some sugar?"

She snorts and tosses her hands up in a resigned sort of gesture.

"Thank you," I say, not wanting to offend her further when clearly my taste in drinks already has. I can't afford to push away any allies, even if they work for Elio. "I'm Deirdre."

"*Si, si,* I know," she says as she unloads the food onto the bedside table.

"What's your name?" I ask her, though she doesn't really seem up for much conversation. I take another swig of the espresso as an expression of goodwill, hoping it will encourage her.

"Rosa. I cook for Mr. Titone. Clean. Keep the house nice." At those last words, she glares at the doorway that leads into the bathroom, noticing the chunks of plaster and flakes of paint left behind by Elio's hammer rampage. She opens the cupboard-like doors on her cart and takes out a small handheld vacuum, marching over to the mess like a soldier. For someone who's got to be at least sixty, she attacks the mess with gusto, grumbling in Italian the entire time.

Now that she's preoccupied and won't notice, I put down the espresso. Thankfully, there's also a glass of ice water, and I chug it. Rosa finishes vacuuming, then returns to her cart for a rag and a spray bottle, heading for the bathroom.

I realize at that moment I desperately have to pee. For some reason I don't think Rosa would take it well if I went in there and interrupted her cleaning process.

Which means crossing my legs and waiting. Or...

Or using his bathroom.

I said I would last night. And he told me to go ahead. Rosa didn't greet anyone on that side when she came through with the tray, so I'm sure that Elio isn't over there.

Now that I'm aware of how full my bladder is, I can't ignore it. I didn't go before bed, and between the champagne last night and the water this morning I'm bursting.

I slide out of bed, padding across the room in my bare feet. I hesitate in the doorway, but a quick glance around tells me I was right. Elio isn't here. I sigh at the lack of door on his bathroom, and swear when I see yet another camera in there, just like the one in mine. I'd hoped that his bathroom wouldn't have one, but no dice. I can't imagine someone like Elio lets other guys sit around watching him on the toilet, so I keep everything crossed that no one's actively watching this feed right now. Even so, I grab a towel from a nearby rack and wrap it around myself as I shimmy my pyjama shorts down with one hand, then perch on the toilet.

I realize too late that the towel is slightly damp. It smells like Elio's fancy cologne, along with another scent, the spice of men's soap. He obviously used this towel after his shower this morning, and now I'm wrapped in it, the same fabric that was rubbed on his naked body covering my bare legs and pussy.

I should fucking pee on it. Use it as toilet paper, I think bitterly. But I don't believe that would send much of a message to Elio considering it would probably be Rosa who has to clean it up.

Holding the towel in place with one hand, I quickly wipe then hop down, flushing the toilet then awkwardly hiking up my shorts under the towel. As I do so, I glare at the camera, not quite brave enough to flip it the bird.

I let the towel fall to the floor and then wash my hands before putting it back on the rack. When I emerge from the bathroom, Rosa is busy stripping my bed.

No, not my bed, I remind myself quickly. *Just the bed I slept in.*

Even though I have nowhere else to go, I feel like I'll be in Rosa's way if I go back in there. Instead, I wander around Elio's room, perusing the books and stopping in front of the music system with its small shelf of CDs. I wondered about those CDs last night. About why he has them. Curiosity getting the best of me, I lean forward to examine the sides of the cases. There are no labels on the sides – they're just generic, plain plastic cases. Frowning, I take one of the cases off the shelf.

And I fucking freeze.

Because I recognize this CD. I recognize the shitty,

almost homemade-looking label on the front with its curly font.

Maeve's Music School

August Performance

Shaking, I take all the other CDs off the shelf, more than ten of them, and sit on the floor, shuffling through them like they're cards. They're all recordings of *Maeve's Music School* performances. The school where I teach violin.

Because I'm a teacher, not a student, I don't perform at every recital or concert. As I look at the dates on the labels, I realize that Elio only has recordings of the recitals I played at over the past year and a half.

These CDs were only available to purchase at the concerts themselves. Which means...

He was there.

At every single public music performance I've had over the past year and a half, *he was there.* Listening. Watching me. And I had no fucking idea.

I drop the CDs like they've burned me, confusion turning my stomach upside down. I wondered why he took me, why he wanted me when he could afford to hire any musician in this city. But more and more I'm starting to understand that, for some reason, it has to be me. Elio has been watching me for far longer than I could have ever comprehended.

Why? Is he a stalker?

Don't stalkers do other stuff, though? Like break into your house and move things around? Steal your panties? Shouldn't they do something other than just skulk in the shadows of your public music performances?

I have no idea what any of this means. I grab all the CDs and shove them back on the shelf, hurrying out of the room. Rosa looks like she's just finishing up, piling bedding in a basket attached to the side of the cart. As she passes me with the cart and heads out towards the hallway, I notice Elio's jacket on top of the heap. With a jolt, I wonder what's become of my ripped dress and panties on the bathroom floor. One look in the bathroom tells me they're gone, no doubt in Rosa's basket.

What was that about stalkers stealing panties?

I grit my teeth, humiliation making my skin prickle and heat. *It's fine. She's just collecting the laundry. She might throw away the ruined dress, but I'll get my underwear back.*

At least, that's what I tell myself.

Chapter 14

Elio

When Rosa pushes a cart into my office, I muse out loud, "She's not eating breakfast."

I'm talking about Deirdre. She's back in her bedroom after visiting mine. But all she's done is drink water since Rosa left, and I frown at the image of the untouched food displayed on my laptop.

Rosa answers me in Italian. "Do you want me to bring her something else? She could barely drink the coffee. She wanted tea."

"Tea?" I ask, raising my brows.

Rosa all but shudders. "I know."

I lean back in my chair, eyes still lingering on my laptop. "Add it to the shopping list. Buy it today. Whichever brands are best – buy a few different ones. No, buy them all."

Tea already tastes like hot garbage, and I have to imagine that buying cheaper or less quality brands only makes it worse.

But the beverage question doesn't answer the *why is Deirdre not eating?* question. I pull out my phone, open a search engine, and use voice-to-text to ask in English, "What do Irish girls eat for breakfast?"

The results are varied. Eggs. Beans. Something called blood pudding.

"You know how to make blood pudding?" I ask Rosa.

"*Sanguinaccio dolce*?" she asks. "The sweet one?"

"No, the Irish one." I flip my phone screen around to her. "It looks like a sausage."

She glances at the image on my screen then nods. "It looks like *sanguinaccio*. I can make it."

"Follow an Irish recipe," I tell her. "And stick a birthday candle in it when you bring it to her." I grimace, the scar tissue at the side of my jaw pulling. "Just make sure it gets blown out."

I wonder what my Songbird would wish for.

Probably to be free of me.

Rosa looks at me like I've lost my goddamn mind. And maybe I have. She knows the rules as well as anybody in this house – no candles. Ever. She's probably also not keen on the idea of straying from her Italian roots in the kitchen, and the irritation is reflected in her affronted gaze. I almost want to smirk at her boldness. Men half her age and twice her weight wouldn't dare look at me like that.

I don't know what it is about old Italian ladies. They aren't afraid of anything. You could have horns and the name SATAN stamped on your forehead and all they'd do is glare, flick *salsa di pomodoro* at you like it's holy water, and tell you to get the fuck out of their kitchen.

"Make it happen, Rosa," I say, giving her a clear dismissal. But she doesn't leave. Instead, she reaches into the basket attached to her cart and pulls something out. My jacket. The one Deirdre was wearing last night. The one I instructed Rosa not to throw away or clean.

"Put it on the desk," I say, jerking my chin to a clear spot on the shining dark wood. Rosa does so, carefully flattening the garment so it doesn't wrinkle, despite the fact there's a fucking bullet hole in the back of it. As she turns to go, I spot blood-stained white satin in the basket and rise from my chair. I'm around the desk in an instant, grabbing hold of the basket so she can't roll it away. I ignore Rosa's questioning look as I fish out Deirdre's dress, crushing the delicate fabric in my fist.

I stroll back around to my chair and sit down. Rosa takes the cue to leave and rolls her cart out of the office, closing the door behind her. I finger the fabric of Deirdre's dress, remembering what it looked like on her.

And what it looked like when I ripped it off.

Something falls to the floor, and I lean down to see what it is, ignoring the pain in my shoulder as I do so. It's yet more smooth white fabric. I lay the dress over my lap and pick it up.

Deirdre's panties.

I spread the white panties in my hands, making them take shape in the air before me, and picture Deirdre in them, her legs spread on my desk. Plump pussy lips nudging the silky lining. I wonder if she's shaved or waxed, or if there's dark red hair there, curling and damp, *soaked* –

Fuck me. It's like my cock's taken on a life of its own since I got Deirdre. No control. I'm popping boners like a teenager who's never gotten his dick wet.

I ignore the absurd urge to shove Deirdre's panties into my mouth.

Instead, I press my nose to the crotch of the tiny garment and sniff.

Madre di Dio.

A couple of flicks over the keys on my laptop and I've

cut off the security feed to this room and unzipped my pants. With the amount of blood I lost last night, there's no way I should be this hard. But the way that girl smells is like fucking magic.

Or maybe like a curse.

I grip my shaft and pump it in hard, swift strokes, still holding Deirdre's panties with my other hand. The worn leather of my glove is raw-yet-smooth friction gliding up and down. I don't take my time or try to draw the act out. This isn't about sensual pleasure. It's about quick release so that I can get my fucking head on straight.

I throb and lean back against my chair, groaning when the pressure on my shoulder adds pain to the flurry of sensation inside me. The tip of my dick is wet already. I'm close.

I want to shoot my load into Deirdre's panties. Completely soak the slippery fabric, stain it with myself the way I stained her skin with my blood last night. But even more than that, I want to preserve the garment exactly as it is now. I don't want to fuck up that perfect scent.

At the last second, I grab some tissues from my desk, wadding them up against my slick tip. I glance at the laptop where the feed to Deirdre's rooms is still displayed, and my hips jerk involuntarily when I see her. She's in her bathroom in those tiny pyjama shorts and tank top, bent over at the sink, washing her face. The view of her sweetly rounded ass in those shorts is fucking glorious. The arched sway of her back as her tank top rides up is a goddamn revelation. I've never really been a back guy. I like big tits, open mouths, and wet pussy. The finer, subtler points of the female form are generally lost on me.

Not lost on me now. Because all I want to do right now is splay my black gloved hand across Deirdre's lower back.

Press my thumb into one of the pretty little indents above her hipbones. Admire the artistry of her spine.

Deirdre stands and dries her face with a towel, then piles her hair on top of her head, twisting it and tying it there. Even the flex of her exposed shoulders as she ties up her hair turns me the fuck on, blood pounding through my groin as I stroke. I can see her reflection in the mirror. Her raised arms make her breasts move, the small but delicious curves bouncing each time she tightens her hairstyle. I remember what it was like to palm her breasts, and for the first time in a long time, the first time I can remember, I wish I hadn't been wearing gloves. The scars on my hands are usually pretty numb to sensation though. I wouldn't have been able to feel her too much anyway.

Unless I'd used my mouth.

That thought has me closer than ever. One last long, deep inhale of Deirdre's scent throws me over the edge. I explode, dick spasming, balls tightening. I completely drench the tissues and part of my glove.

After my breathing has somewhat returned to normal, I strip off my gloves and toss them in the trash along with the tissues, then head for the bathroom that's attached to my office. I wash and dry my hands without looking at them, because I never look at them, then fish out a new pair of leather gloves from a drawer and slide them on. These ones are stiff, not as broken-in as the pair I just tossed. The tough leather reminds me of my own scarred skin. It's taken multiple surgeries just for me to be able to use my hands mostly normally, to ease all the tightness.

When I return to my office, my gaze goes first to the laptop, where I see that Deirdre is now dressed in jeans and a white T-shirt. She's pacing the room like a caged animal. I wonder if she'll try to leave through my room. I've told the soldiers stationed all over this house that she can roam if she wants to, as long as they keep her under constant supervision and don't let her go outside. I haven't explicitly told her she can leave the room, though, and I watch her to see if she's brave enough to do it anyway.

The sound of my phone buzzing distracts me, and I pick it up. It's a text from Valentina.

Don't forget the gala. 8pm. Are you bringing Natalia with you? She's on the guest list.

Natalia Rizzo. She's not my girlfriend or my mistress but she's good for a quick fuck and she loves attending snazzy shit like Valentina's galas. I have a feeling she wants to be more to me than what she currently is, though, and that thought makes me want to put a knife through my eye. I don't particularly like her, nor her me, but we get what we need from each other. Sex. Status.

Maybe I should bring her. The rushed jerk-off session at this very desk proves I need to fuck someone. Get this out of my system. Natalia would enjoy it, too, especially after the gala. Being around all that glitz, glamour, and cold, hard cash always makes her horny.

But the thought of Natalia, with her gorgeous curves and long, bleached-blonde hair does nothing for me now. Not even the slightest hint of desire stirs through me, and I know it's not because I just came. Because when I think of someone else, someone with freckles and blue eyes and red hair, hair that I normally hate, the desire comes roaring back.

I use voice-to-text to reply, *No.* My phone has a resistive screen, so technically I can type on it wearing the gloves, but it's a pain in the ass.

Thank God, my cousin replies. Valentina gets along with Natalia about as well as I get along with her outside of the bedroom. Which is to say, she doesn't. *Are you bringing someone else?*

I'm about to reply, *No*, again when I freeze. A slow smirk unfurls on my face. Because I am bringing someone. Someone who will make the night a lot more bearable, maybe even interesting.

Deirdre, I reply. *Get here a few hours early to help her get ready. Nice dress, shoes. Jewellery. The works. Use my credit card. I want her flawless.*

She looks flawless in her fucking T-shirt and jeans, to be honest, but that's not what I'm telling Valentina. There's a long pause without response, and I know it's because she's absorbing what I just said. Absorbing the fact I want Valentina to dress Deirdre like she's one of us.

I want her to look like a fucking *principessa*.

It's the perfect opportunity. The perfect, public place to put Deirdre up on display and to let everyone in this city know she's mine. I'll give Severu his money, and even if no Irish are there, no doubt word will filter back to Darragh quickly that Deirdre belongs to Elio Titone now.

And Elio Titone keeps what's fucking his.

I'll have her at my side, dripping with diamonds and pearls, just within reach and yet completely untouchable.

Untouchable to everyone but me.

Valentina's reply flashes across my phone. *I'll be there.*

I send one last reply before sliding my phone into my pocket and letting my gaze once again land on Deirdre in her room.

Good.

Chapter 15

Deirdre

Other than Rosa coming to bring me the weirdest possible lunch I could have imagined – some kind of dark-coloured sausage with a single burning candle stuck into it – I've been alone all day. I haven't heard from Willow. Or my father. Despite the fact that he's the one who's put us in this situation, I can't help but worry about him. I wonder where he is. And I wonder if Elio knows.

But I don't get any answers, and the day ticks by into afternoon. Around 4pm, a quick knock sounds at the door that leads from Elio's room into the hallway, and then Valentina breezes in.

At least she knocked, I think with an internal sigh. And honestly, I'm glad she's here. The isolation was killing me.

Her arms are loaded with stuff. She's dragging a suitcase on wheels, along with what looks like a few garment bags slung over her shoulder. She gives me a dazzling smile and strolls through Elio's room into mine, dumping all the garment bags on the bed that Rosa made when she came in to deliver the lunch I didn't eat.

"Hellooo," Valentina says in a sing-song voice as she turns to face me, hands on her hips. She looks drop-dead gorgeous, with perfect contouring, smoky eye-shadow, fake eyelashes, and bright pink lips. Her hair looks like it's been professionally done – freshly blown-out in big, luscious waves. Her outfit seems slightly out of step with her hair and makeup. She's wearing simple black leggings and a plain black T-shirt.

"Hi," I say, confused by the sudden apparition of her. "What's all that?" I ask, jerking my chin at the stuff she's put on the bed.

"Dresses and shoes. I would have brought makeup, but I've already filled your bathroom's drawers with it."

I hear her words and absorb their meaning in a literal sense, but find myself staring at her with a complete lack of understanding. She doesn't seem bothered by my lack of response. She just bends over, lays the suitcase flat, and opens it. Inside are about ten lumps wrapped in paper. As she unwraps them, I see that these are the shoes she was talking about. Each pair looks brand-new and unimaginably expensive.

"I don't know your size, so I aimed for the middle. Most of these are between seven and eight, but I have a couple size six pairs, and even a nine somewhere in here."

"Those... those are for me?" I ask, frowning and staring down at the beautiful shoes she's unwrapping like presents. "Why?" Is this some kind of weird work uniform Elio wants? I usually wear flats when I play. Wearing heels alters your posture, and can change the quality of the performance if you're not actively aware of it.

"For the gala tonight!" Valentina straightens. "Elio didn't tell you?"

I snort at that. The guy hasn't told me anything besides the fact that he basically owns me now.

Valentina rolls her eyes. "Typical. Titone men hate opening their mouths unless they're discussing business." She turns to the bed now, unzipping the three garment bags. "There's a gala at the AGO tonight. We paid for a new wing and tonight's a private opening night. Elio wants you there."

Nerves flutter in my stomach. I squeeze my hands together and press them against my belly.

"Am I the musician playing tonight?" God, I'm completely unprepared for this! Playing for the duration of an entire gala... That's *hours*. I don't have songs picked out or rehearsed, and I don't know if there's a band I need to fit into. The thought of performing at an event of that calibre with less than a day's warning makes me feel like I'm going to throw up. Having consumed nothing but water and two sips of espresso probably isn't helping in that department, either.

But Valentina shakes her head and turns around to face me again.

"God, no!" she says, sounding shocked. She shakes her head again and hastily adds, "No offense. But I booked the band months ago."

"Oh." It comes out more like a relieved sigh than a word. "Then what will I be doing there?" Maybe they need a last-minute server or something.

Valentina taps a long, polished beige fingernail against her chin.

"You'll be there as Elio's... Honestly, I don't know. Date?"

Date.

The word skewers me, and the relief I felt a moment ago vanishes, replaced once again with nausea.

"That's not possible," I sputter.

She shrugs. "I don't know. I asked him if he was bringing anyone and he said you. He wants you all dolled up, too. I brought some dresses to try..." Her words trail off as her eyes widen. "Fuck me, you're pale. I mean, you're already pale, but I didn't know somebody living could get that white. Good thing I've got a shitload of blush and bronzer in the bathroom."

I can feel what she sees – the quick exit of blood from my face.

Valentina's eyes narrow, her thick lashes fluttering heavily.

"What have you eaten today?"

"Eaten?" I echo woozily.

She mutters something under her breath and quickly closes the distance between us. She's shorter than me but surprisingly strong as she grasps my elbow and leads me to sit on a small chair over by the desk and music stand.

"Don't tell me my cousin hasn't been feeding you," she snaps.

"No, no," I say, bending to put my head between my knees. "Rosa brought me stuff."

Not that I could bring myself to eat any of it.

"Hold on," she says. I hear her heels tapping as she moves away from me. From Elio's room, I hear her calling into the hallway. "Hey! Robbie! Tell Rosa we need snacks, would ya?"

Her voice gets louder, aimed back at me.

"You're not a vegan or something, are you? Gluten free?"

I weakly shake my head, bumping my own knees as I do so.

"OK. Good. Because if you were, you really would starve in this house. There's no escaping the meat, cheese, bread, and pasta."

Normally, those are all things I like eating. But this is not normal. Not for me.

Just as I'm getting the strength to lift my head back up without feeling like I'm going to fall off the chair, Valentina's returning with a cart like the one Rosa uses, a tray perched on top. Actually, it isn't a tray, but a charcuterie board, laden with thinly sliced meat, olives, sliced mozzarella, tomatoes drizzled with balsamic vinegar, and fresh bread. There's more olive oil and balsamic in a small dish for dipping the bread, and my mouth waters. Beside the charcuterie board is a large glass pitcher of ice water with lemons and some sort of leaves floating around in it, along with two glasses. Valentina pours a glass full, then thrusts it at me.

"Here. Drink this, then have some food."

She may be smaller than me, and I'm sure she's younger, but there's an undeniable edge of authority in her voice. But I guess that comes with the territory when you're the only daughter of a mob boss. I take the glass and have a sip. While I'm drinking the water, Valentina busies herself loading up a small plate with all kinds of stuff from the charcuterie board. When it's done, she holds it out to me.

"Come on. You don't want to attend one of my and Mamma's events on an empty stomach. The booze flows like fucking water."

I can't imagine I'll be drinking at the event, but then again, I didn't imagine I'd be attending on Elio Titone's arm, either. *Just what am I to him? What does he want me to be?*

She's right, though. I need to keep my wits about me and maintain my strength here. I can't waste away and starve.

I start with the bread, because I feel like that will go down easy on my roiling stomach. I dip it into the olive oil and balsamic and take a bite. It's possibly the best bread I've ever had, slightly warm and fluffy, with a crunchy crust softened by the oil and vinegar.

That bite seems to have awakened my appetite, and I quickly scarf down the bread, then move onto the tomato and mozzarella salad, then the prosciutto and salami and olives. The entire time, Valentina watches me with a satisfied smirk. Even though she's so young, she's giving me total Italian grandma vibes. She clearly enjoys feeding people.

After clearing my plate, I chug some water, then wipe my mouth with the back of my hand.

"Thank you," I say, meaning it. "I didn't realize how much better I would feel after some food."

"Carbs solve everything," she says with a nod.

"Well, I wouldn't go *that* far," I say. My stomach may be full now, but I'm still stuck in this goddamn house, and now I'm apparently going to an event with Elio, which makes no sense. So, I would say that things are very much *not* solved.

"OK, you're right. But they help a little," she says. Her gaze falls to the giant pink diamond ring on her finger and lingers there for a moment before she jerks her head back up to look at me. In a voice that feels falsely cheery, she says, "Alright! You're fed! Now it's makeover time."

I should have known based on how perfect Valentina's hair and makeup look that *makeover time* is serious business for her. I'm completely unprepared for the thoroughness of her onslaught. And it does feel like an onslaught – my hair pulled tightly into rollers, eyebrows plucked, my skin smudged and sponged and powdered. She even makes me shave my legs and armpits to eliminate the one-day stubble there, instructing me firmly not to tell Elio before taking the razor away again after.

We do all the makeup and hair stuff in the bathroom. It takes a long time – Valentina is a total perfectionist. But after a few hours, she seems satisfied with the state of me.

"Now, the dresses," she says, marching back into the bedroom. I stand from where I was seated on the toilet and move to follow her. Before I leave the room, I catch sight of my own face in the mirror and halt.

A shimmering, polished woman stares back. I don't look like myself. Even my freckles are gone, hidden under foundation and bronzer. My cheekbones look sharper, my nose narrower, my lips darker and fuller, my lashes longer. I like makeup and I do wear it, but not to this extent. I've never seen myself like this.

The big curlers are still in my hair, giving my head a weird, bubbly look, but even that can't take away from the stunning effect of the makeup.

Looking so different is jarring. But strangely, it's also comforting. I can pretend it's not me, Deirdre O'Malley, but somebody else in this bathroom, in this life. This new look is like armour, a mask between Elio and me, a barrier like his leather gloves.

Feeling just a little bit stronger, I turn and catch up with Valentina.

She's standing by the bed, staring downwards. The three garment bags are open on the bed, each one containing a dress of a different colour.

"That one's mine. I have to change, too," Valentina says, pointing to a pink sequined dress. "You can try those other two on and we'll see which one is better."

I shift back and forth on my feet, eyeing the camera in the ceiling. Valentina twists to follow my gaze, then sighs.

"Yeah. You'll get used to that."

I scoff. "I doubt that."

Valentina gives me a serious look. She's clearly enjoyed her role as my snack-provider and makeup/hair artist, and she's been chatty and relaxed most of the afternoon. But now, she looks grave.

"You have to get used to it, Deirdre. This is your life now. *This is it.* It's not safe, and it's not easy, but it's what you've fucking got."

The speech seems practised. I wonder if she's said these exact words to herself.

"This isn't my life," I mutter, crossing my arms and shaking my head so hard that the rollers wobble and tug at my hair. "I have a life."

"*Had,*" Valentina corrects me. "You may still be in Toronto, but where you've come from and where you are now are two completely different worlds. The sooner you accept that, the better."

"How can you say that?" I cry. I've started feeling a sense of comradery with Valentina, but it comes crashing down. She's not here to be my friend. She's here to make sure I serve Elio in whatever fashion he chooses.

But maybe I'm wrong. Because the look she gives me isn't cold, but pained.

"I say that because it's true. Because it's a lesson I've had to learn over and over again." Once again, her eyes go to her ring, and for a second she looks like she wants to cut off her own finger.

"How old are you?" I ask her softly.

"I'll be nineteen in June," she replies, closing her hand into a fist and letting it drop.

Jesus. Only eighteen, engaged, and clearly unhappy about it.

I guess being the boss's daughter doesn't afford you as much power over your own life as I thought.

"Who's your fiancé?"

"God, I don't want to talk about him," she moans. "I'm already going to have to see him tonight." She sighs, twirling the ring on her finger, then meets my gaze steadily. "Look, this is shit. I know it is. You didn't choose to be here, and I get it. I've had eighteen years to get used to these men and you've barely had a day. It's fucking garbage. But you're strong. Just like me. I can see it in those baby blues." She smiles. "And if there's anything strong women are good at, it's surviving absolute trash heaps of situations like these."

I'm not sure I feel that strong right now. I've thrown up walls, but they're all being chipped away at. By my father, with his betrayal.

By Elio with his hammer.

But I have to be strong. I'm a survivor. Even if being a survivor has filled me with guilt for half my life.

I wonder what Mom would say if she were here.

No. If Mom were alive, I wouldn't be here at all. She never would have let this happen.

"Alright, then. What kind of dress should I wear to get through an 'absolute trash heap of a situation'?" I ask.

Valentina grins and wraps an arm around my waist, leaning in and squeezing. "That's the spirit!"

I swallow, unexpected tears threatening to ruin my makeup. This is the first time I've been touched by another woman in a long time. I try to remember the last time I hugged Willow and want to cry even more.

"Are you able to get a message to someone for me?" I ask, spinning in Valentina's grip. "My best friend Willow.

She's worried about me but her dad took her phone and won't let her contact me."

"No tears! Ah! Your makeup!" Valentina says, fanning her hands over my face in a frantic motion. "Is she Irish?"

I know what she's asking with that question. She's not asking just about her family background, but asking if Willow is in the life.

"Yeah," I say. There's no point in lying. "Her dad runs a pub called *Briar and Boar* for Darragh Gowan."

"Hmm. How about a letter? I could send it for you."

"Like, mail it?" That will take days, and who knows if I'll even get a response? But Valentina nods to confirm.

"From what I understand, Darragh is just about foaming at the mouth to get his hands on your dad. Or, in his place, you. He likely already knows we have you, so it's not like any of us can just go waltzing into his territory right now. I think mailing a letter is your best bet to actually get a message to Willow without everything blowing the fuck up."

"OK. That works," I say hurriedly. I don't want Willow in danger if some of Elio's men show up at the pub. And now that I think about it, maybe a letter is perfect. If I don't put a return address on it, there's no real reason some mail for her would arouse Paddy's suspicion. She can burn it when she's done.

I don't even know what I'll write. I'm alive? I'm trapped? Save me? Forget you ever knew my name?

I promise myself I'll figure it out as Valentina tells me she'll bring me envelopes and paper. She puts a note in her phone about it and then gasps.

"Oh, shit. We're behind schedule. Time to get dressed and go!" She pins me with a look. "Seriously. Chop chop. No more worrying about the camera."

It amazes me that she doesn't worry about the camera. When she sees my look, she groans and runs to the bathroom, returning with a towel.

"Here. I'll hold this around you."

I'm grateful for her as she opens up the towel and blocks the view of the camera while I shimmy out of the jeans and T-shirt I'm wearing. "Which dress?" I ask.

She cranes her neck to look at the bed.

"We don't have time to try them both on. Go with the blue one. That's the one I really wanted to see you in."

For a second, I'm not sure what she means. One of the dresses is green, the other is black. But then I realize the black one is actually the deepest shade of blue you can get before black. Deep, inky blue silk. I reach my hand out of the towel and snatch it, then step into it.

There are no zippers or buttons to do up. It's a simple cut with two straps, a deep V-neckline, and a plunging open back. I feel the air on my exposed back and I'm about to ask Valentina if I can wear the other dress instead when she whistles.

"Holy fucking shit, Irish. That's the one. Fits you like a glove."

The word glove makes me think of Elio, and my stomach tightens. I look down at myself, at the cling of fabric at my waist and hips, the long skirt with a high slit up one side. Before I can stop the thought and tell myself I'm absolutely insane, I wonder what he'll think when he sees me.

As his date. What the fuck is happening?

Valentina flings the towel away.

"Take out your rollers while I get changed! And pick some shoes!" she says. She undresses in a frenzy, and I can't help but gawk at her confidence while I yank the curlers out of my hair.

"You really don't care about the camera?" I ask. At least she's got a strapless bra on, unlike me, so she's mostly covered.

"I'm used to it," she says, stepping into her sequined pink dress. In contrast to mine, the skirt on hers is super short. "It's the same in our house. But the security feeds for the family bedrooms don't go to the main hub."

"What does that mean?" I say, running my fingers through my hair now that all the rollers are out.

"My papà's the only one with access to the family bedroom feeds. He's a lot of things, but he's not pervy enough to watch his own daughter getting changed or taking a dump. It's mostly to make sure I'm not sneaking guys in there or something, especially now that I've got this." She flaps her left hand in the air, and I know she means her engagement ring. "It's the same here, you know. Only Elio has access to the cameras in here and in his rooms."

"He didn't mention that," I say slowly. I'm not sure how I feel about that. I knew that Elio would have access to the cameras. It's his house, and he has all the power. But I didn't know he was the *only* one who'd see me in here. I can't tell if I'm comforted or not, and I don't have much time to think about it, because Valentina is urging me to get some shoes on, stat.

I grab a pair of strappy silver heels in my size and try them on. They seem to fit alright, but the heel is astronomically high. Far higher than I'm used to. A quick look at all the other shoes tells me I won't get anything lower, and I may as well just stick with what I've got.

"Zip me up?" Valentina spins, and I do up the zipper at

the back of her dress. Hers is strapless. Once she's done up, she turns and fluffs my hair a bit.

"You look like a goddess. Let's go!"

Go. Go to an event. With Elio.

At least it's in a public place. Nothing bad is going to happen to me surrounded by other people. A small, stupid part of me is still holding out hope that somebody might even save me from all this.

I turn towards the door, ready to leave, when Valentina stops me with a cry.

"Oh, my God! Your underwear!"

"What?" I ask, twisting back to look at her. I have no clue what's happened to my panties from yesterday, so I'm wearing one of the pairs I found in the closet.

"The back of the dress is too low. You can see the top edge of them."

"I'll put on the other dress and-"

"No time," Valentina interrupts. "Just take them off."

My cheeks flush hot. She cannot be serious. She wants me to go out in public, to come face to face with Elio, wearing *no fucking underwear?*

But her face tells me she absolutely is serious. She's practically dancing with anxiety about the time, and as much as I hate this whole situation, I don't want to make problems for her if I can help it. Besides, it's not like Elio hasn't seen me even more exposed. At least my dress is all in one piece this time.

"Fine," I grit out. I don't have to worry too much about the camera, because my skirt is so long it completely covers me as I wiggle out of the underwear. "Better?" I spin around.

"Perfect!" Valentina says, shoving her phone in a small gold clutch. "Now let's go!"

Chapter 16

Elio

I've just emerged from my office and am crossing the main floor of the house when I hear the clatter of high heels on the stairs. I reach the front door and turn just in time to get punched in the face.

That's what it feels like. That's what my Songbird *looks* like, coming down the stairs. So beautiful she's a blow to the fucking head.

I barely notice my cousin beside her as Deirdre descends the stairs. Her steps are quick but wobbly, and she's looking down like she's afraid she's going to fall and snap her neck. Which, considering the shoes she's wearing, is probably a valid concern. My gaze slides from her silver shoes, up the tantalizing line of her leg appearing at the slit in her dress, to her hips, her sweet little waist and tits. That dress is a goddamn dream on her, encasing her body in silk so dark blue it makes her eyes look like midnight instead of their usual midday sky.

Those deep blue eyes meet mine, and Deirdre freezes on the stairs. Valentina just keeps on going, practically

118

sprinting even though her heels are even higher than Deirdre's.

Deirdre and I stare at each other for so long I wonder if she's planning to stay on that step all night.

"Need me to carry you again?" I ask.

She inhales sharply, her lush mouth tightening.

"No, thank you," she says, her tone clipped. "I don't need another dress ruined by your blood."

Valentina tenses beside me, no doubt fearing my anger. But I surprise them both by letting out a chuckle.

"I'm all stitched up, remember, Songbird? Good as new."

Not exactly true. My shoulder's going to be a pain in my ass for a while. But Morelli checked my stitches today and put new bandages on earlier, at least, so I won't be bleeding all over her. I stare at her cleavage, her collarbones, remembering what my blood looked like smeared there, and the crotch of my pants feels suddenly tighter.

Deirdre starts walking again, descending the last few steps. My gaze is stuck on her chest, and I frown, feeling like something's missing before I realize what it is.

"Where's her jewellery?" I ask my cousin.

Valentina smacks the palm of her hand to her forehead.

"Ah, shit. It's upstairs with the shoes."

"Go get it," I tell her, keeping my eyes on Deirdre's bare neck.

"But we're late! Mamma's already there and pissed about it. I've got about a dozen texts from her and-"

I tear my gaze from Deirdre's skin long enough to give Valentina a look that sends her running for the stairs.

"I'll be right back!" she calls. She's like a tiny fucking track athlete even in those shoes. She's running like it's her job.

I'm alone with Deirdre now. There are a few soldiers scattered around the main floor of the house, and Curse and Enzo are both outside ready to go, but in this space by the door, it's just the two of us.

Deirdre looks everywhere but at me when she finally speaks.

"So, how does this work? The jewellery, the clothes. Is this all getting added on to my debt? Because I'd rather not have it at all."

I pause, drinking in the sight of her in a dress I paid for, already imagining the tens of thousands of dollars of gemstones I'm about to wrap around her throat. A collar with *Titone* spelled out in the language of diamonds.

"I'm feeling generous. Consider it a birthday gift," I say. Her gaze snaps to me, and I don't miss the way it slides up and down my body in my black suit and black shirt. The only thing not black on me is my pocket square. A slight wrinkle appears between her eyebrows when her gaze snags there, and I wonder if she recognizes it.

I almost ask her, but Valentina is back, panting as she careens down the stairs.

"Here, quick, quick!" she says to Deirdre, holding out sparkly stuff. My cousin's frenetic impatience is grinding my nerves raw. I hold out my hand for the jewellery and tell her, "Go ahead. Curse and Enzo will take you."

Valentina dumps the shimmering gems and metal into my hand without a moment's hesitation before running for the door, pulling it open and disappearing. Deirdre flutters, looks like she'll call out something like "Wait!" But it's too late. Valentina is gone and it's just us again. Her eyes fall to my hand, where bright, clear diamonds and white gold shine in stark contrast to the black leather of my glove. Her mouth primly puckered, she reaches for my hand, but I pull it back.

"I'll do it."

"What do you mean, you'll do it? If I have to wear it, I'll put it on myself."

She reaches forward again, but once again I move my hand, curling my fingers into a fist.

"We aren't leaving until I put this stuff on you."

She doesn't understand. She doesn't understand what showing up in public wearing my finery, my diamonds, means. It will tell the entire fucking city that she's mine now. Not as a debtor, someone to torture or to kill over what she owes. Not as someone I couldn't care less about losing.

But someone possessed.

Someone protected.

"Then we won't leave at all," she snaps.

I don't say anything else. I step towards her. She steps back. We do this over and over until she collides with the wall. She's trapped by my body, and I hold up my fist between us, loosening my grip slightly until a white gold chain slithers out and dangles in the air. It swings like a pendulum, and her blue eyes track the movement.

"You'll find that things will be much easier for you if you don't disobey me," I mutter.

Her eyes flash. "Maybe I don't want this to be easy."

"What do you want this to be, then?"

Her reply is flat and grim. "Over."

A concoction of emotions I don't like and won't name floods my body. I feel like I could crush the diamonds in my fist.

"Put your fucking hair behind your ears."

She stares at me in mute defiance, and I grunt as I lift my left hand, ignoring Morelli's instructions not to use that arm as much as possible. Deirdre gasps when I grasp all her hair at the nape of her neck and tug, forcing her head back, baring her throat. Her heart beats a rapid-fire rhythm there, poetry of the body and of blood. It's a song in and of itself. I want to put my fucking tongue there.

Instead, I reach to the side with my right hand, depositing the jewellery on a small stand near the wall. From the pile, I grab one earring. It's a dangly diamond thing with a simple hook to slide through her earlobe. No back or clasp.

Deirdre can't move much with her hair bound so tightly by my fist. She breathes rapidly, staring at the earring like it's a murder weapon. Her body vibrates with what I assume is fury. She doesn't look afraid. She looks fucking pissed.

But something changes when the leather of my glove brushes the shell of her ear. She makes a sound, between a whimper and a gasp, that jolts straight to my dick. Her entire body goes taut, her breath catching as I skim a single knuckle over her earlobe. I stop looking at her ear for a second and see that her eyes are scrunched shut. Her back is arching away from the wall, and it's not because I've started pulling her hair. And...

Her nipples are hard.

I couldn't see them through the dress before, but I can see them now. The temperature hasn't changed. It's toasty fucking warm. Honestly a little too hot for my liking, now that my blood is boiling inside me.

"Sensitive, Songbird?" I mutter quietly, brushing my knuckle down her ear again experimentally. I watch her as I do it. Watch the flutter that goes through the muscles in her face, the tautness that spreads down her body. Watch the way her nipples swell and tighten further, begging me to mouth them through the slippery fabric of her dress. Her hands are plastered to the wall at her back.

"Can you just get this over with?" she breathes, her eyes still closed, as if she can't stand to look at me. Can't stand to acknowledge what she might be feeling in response to my touch.

But now I want to take my fucking time. Unlike Valentina I don't really care when we arrive at this event. I don't plan to stay long, anyway. Just long enough to give Sev his money and make sure everybody sees Deirdre at my side.

Slowly, I release my grip on her hair. I don't think she needs me to hold her there anymore, and I'm right. She's completely bound by tension, just from that slight touch at her ear. She's definitely beyond sensitive there. Which is damn good information to have. I gently take her plump earlobe between my left thumb and forefinger and guide the earring hook to the small hole there. I press it slowly in, penetrating the silky flesh, while Deirdre remains perfectly still except for her ragged breathing. Bent this close to her face, I wish I'd told Valentina to go a little easier on the makeup. I can't see her freckles now, and that bothers me.

I let go of the earring, watching the long line of diamonds dangle and bump the side of her throat. Then, I ease my fingertips under her chin, tipping her head to the other side to do the same on the other ear. Her eyes flare open, and she stares at me, gaze sparking, as I reach for the other earring.

"Like to watch when men put things inside you?" I ask, feeling her gaze on me as I slide the second earring into place.

"Wouldn't know," she hisses. "I've never let a man put something inside me."

I freeze, and so does she. Her eyes widen, her lips clamping together as if she didn't mean to say that. Now that the earring is in, I release it. My fingers skim down her throat, and she swallows.

"You're a virgin?"

My fingers keep sliding down her neck, tracing her collarbones, then brushing a knuckle between her breasts.

I can barely see the red blush beneath all her makeup, but I know it's there, because it creeps up her neck, too. I slowly rub my knuckle up and down the valley between her breasts. I can't stop staring at how much she reacts to me. How flushed her fair skin gets, just from this slightest touch.

"I don't see why that matters!" she stammers.

I don't know why it matters, either. I've never cared about virginity as a concept before. A lot of men in our world do, want their mafia brides untouched, but I couldn't care less. If anything, getting saddled with a virgin who doesn't know what she's doing seems like an easy way to guarantee a boring night in the sack.

But now...

Now, I find I do care. Care that nobody else has been inside Deirdre. If I wanted to, I could be the first man, the last man, the only man who's ever fucked her. A possessive satisfaction rises up inside me, telling me that she's mine in all ways now, even if she fights it.

"I don't even know why I said that," she groans. "Well, at least it proves that I'll be useless to you in that department if you ever decide you want me for something other than violin. Since I have no idea what I'm doing."

"You'd have an idea of what you were doing if someone taught you."

She breathes in sharply at my words. She's about to say something else, but I silence her with a feather-light but unmistakeably intentional brush of my thumb over her hardened nipple.

And then I do it again.

"What are you doing?" she whispers thickly.

I don't answer her with words, instead drawing an achingly slow, firm circle around the outer edge of her nipple. Teasing, not coming close to the sensitive bud of it again. Her breath is coming in short little pants. Fuck, I want to take her breast roughly in my hand, knead it, draw up the skirt of her dress and pin her to the wall.

I don't. Jaw tight, I keep circling, slowly, so fucking slowly, until I think Deirdre is going to come apart at the seams. She's too proud to ask me to do it, but I can see she needs it.

"Do you want me to touch you there again?" I murmur against her ear. She shudders at the cascade of my breath over her skin.

"Fuck you. Let me go," is all she says, but it's practically a whine. She may not be begging me with words, but she is with her body. Her back is arching towards me, seeking my touch.

"I think you do," I say. "Right now, I bet all you can think about is what this leather will feel like sliding across your bare skin."

She jerks beneath my touch, and I know I'm right.

It would be so easy, too. To slide the silk of the dress over, maybe even rip it like I did last night. Rub the puckering berries of her nipples between my gloved fingers. Take one and then the other in my mouth so I could feel her properly, no fabric between us. My cock pounds at the thought, my tongue lashing the backs of my teeth.

I want her to beg me to do it.

Even though I know she won't.

With an impatient growl, I give her what she needs but won't ever ask for. I press my palms to the sides of her breasts, moving my thumbs across her nipples in demanding strokes. She lets out a soft moan, then clamps her mouth shut, as if pissed off by the escape of the sound. Like that moan is a betrayal.

She doesn't want to feel what she's feeling. To react to me the way she's reacting. All I'm doing is playing with her pretty little nipples, and she's getting all twitchy and wiggly, her hips bucking forward before she stops the movement, fighting for control.

She's not just sensitive around her ears. She could come like this, is probably already fucking close. The thought inflames me, makes me forget every rule, everything I've told myself about why I've brought her here.

My lips touch her ear this time when I growl, "If I pulled your panties to the side right now, I think I'd find that virgin pussy soaking for me, Songbird."

Her hands, hands that this entire time have been plastered to the wall, not touching me or pushing me away and pretending to be neutral participants in all of this, rise between us. She plants them on my chest and shoves, eyes burning me with blue fire.

"So everything you told me before is a lie, then," she snaps, shoving again. "You do want a whore. You just want me for my body."

I drop my hands from her breasts and capture her chin in my fingers, forcing her gaze to remain on mine as I lean in and tell her, "I want everything. I want your fucking *soul*."

She tries to shake her head but can't.

"Six million dollars for a soul," she whispers, and she doesn't sound angry now, but sad.

I let her go, flexing my fingers inside my gloves and

shrugging, sending lancing pain through my shoulder, and simply reply, "Small price to pay."

I would have paid millions more. There's something in her that speaks to me in a language I've half-forgotten. It's like an itch at the back of my mind that I need to locate so I can scratch it until it bleeds.

I'm about to turn towards the door and take her out of here when I see something glittering. The necklace. I pick it up.

"Turn around," I say.

She just stares at me, arms crossed over her chest as if to keep those pesky, sensitive nipples of hers in check around me. I hold up the necklace, and she merely lifts her chin and narrows her gaze.

Fine by me. I can put it on like this.

I lean close to her again, and at the last second she decides to finally listen and does turn around. Maybe she thinks this is all a little better if she doesn't actually have to look at me.

I sweep her hair forward over one shoulder, doing my best to ignore the crackling colour of it. Fucking hell, she's got a lot of it. Long and thick. It completely hid her back before, but now...

Now I can see everything.

Valentina may have gone overboard on the makeup, but I have to hand it to my cousin. She chose the perfect dress.

The back of the dress isn't even a back at all. It's a gaping plunge of silk, exposing Deirdre from shoulder blade to hip. I let the chain of the necklace dangle from my hand, letting the thin end of it drag up the curve of her spine to her neck. I can see the goosebumps as they rise. See the way Deirdre's arms tighten around her body.

I move in closer behind Deirdre, taking a moment to

look at the necklace to figure out how it clasps. It has a short, wide band of diamonds with a central large stone that must go at the front. I sweep it around the front of her neck, then do up the clasp at the back. I pause to admire the effect, and the effect goes straight to my balls.

Because the necklace looks like a diamond collar, fitted tightly around her throat. And the white-gold chain dangles down Deirdre's back like a glittering leash.

I finger the chain at the back, tugging lightly, and smirk when Deirdre vaults backwards in response, stumbling in her heels until she crashes into my chest. She rights herself quickly, trying to pull away from me as fast as she can.

But I don't let go of the chain until she's in my car.

Chapter 17

Deirdre

What is happening?

That's the question running through my head over and over again as I sit motionless in the front passenger seat of Elio's car. It's a different vehicle from last night's black SUV. It's still black, but it's smaller, some kind of Porsche I'm pretty sure.

What is happening? What is happening to me?

The place between my legs still feels achy and damp as I squeeze my thighs together. Elio, the arrogant violent stupid fucking *bastard*, almost made me come. Just from touching my nipples.

What is happening to me?

I shouldn't like his touch on me. No, I *don't* like it. But something in my body reacts to him in a way I can't control. And the shame of it makes everything burn hotter. Makes every touch into something toxic, nearly drugging, something I'm terrified I'll start to crave if I'm not careful.

But how the hell can I even be careful? Everywhere I go, there Elio is. He houses me. Even fucking dresses me now. My fingers rise to the diamond collar at my neck, a beautiful and terrible symbol of what's become of me.

"Why are you bringing me to this event?" I ask, tracing the intricate lines of diamonds that lead into one huge one at the centre. I've got to be wearing tens of thousands worth of dollars of gems right now. Maybe even more.

I don't expect him to answer, but he actually does.

"It's the most public and efficient way to show the other people who want you that you're mine."

The other people who want me. I guess he means Darragh and the Camorra.

I let my hand fall away from the collar and rub my temples.

"Do you know where my father is?" I ask dully. Once again, I don't expect him to reply.

And once again, he surprises me.

"Bermuda."

I whip my head towards Elio, a dizzying array of emotions flying through me. The first is relief that my father is alive and he's escaped.

The second is despair.

Because he really has left me here.

Maybe he's just hatching a plan, I tell myself, chewing on my lip. *Maybe he can't figure out how to help me here with so many people after him, so he left to figure out his next move.*

I wonder if Elio can sense the hope inside me. If he can smell it the way a dog smells blood.

"He's with Bridget. She flew out there this morning."

Bridget. The name is familiar, though it takes me a second to place it.

"Bridget, like, our cleaning lady? That Bridget?"

She only worked for us for a couple of weeks a few years

ago before she was mysteriously replaced. I always wondered what became of her, but she was so young, only a few years older than me, so I figured she'd just gotten a new opportunity or maybe had college to deal with. I remember her being chatty and sweet and extremely pretty. *Why would Dad need a maid in Bermuda?*

I'm embarrassed that I don't figure it out until Elio tells me.

"She's his girlfriend. Or maybe sugar baby is a better term. Has been for years."

I feel like somebody's punched me in the stomach. I lean forward, breath practically knocked out of me as it truly sinks in. My father created this entire mess and left me to pick up the pieces without a fucking thought. Clearly, he still has money on hand if he can jet off to tropical islands. And instead of using that money to try to pay his debts and save me, he flew out the woman he's fucking instead.

How did I not know any of this?

Head spinning, I try to comb through the past few years, wondering if I've missed any signs. How dense am I that not only did I not realize what was happening with the money situation, but I didn't even clue in that Bridget stopped working for us because she became my dad's girlfriend instead? His expensive little secret?

Turns out Dad had a lot of expensive secrets.

The sense of betrayal goes deeper than just me. I feel like Dad has betrayed Mom, too. Betrayed her memory in the worst possible way. I obviously didn't expect him to be alone forever after her death, but this? Banging some college-aged girl and protecting her instead of me when shit hit the fan?

This is a nightmare.

A nightmare that Elio just keeps on making more real. Adding more and more details.

"She's got expensive taste, from what I hear," Elio says. He speaks casually, as if each word isn't shattering everything I thought I knew. "She doesn't work but lives in a fancy condo in Yorkville. Drives a Range Rover. Or, she did. I wouldn't be surprised if Sev's men have already seized the vehicle."

"Please stop," I whisper. I don't even know why I bother. My father may be greedy and a coward, but Elio is cruel, and begging him won't get me anywhere.

"The truth hurts, Songbird," he replies, proving just how right I am. How cruel he is. What he says may be the truth, but he's the one wielding it like a knife, digging it right into my heart.

"But what else is it they say?" he continues. "The truth will set you free."

I stare at his profile, dumfounded.

"Free?" I echo in disbelief. The diamond collar around my neck tingles. I want to rip it off, dangle it in front of his face and ask him, *Does this look like free to you?*

Neither of us speak for a while. There's no music on in the car, and the only sound is the bleating of my broken heart in my chest. I watch the lights of downtown Toronto pass the window like fallen stars and wonder how the rest of the world can just keep on turning, just keep on being beautiful, when mine has entirely collapsed.

When we get close to the AGO, Elio finally speaks again. A sudden, casual declaration.

"You can always put a bullet in his head. That's what I did."

My hands squeeze into fists in my lap.

"You killed your own father?" I shouldn't be surprised by that. Elio's ruthless. It's what he's known for.

He laughs, but the sound is dark and brittle.

"Trust me, he deserved it."

"Trust you?" I respond with my own bitter laugh. The laughter dies in my throat when leather brushes the back of my neck. Elio fists the chain of the beautiful collar beneath my hair.

We're at the AGO now, and he stops the car. Outside, a young valet jogs through lightly falling snow towards us.

Elio leans in at the same time he tugs the chain, forcing me sideways towards him. He speaks close to my ear, not touching it, but even so a shameful shiver runs through me, zinging in my nipples and my clit, rekindling the earlier arousal.

"You're going to have to trust me, Songbird."

His breath is the barest brush of sensation on my skin, but it explodes through me. His leather-bound knuckles rest against the top of my spine, prickling and hard and soft all at once.

"This city is a snake pit. And the only one who can keep you safe here now is me."

Chapter 18

Deirdre

The cold air feels good on my skin when I step out of the car. Elio holds the door for me, his gaze a hot contrast to the winter night. Plump snowflakes hit my shoulders and hair, and I know if I'm out here too long I'll freeze my ass off. But for now, it's heaven.

Curse appears seemingly out of nowhere, startling me as the valet drives the car away. The two brothers bracket my body, both of them keenly alert, like bodyguards, reminding me of the other dangers that still lie in wait for me.

Elio's gloved hand finds the back of the necklace again, and I buck against his touch.

"No way. You're not walking me in there like a dog," I say. Elio doesn't look at me, his gaze sweeping back and forth over the snowy street. But shockingly he releases the chain.

Only to settle his hand on my lower back. My *bare* lower back. So low his fingertips dip beneath the fabric of the dress and settle on my hip.

"Better?" he asks as we enter the art gallery.

No. It's ten times fucking worse. Because instead of just humiliation, now I'm once again feeling the electric bite of arousal. The surface of his glove is cool at first, but the longer his hand is on my skin, the more heat I feel penetrating the leather. Seeping into me. Branding me. This is insane, getting turned on solely from his hand on my back. *His* hand! The man who took me, who caged me, who claims he owns me. But though I try to fight the sensations, I can't deny them. It feels like his hand is sinking right through my spine and into my pelvis, stirring and squeezing inside with cruelly expert precision. With the mere press of his palm, the claim of his fingers, he's playing my body with a mastery I could never hope to achieve at the violin. Not in a hundred fucking years.

We head towards the entrance tables, and the brothers don't even toss a glance at the two young women collecting tickets. There's a line-up of attendees waiting to hand over their tickets, and I burn with their gazes as we pass right by the line. I wonder which of the dazzling women and men in suits are part of Elio's world, and which are just regular rich people out for a night on the town. Do they know who Elio is? Do they know who I am?

Can any of them help me now?

I think about twisting and looking back at those people, waiting so patiently in line. The people following the rules while Elio ploughs right through them, dragging me along with him. I think about calling out to them, begging them to save me. But I don't, because maybe I'm a coward like my father has turned out to be.

Or maybe I'm weak in other ways. Worse ways. Because Elio's hand is still there on my back, and it's like he's bound me with that simple touch. It's like I can't speak, can't even breathe if he doesn't allow it. I let him guide me further into the building, and I want to pretend I walk numbly, like an automaton. But I'm not numb. Every nerve is ragged and raw. My whole body in turmoil. Tumultuous waves of quivering heat rise, fall, *crash*. I hate it, and hate him for making me feel it.

But even the hate doesn't ease my aching clit. My oversensitive nipples.

I wonder if the hate makes it worse.

Though it's a nearly impossible task, I try to focus on the surroundings to take my mind off my hideous reactions to Elio. Curse is still on my other side, but I'm barely aware of him or anyone else as we walk. Elio commands everything, including my attention.

We end up in a space I don't recognize. I've been to the AGO before, but it's been a while. I know it's been under construction recently, and this must be the new wing Valentina mentioned. It's a vast, glittering space with pure glass all along one towering side, leaning inwards at the top, creating a half-pyramid effect. The space is dotted with beautiful people admiring various art installations, sculptures and other three-dimensional pieces in the centre of the space, with paintings and sketches and textiles on the inner wall. At the far end of the space, there are long tables with food as well as a bar with a bartender handing out drinks. Near the food is an area free of tables and art pieces, and a few couples are dancing to music played by a small string quartet.

"There you are!"

A familiar voice cuts through the music and the chatter. Valentina hustles over. You'd never know based on how she moves that she's wearing shoes that should be considered hazardous to human health. My own feet are already aching, my arches contorted. If I tried to run like her, I'd break an ankle.

Or my neck.

Elio doesn't move his hand as his cousin joins our group. Valentina's lashes are so long and fluttery it's impossible to miss the way her gaze dips there before bouncing right back up.

"Oh, shit, your hair! I didn't have time to spray it after you took out the rollers!"

I reach up, wondering what she's talking about, then remember the snow that fell on me which has no doubt melted and changed the style. My natural hair is a weird combination of straight and wavy at the back and curly at the sides and front. A quick brush of my fingers lets me know that little baby hairs are springing up into ringlets around my face. I try to smooth them, then stop. I shouldn't care what I look like. If my hair is presentable enough. I don't even want to be here at all.

But when I stop fussing with my hair, Valentina takes over. Even in her heels she's shorter than me, because my own shoes negate any height hers add. She stretches, frowning and smoothing, muttering about hairspray. I'm about to ask her to stop, to shy away from her touch, when something happens that makes me freeze.

It's the brutally slow and unbearably erotic movement of Elio's hand against my skin. He glides his hand in a smooth, small circle against my back, his fingers caressing my hip until I can't make a sound, can barely breathe. I squeeze my inner thighs together and close my eyes. The sensations of Valentina fiddling with my hair die away, along with everything else, until there's only Elio. Elio and the leather-smooth slide of his hand on my blistering skin.

His hand dips slightly lower, and I feel a new tension

enter his grip, jarring him into sudden stillness. *Fuck.* He's realized I have no underwear on. There's no way he hasn't. His fingers are well beneath my dress now, past where the top of panties would sit on my hips, and even with the gloves he'd be able to tell there's no extra fabric down there.

We both remain still but not still, frozen but vibrating beneath the silence. Then, there's a tiny movement from him. The cricking of his index finger against my hip – oh, hell, it's basically the top of my ass, who am I kidding? I think that slight nudge of his finger is to make doubly sure what he felt was real. Or rather what he *didn't* feel, what isn't even *there* to feel.

He does it again. It feels like he's cricking that finger inside me.

I constrict around nothing.

"Jesus, you don't need to squeeze your eyes shut and screw up your face like that," Valentina admonishes. "You'd think I was pulling your hair out or something."

My eyes fly open, and the world rushes back.

Valentina's hands fall away from my hair, and she shrugs. "That'll have to be good enough for now."

Elio doesn't say anything, merely increases the pressure of his palm, and I'm suddenly propelled forward. Valentina lunges out of the way so that we don't collide as Elio steers me forward.

"Where are we going now?" I ask as we move through the room. He doesn't answer with words. He simply stops and turns to face me on the dance floor. The quartet is playing something slow and lovely, a song I don't recognize. Hand still plastered to my skin, he nudges me until I stumble closer to him, my hands rising to land on his chest. And I hate it, hate that I'm using him to steady myself, to keep my balance. I'm about to rip my hands away when Elio bends and gives a single word of command:

"Dance."

Un-fucking-believable. He expects me to dance with him? I feel like a marionette, like I'm nothing to him but a prop to perform at will. And when his hand starts doing that slow circle thing on my back again, making my insides turn viscous and poisonous and hot, I realize that if I am a marionette, he controls more of my strings that I do.

Maybe even all of them.

"Put your arms around my neck," he commands. With a soft grunt, he raises his left hand to my hip. With his shoulder injury, I wonder if the movement hurts. I hope it does. I hope the simple act of holding me hurts for the rest of his life.

And at the same moment, I hate the hurt. And the guilt.

You don't walk away banged-up but generally unin-jured from the car accident that killed your mother without guilt imbedding itself in your bones like shrapnel. I didn't realize how deep that guilt went, how much it's screwed me up, until now. Because I can't even be fully satisfied that Elio's injured. I know it was only because he didn't want to let someone else damage what belongs to him, an act of pure possessiveness rather than protectiveness, but that act, that injury, twists inside me now. Makes me feel like I owe him something. Something far greater than the millions of dollars I already do.

Elio's grip tightens on me, and his tone is dark when he speaks again.

"Don't disobey me, Songbird. Not in public. Not here."

I still haven't put my arms around his neck like he told me to. I wonder what would happen if I pulled away. If I screamed and caused a scene.

Elio's earlier words come back to me in a haunting rush.

This city is a snake pit. The only one who can keep you safe here now is me.

I stare at my hands, starkly pale in contrast to the perfect black of his suit's jacket. My fingers feel frozen. I can't pull them away or move them up to his neck. Either choice feels like it will have permanent and devastating consequences. Disobeying him, extricating myself from him, and putting myself at the mercy of the other men who want me.

Or submitting to him. Admitting that I need him now.

I wonder if I do. Need him. If the only way to avoid being torn apart by prowling coyotes is to put myself at the mercy of the wolf instead.

I can feel Elio's hard stare on my face as I watch my own hands. They move like they belong to someone else. Sliding slowly, then more quickly, up to the base of his neck. He's so tall, even with my shoes, that I can't wrap my arms around his neck, so I just let my hands rest there.

Elio breathes out quietly, draws his thumb up and down the shuddering place where my spine meets my tailbone, and murmurs, "Good girl."

I don't know if it's his hands on me, or the way my nipples are pressed achingly to his front, or the dark rasp of his voice around those words, but my core pulses, and heat floods my skin.

I wonder if Elio's going to try to lead me in some kind of elaborate waltz, but he doesn't. He guides me back and forth in a circling, hypnotic sort of sway.

"But maybe not such a good girl," he suddenly says, his fingers digging even lower beneath my dress. One of his fingers brushes my ass, teasing the cleft there. "Why aren't you wearing panties?"

His question grows gruff at the end. Quiet, but rough and demanding. Humiliation churns alongside the arousal. And so does anger.

"That wasn't my choice," I whisper fiercely. "It's this dress! And Valentina was rushing me and just told me to take them off and-"

"And you did it," he growls, cutting me off. "Don't blame the dress or Valentina. Take responsibility, Songbird. Acknowledge the fact that a part of you wanted to come here with me without panties. You wanted to flaunt your bare little ass and pussy."

A shift of Elio's swaying stance drives the unmistakeable bulge of his cock against my belly. My mouth goes dry.

"That's not true," I whisper. But now I'm second-guessing myself. Why didn't I fight Valentina harder on this? Why didn't I hold my ground? Am I that much of a push-over?

Or did some subconscious part of me, a part of me I didn't even know is there, want this? Want this humiliation?

"If it's not true then tell me why you're so fucking turned on right now."

I gasp, feeling like he's blinded me. Like I've been hiding in the dark and he just threw on the floodlights. Exposing me completely, leaving me stunned and breathless and blinking. Another swaying shift nudges the top of his thigh between my legs, and a riot of aching pleasure so intense it almost feels like pain shoots up my spine.

"Does this make you feel more in control?" Elio murmurs against my hair as my clit throbs needily. "Knowing that you're making me fucking insane right now?" His hands guide my hips in a slow grind against his thigh. "You're playing a dangerous game. I don't like being taunted."

Only someone with a death wish would taunt this man.

"I didn't," I pant, wriggling in his grip, and I don't know if I'm trying to get closer or get away. "I, I..."

I'm going to come.

Dear fucking God, I can feel it. A fevered pulse, a quickening between my legs. In Elio's arms, against his leg, surrounded by other people, *in public*.

What is happening to me?

Panic claws at me, and for some stupid fucking reason I feel that panic most between my legs. It sharpens every sensation. Makes the roll of my swollen clit on Elio into a bright, ecstatic point of pressure that I couldn't pull away from if I tried now. He isn't even moving my hips for me anymore, just the slow motion of our dancing is enough to bring me closer and closer to that edge.

"Fuck, Deirdre," Elio groans quietly, voice roughened. "I should spank your sweet little ass for this."

It's a shocking image. Me, bent over a table. Or his lap. That black glove coming down over and over on my bare skin, stinging, marking, claiming. It's degrading. And – God help me, what is *wrong* with me – alluring. *Shit*. His fingertips press there now, a stark and silent warning.

"Or maybe this is punishment enough," he says. "Coming in public the way you're about to."

"Stop," I whisper, screwing my eyes shut. But I don't even know who or what I'm saying it to. To Elio. To myself. To the treacherous orgasm that's building, rising, cresting inside me. There's no stopping it now, no matter how much or whom I beg. No matter who is watching. That burgeoning sweep of sensation is taking over, surging inward and crystalizing like a knife, drawing blood before it shatters. I cling to Elio, shuddering and coming hard, knowing that without his shoulders under my hands and his fingers on my ass that I'd collapse. And maybe that's what he wants. To show me that I can't even fucking stand without him now.

But now his hands are dragging upwards to my waist, and he's creating space between us like he's about to let go.

Did he hear me say "Stop" and actually listen?

Or does he just want to see me fall?

"Take her," Elio says above my head to someone else. My pussy still squeezing with the shameful aftershocks of my orgasm, I pant raggedly and swallow, dizzily wondering what he's talking about. I curl my hands into fists and let them slide away from Elio's shoulders as he releases my waist. Luckily, my rubbery legs hold. He was speaking to Curse, I realize, as his brother nods and moves in close to my side.

My gaze digs into Elio's back as he turns and cuts through the crowd, walking away without another word. He said all those terrible things to me, held me hard against him while I came in the middle of this fancy event, and now he's *leaving*? Leaving me here with his silent, brooding brother while I'm soaked and shaking and still pulsing inside from what just happened?

My breath burns my throat, and I don't know if it's because of how hard I'm breathing or because of the fury.

Chapter 19

Elio

I saw Severu Serpico enter the room the same moment my desperate little Deirdre came against my thigh. Piss-poor fucking timing. Because I'd been about to say fuck it. Fuck Severu, fuck the money, fuck the event. I was about to drag Deirdre back to my car, toss her down in the backseat, and smack her ass for coming here with no panties.

Either that, or worship her pussy with my tongue.

Maybe both of those things.

It's a needy little cunt. I can already tell. Could tell from the way she came apart just from the slight bumping grind of our slow dance. She's needy all over, I'm discovering. Her ears. Her nipples. Her beautiful lower back.

Her clit.

I can't stop thinking about her clit, nestled between her legs, naked and so swollen beneath her dress, as I stalk across the gallery. But Severu is watching me, flanked by two of his men. He's waiting, and I have to get my head on straight to deal with business now.

I really don't like interacting with other bosses with half

my body's blood in my dick. Doesn't leave enough for my brain. Sev Serpico is one smart motherfucker, and there's no room for mistakes where Deirdre is concerned. I approach him in measured strides and come to a stop before him.

"Severu," I grunt in greeting.

"Elio," he responds smoothly. He swirls a small glass with golden liquid in his hand. Despite the tension simmering between us, he's perfectly composed, cordial even, looking sharp in his charcoal suit. He's older than me, in his early forties, and there are strands of grey at his temples, but I don't think that matters much. He's got the kind of face that women go nuts for. The kind that seems to only get better with age. The guy looks like he should be playing a mob boss on TV or something, like he's an actor instead of a criminal, but there's nothing fake or performed about the lethal power he carries. His eyes are a warm amber colour, but his gaze is ice cold. So observant it's almost cutting.

In half a second his gaze has gone to the too-tight crotch of my pants, then back up to my face, and I know he's already figured out what's happening.

"You're keeping the O'Malley girl."

It's not a question, but I answer anyway. So there won't be any room for doubt.

"Yes."

"Her papà owes me money."

"He owes me more."

"You and Curse killed three of my men and maimed another."

"And one of them shot me."

This surprises him. Clearly, the one soldier I left alive didn't notice my injury through the agony of his own.

I can tell Sev is weighing what he wants to say next very

carefully. No doubt the fact one of his men shot me has thrown a wrench into whatever negotiating power he thought he had here. He knows as well as I do that if I had been killed that night, there would have been a fucking war and his head would probably already be on a spike somewhere in my uncle's house.

I almost wonder if he's going to apologize, but instead he asks mildly, "How are you healing?"

"Like you give a fuck," I grunt. "Here. Take this. It covers O'Malley's debt plus some extra for the soldiers. A courtesy." I take the cheque out of my suit jacket's inner pocket and hold it between us. Sev's eyes flicker over the million-dollar sum scrawled on the paper. He grasps the edge of the cheque, but I don't let go yet. I draw the cheque back towards myself, pulling his hand with it, and lean towards him.

"I don't care what you do with this money," I mutter. "Give it to the widows. Invest it. Blow it on coke." My pinching grip on the cheque grows tighter. Sev doesn't let go or pull back, meeting my dark gaze steadily with his paler one as I continue speaking. "But any claim you had on Deirdre Elizabeth O'Malley is gone now. Fucking annihilated. I don't want to see any of your men within a hundred metres of her. If I do, they'll get the same treatment as the soldiers who came to her house. And there won't be a fat cheque for you in recompense this time."

Sev cocks his head, his eyes narrowing slightly. Finally, I release the cheque. He slides it into his jacket and coolly replies, "Noted." He raises his drink as if toasting me, and light glances on scotch the same colour as his eyes. "Enjoy your new plaything. You've certainly paid enough for her."

As he turns and leaves with his two men, I suddenly think he maybe isn't as smart as I thought he was. Because if he can't tell that Deirdre is worth ten times what I've paid for her then he's a damn fool.

I scan the room for Deirdre, finding her with Curse. I'm satisfied that she's safe, but I want to get her home soon. I've staked my claim on her publicly, paid Sev off, and I don't need to waste much more time here.

I take a step, the first of many to cross the gallery floor towards her, but someone blocks my path.

"Elio," says a high, syrupy voice.

"Nat," I grunt in irritated reply. I take Natalia in with a quick glance. Long, bright blonde hair swishing around her shoulders. Tight golden dress that makes her tits and hips look fantastic. Lips so lubricated with gloss they'd slide up and down my shaft like a fucking wet dream.

And I don't feel a thing.

The seductive smile on her face hardens at my lack of reaction to her. She wants me to want her and can tell that I don't.

"What's with the ginger?" she asks. And I feel something now, alright. Rage.

"None of your concern," I warn. But she ignores the deadly edge to my voice, pouting and crossing her arms until her boobs practically reach her throat.

"I thought you didn't fuck redheads," she snaps. "Didn't you tell me that last year when I dyed my hair red? I changed it back to blonde the next week and fried my fucking ends off."

It's not just red hair I don't like. It's the colour in general, especially when it veers into orange. Too garish, too hot, and most of the time I don't want to fucking look at it. Unless it's red wine, or blood, but both of those things are too dark to be confused with fire.

Deirdre's hair looks like fire. A riot of orange-red flame

tumbling down her back. I stare at her, jaw working, my fingers flexing inside my gloves. For a single, mind-numbing second, I think I smell smoke, and I wonder how fast I can cross this crowded room and grab her.

But then I breathe out between my teeth, realizing it's the scent on Natalia's hair and clothing. I'd forgotten she smokes. She knows better than to do it in front of me, but she must have had a cigarette recently, because the smell is fresh and not covered up by the cloud of hairspray and perfume around her. It sets me on edge.

"Who says I've changed my rules?"

Nat's shiny lips part in an O of affronted surprise.

"Are you shitting me, Elio? I just watched you basically fuck her right there on the dance floor. It looked like you were practically inside of her! And she's dripping with goddamn diamonds. Don't tell me that they're hers."

"You and I aren't together. Why do you give a shit who's warming my bed?" I ask.

"*Warming your bed?*" she hisses. "I've never even been allowed to step foot in your goddamn house! You only ever want me to suck your dick in your car, or in hotels!"

"They were nice hotels," I remind her flatly. The most expensive Toronto has to offer. She can't complain on that front.

"That's not the point and you know it!"

She's right. I do know it. I know exactly why she's pissed and I should have seen this coming. She's the daughter of a capo loyal to our family. But she doesn't just want to be somebody important's daughter.

She wants to be somebody important's wife.

She switches tactics, going from pissy to sultry.

"Come on, Elio," she murmurs, laying a hand on my

chest. "Let me take care of you tonight. Suck you." Her tongue touches her glossy lips. "Ride you."

My cock twitches, not because of Nat, but because of the image her words create. The image of a woman's head bobbing between my spread thighs. When that woman's eyes meet mine, they're not Nat's brown ones, but blue. Burning with hate and defiance and inescapable need, all at once.

Then I imagine Deirdre riding me. Fuck, she's a virgin. So innocent she probably wouldn't even know how. Would need my hands on her hips, rocking her, guiding her, just like I guided her greedy little clit against my thigh tonight.

I look over Nat's head and find Deirdre's eyes fastened on me from across the room. All the things to look at in here – the well-dressed people, the beautiful art – and I'm the one her gaze seeks out. *Eyes on me, Songbird.*

Nat is still touching me. I grip her wrist and pull her hand from my chest.

"Get out of here and take a fucking shower," I mutter, dropping her hand. "Don't ever come before me reeking of smoke again."

Nat balks and looks at me like I've slapped her, but I ignore her reaction. There's only one woman not related to me by blood or marriage in this building I actually care about.

She watches me with wary blue eyes as I approach.

Like she cannot turn away.

Chapter 20

Deirdre

I stay, shaky and silent, with Curse as Elio threads his way through the event's attendees. After he's out of my line of sight, I find myself staring at my own shoes, unable to look up and meet anyone's gaze. How many people here know what I just did? How many of them know that I just came in my captor's arms? My cheeks are hot. So is the place between my legs.

Elio is gone for a while, and I can't stand that I do it, but eventually I can't help myself from looking for him. Maybe it's the prey needing to know where the predator is. A self-preservation instinct.

He draws my attention with magnetic power and I find him instantly. He's taller than basically everyone here, a prowling wall of a man in an all-black suit. All black except for the snowy white of his pocket square, which I once again notice looks slightly out of place.

There's something else not black on his chest, I see suddenly. A hand, resting in the area of his sternum in an intimate, possessive gesture. That hand is attached to an absolute bombshell of a woman standing almost as close to him as I was a few moments ago. My insides twist when Elio's gaze meets mine over her head.

Just how many women does he have in rotation?

I'm probably just one of many. That should be a relief. Relief that Elio's attention might not always be so fiercely pinned on me.

But... it's not. It makes me feel shitty and small and pathetic. Makes me feel even worse for reacting to him the way I do, reacting to him the way I've never reacted to any man, when for him I'm just one idiotic girl out of who knows how many.

His eyes still on mine, Elio grasps the woman's wrist and pulls her hand off of his chest. He lets it drop, says something, then cuts around the blonde woman, heading straight for me. Instinctively, I try to move backwards, but my ass hits the table, rattling glasses, which makes Curse's eyes snap to me.

"What does your brother really want?" I ask as Elio approaches, taking up so much space in my vision I know he'd blot out the sun if it were daytime.

Curse watches me silently, and I decide he probably won't answer. Maybe even he doesn't know.

But then, he says something. I'm pretty sure it's the first word I've heard him speak this entire time.

It's a short reply. One single word.

"You."

There's no time for clarification, because Elio is back. I cross my arms and look away from him.

"Sev's got his money."

I'm not sure if Elio is talking to Curse or to me. Maybe both of us.

Sev's money... A million dollars, handed over like it's nothing.

Handed over for me. Elio buying me and protecting me all at once.

But who will protect me from him?

Elio's hand once again settles on my lower back, and I nearly jump out of my skin at the contact. It's like my skin is electrified. Even the softest touch jolting through me.

"Are we leaving?" I ask tightly as he steers me through the room once more. But we aren't heading for the exit. We're walking towards another table of food.

We stop in front of it, and before me is the biggest, most beautiful cake I've ever seen. It looks like a wedding cake you'd see in a magazine. Three creamy white layers decorated with elaborate blue buttercream flowers and sugar beads that look like real pearls. My stomach grumbles, and I grimace. I wish I could turn my body into a block of ice. That I had no needs. No need to eat. No terrible need between my legs. If I could somehow disconnect myself from my own inescapable physical impulses, I could be just a little more in control.

But I can't. I'm hungry. My pussy aches. My skin crawls and tingles and burns under the firm stamp of Elio's hand.

It's odd the cake is still in one perfect piece while the rest of the food has been picked away at over the evening. It's not like the event just started, and we got here late.

Almost as if reading my thoughts, Elio slides his hand off my back and grabs a large metal cake server. Some strange impulse takes hold in me.

"Wait! Don't cut it," I burst out.

Elio quirks a dark brow at me, and I flush under his gaze.

"I feel like... I feel like we're not allowed," I say, feeling incredibly stupid as I do so. But this cake is just sitting here untouched, like it's for later or something. Like someone else is supposed to take the first piece.

Elio stares at me for a long moment. Then, he turns back to the cake, lifts the cake server, and plunges it into the top tier. He does it again, creating a huge slice, then puts that slice on a plate and holds it out to me.

"Why don't you think anyone else has cut into this, yet?" he asks. I stare at the slice of cake. Red velvet. "Just who, exactly, do you think this cake is for?"

"For... for the event. I thought Valentina was going to do something with it, or..."

My brows wrinkle inward as I notice something on the piece Elio holds out to me. Thinly piped blue frosting, a tiny slice of a letter.

I crane my neck to see the top of the highest tier, my eyes dragging over words I hadn't noticed before.

Happy birthday Songbird.

"It's a birthday cake," I say, stunned. It's a pointless observation. He obviously knows what it is. It's spelled out on the fluffy surface. "How does Valentina know today's my birthday?"

"She doesn't."

My throat tightens. The only one who's mentioned my birthday in the past twenty-four hours is...

Elio.

"You did this?" I turn back to him, finding him still holding the plate out to me, his eyes boring into my face. His stance, holding up the plate, makes his suit jacket gape ever so slightly. It shifts the white pocket square, revealing an edge of lace that looks oddly familiar.

My breath explodes out of me.

"Your pocket square!" I hiss, my body alight with confused embarrassment. "That's my... my..."

I can't get the words out. But I know exactly what I'm looking at now. Carefully folded and lovingly tucked into Elio's luxurious, expensive pocket is my *fucking underwear*. The panties I was wearing the night he took me.

A smirk tugs at his mouth, the scarring along the left side of his jaw making the expression crooked.

"Probably a good thing I've got an extra pair on me, considering you seem to have forgotten yours," he drawls. "Maybe I should pull them out right now, unfold them, and slide them up your legs. Although, they haven't been washed."

"*Haven't been washed,*" I echo in astonishment, shaking my head back and forth so hard it makes my brain feel like it's colliding with my skull. He's not just using my panties as his pocket square at a very fancy, very public event, but he's using my *dirty* panties. "Why... What the hell?" I stammer. "Why wouldn't you at least wash them?"

It's an absurd question. Like I'm trying to tease some sort of rationality out of completely unreasonable behaviour. Oh, yes, panties as a pocket square. That makes sense, as long as they're clean!

Not.

Elio's smirk extends to a grin.

"Now why would I do that?" he asks, his voice like silk and smoke. He takes in a deep breath through his nose, filling his chest, then lets it out with a satisfied *ahh* sound. Like he's just taken in a lungful of pristinely fresh air on a mountainside hike. "Don't need cologne when I can smell like Songbird instead."

Oh my fucking God.

I absorb his words, still shaking my head in disbelief. My disbelief only deepens when I remember the scent of his cologne on him from dancing earlier, and I realize he just made a joke.

Elio Titone, a man with more blood on his hands than a butcher, has a sense of humour.

For some reason, that's even more disconcerting than his violence.

This is too much. I'm overcome with the almost feral need to get my panties back. To lay claim to them, because they're fucking mine. My hand snaps upward to tear them out of Elio's pocket, but he's faster. He blocks me with the plate, and my hand sinks into buttercream and dense red velvet, coating my fingers in sticky softness.

"Shit," I mutter, pulling my hand back and staring at the mess.

"Lick it off."

"What? No!"

He sets down the plate then grips my wrist.

"Lick it off or I will."

I stare at him mutinously, just daring him to do it. He may be insane enough to use my underwear as a goddamn fashion accessory, but he and I are the only ones who actually know what it is. That panties pocket square was a private message just for me. But standing in the middle of a public event and licking my hand in front of everyone? No way, that's-

He sucks my pinky into his mouth.

My breath catches as hot wet suction works over my smallest finger. Elio's tongue swipes along the line of my knuckles, the strokes demanding and so sensitizing I almost forget where we are. But, oh, *God*, there are people everywhere, and it feels like the whole world is watching me vibrate under this man's mouth. The thorny shame of it pulses in my clit.

I try to tug my hand away.

Elio lets my finger out of his mouth, sucking up the length of it as he does so until it's released with a wet popping sound. But he doesn't let go of my wrist.

I yank harder. He grasps me more firmly.

"I told you what would happen," he said, his voice quiet but hardened with a dangerous edge. "I told you that if you didn't lick this sweet mess off of your fingers then I would. You need to learn that when you disobey me, there are consequences."

Why do I feel those words deep in my core? Why do my nipples harden in response?

Why do I feel anything, *anything* towards this man besides pure fucking hate?

And how do I make it all stop?

Elio moves to start sucking my next finger when I cry out, "Fine!"

The word is out before I've even realized I've said it, but there's no backing down now. Because Elio is guiding my hand towards my mouth, a look of challenge in those obsidian eyes. I lick my lips, and his gaze falls to my mouth, muscles in his jaw flexing.

I start to lick my hand.

I try to do it fast. Get this over with. My tongue laps at my sticky skin, and I swallow the sweet cake and frosting down. This is hands-down the most delicious cake I've ever eaten, and that annoys me. It annoys me that the best birthday cake I've ever received came from *him*, and that it has to be licked off my own skin with *his* fingers on my wrist and *his* eyes on my face.

I try to ignore the fact that I could have just taken the plate when he'd first offered it and eaten it with a fork. Try to ignore the fact that he actually did give me a chance to eat this stupidly amazing cake like a normal person. But nothing about this situation is normal. Not the cake. Not him. And definitely not me. Not anymore.

I'm mostly looking at my own hand, trying to get every crumb and smear of frosting as quickly as I can. But when I do flick a glance up at Elio, his face has completely changed. The look of challenge there is gone, replaced by something so intense it alarms me. His jaw is set hard, his nostrils flaring, and he almost looks angry. Angry with me for doing exactly what he told me to do.

"What?" I ask, shaken by his expression. "You're the one who told me to-"

He doesn't let me finish. Face thunderous, he pulls me by the hand and says, "Let's go."

Chapter 21

Elio

I thought her submission would be better. That it would soothe something inside me, make me feel like I was getting back on track with her somehow. That it would be what I wanted.

I should have known that it would be worse. So much fucking worse. Deirdre glaring at me and hating me and telling me *no* is one thing. Deirdre obedient, sucking frosting off her own skin because I told her to, her wet pink tongue gliding all over because I've cornered her, is practically catastrophic. It turns my insides dark and hungry and twisted. It makes me want to push her harder, until she buckles. Until she breaks. Until all she can do is exactly what I tell her to because there isn't a single fucking thought in her head that I didn't put there.

Deirdre obeying me is addictive.

I'm already addicted to her music and her scent. If I get in this any deeper, I'm fucking done for.

The cold air outside helps clear my head a little, but it doesn't last long, because then we're in my car, the space so small and confined. So fucking close, so easy to tell her to take out my cock and suck it the way she just sucked her slender fingers.

I focus on the road as I drive, gripping the steering wheel hard with one hand, knowing that Deirdre's watching me.

"Am I ever going to get my panties back?"

"No," I reply curtly. I think about the intimate white fabric tucked into my pocket and want to pull it out. Stroke it. Want to press it to my face and inhale hard, but I'm pretty sure at this point if I try that I'll veer right off the goddamn road.

"Alright, then," Deirdre says. Her tone turns cool, almost business-like. "How much are they worth? Are you buying them? Does that wipe out some of my debt?"

"I loaned your family millions of dollars. You don't think I've already paid for these?" I grunt. "They were mine the second they touched your skin."

"No," Deirdre says firmly. "I have my own job, my own bank account. I bought almost all of my own clothes with my money, not my dad's. So, I'll repeat my earlier question. How much are they worth to you?"

Fucking priceless, is what I want to say. But telling her that I'd wipe her entire seven figure debt for a sniff of her used panties is not exactly going to put me in a position of power here.

But even so, I have to admit I'm impressed by her right now. Trying to negotiate with someone like me, in a situation like this.

"Name your price," I say, turning the car onto Brindle Path.

Deirdre pauses, as if she didn't actually expect me to agree to this. I can practically hear the gears turning inside her head.

"Twenty thousand dollars."

"Done."

"Wait, what?" She sounds stunned, her coolly confident business-woman mask slipping away, and I smirk.

"Should have asked for more, Songbird."

The guard opens the gate to the house, and I drive up and put the car in park.

"Fine, then," she says as we emerge from the vehicle. "What about my rate per performance? Per song?"

The answer is the same as before. *Priceless.*

I don't speak as I open the door. I start mounting the stairs and she follows without needing to be told, which makes my cock hard.

Clearly, she's learned from the negotiations in the car, because her proposed sum this time is much higher than before.

"A million dollars per song!" she declares.

I let out a bark of a laugh at the balls of an offer like that. At that rate, her debt would be paid in less than a week. It could be paid off in a single fucking night.

"Nice try," I tell her as we reach the top of the stairs.

"Fine. A hundred thousand per song."

"Not if you're going to pull more of that *Twinkle Twinkle Little Star* shit," I reply as we enter my bedroom. We both stop walking, and she looks at me, her face determined and so damn pretty it makes my fingers twitch.

"I won't," she says firmly. "You can pick the songs. I don't care. I'll learn anything, play anything."

I hear the rest of the sentence without her having to say it out loud.

I'll do anything to get the fuck away from you.

"A hundred thousand per performance, not per song," I counter. "If the performance meets my standards."

She presses her lips together, considering.

"Define performance."

"A set, unbroken period of playing. An hour. An evening. However long I say it is."

She nods slowly.

"OK. So that's, what, about sixty performances? If I play for you every day my debt will be paid in two months."

My teeth grind. I can see how smart she is. The clever, iron will driving her to save herself. I admire it, I do.

But I also want to strangle it. Want to remind her that no matter what she does, no matter how much money exchanges hands, she's mine until I say she's not.

And I can't see myself saying that anytime soon.

Or ever.

"Not so fast," I murmur, and I both loathe and love the look of unhappy doubt that flickers over her features. "I won't be hanging around here every day and night waiting for you to play for me. You won't be earning a hundred grand a day. And maybe I should bring that contract out again and remind you of the interest rate. Forty-two percent," I explain when she cocks her head in confusion.

She blanches.

"Forty-two percent," she says in disbelief. "That's outrageous. That's-"

"That's what you get when you borrow money from fucking loan sharks," I tell her. "I'm not a bank." I take a step towards her. "I'm not your friendly neighbourhood credit union." Another step, until I'm close enough to grasp her chin and tilt her face up to mine. "And I'm certainly not a charity."

"Fine," she hisses, jerking her chin from my hand. "Then let's start. Right now."

She moves away, then returns a moment later with her violin. And without her shoes.

The straps from her shoes have left criss-crossing red lines on her fair skin, and the marks make my blood heat.

"What do you want me to play?" she asks. I can tell she's trying to assume a look of professional neutrality. But that spark of defiance in her eyes is still there.

"Something good," I say, sitting on the edge of my bed and spreading my thighs. "Something Irish."

Her slender orange eyebrows rise at that, but she recovers quickly with a nod. She lifts her violin and bow, and is about to start, when I say, "Not like that."

"Not like what?" she asks, frowning.

"Not way over there." I point downwards, to the space between my thighs. "You'll play right here."

"I... I can't do that. It's too close. I won't be able to focus. I-"

"I told you that you'd earn one hundred thousand dollars per performance if the performance meets my standards," I remind her. "I get to choose where and how and what you play. Now come here."

She shifts on her little bare feet, and I wonder if she'll disobey me, if she'll fight. But she doesn't. She comes to me, with small soft steps, and there it is again, that darkness that almost feels like rage when she obeys me. A darkness that tells me to order her to kneel, right now, so I can jam my cock down her throat.

But more than anything right now, I want to hear her play. It's why I've brought her here, after all.

Deirdre stops between my knees.

"Closer," I urge her. Her breath gets shaky, but she does it anyway, stepping forward until her hips are a mere inch from my crotch.

"Now play," I rasp.

She does.

She starts slowly, the notes almost melancholic, before everything intensifies, rising and quickening into a relentlessly, tragically beautiful rhythm. I groan, letting my eyes fall shut. This is what I wanted, what I needed. This luminous, ravenous, drugged-up feeling. The bleeding, brutal beauty that Deirdre wields with the precise yet wild artistry of an angel. I fist the bedding, tilting my head back, letting the notes fall over me like snow, like rain, like a blessing and a curse. Sacred and profane. Salvation and ruin. Celestial, ethereal, and deeply, primally human.

How the fuck does she do this?

I've listened to violin on endless repeats for the past year and a half. I'm pretty sure I've even saved this exact song to a playlist somewhere. But it's not the same. Nothing touches what Deirdre does to me, and I need to fucking know why.

I crack my eyes open, as if that will help me understand somehow. But that just throws me into chaotic, lustful turmoil, because I'm about eye-level with her breasts, and every time she moves her arms, they bounce and strain the silk of her dress.

Having her this close and hearing her play, properly play, while one breath away from her skin is too fucking much. I've wanted her for too long tonight, and my dick is paying the price. My eyes glued to her chest, my ears and brain and lungs and whatever's left of my heart flooded with her song, I undo the buckle on my belt.

The sound makes Deirdre's eyes snap open. Her playing slows, then stops altogether when I take out my throbbing shaft and start to stroke it.

"What the hell are you doing?" she breathes, her eyes huge and glued to my hand on my dick.

"Keep playing," I command her, fisting myself harder.

"I... What? While you're doing *that*? That's way too distracting!"

"Then close your eyes," I grunt. "Then maybe you won't be so affected by me and the sight of my cock."

She blushes so hard that I see it through the makeup this time.

"I'm not *affected* by you!" she exclaims.

I could tell her all the ways I know that isn't true, starting with how she fucking came on my leg at the gala tonight. But instead, I just spread my thighs wider, stroke myself faster, and tell her, "Prove it."

She swallows so hard the muscles in her throat visibly contract, and fuck, does that make me feel like I'm already close.

"Keep playing," I order. I run my thumb over my agonized tip and add darkly, "Every time you stop before I tell you to, I'll dock your pay by ten thousand dollars."

That gets her attention real quick. Jaw tight, she scrunches up her face and starts to play again.

"Good little Songbird," I groan. The music roars through my blood just like desire. Velvety sensation expands in my groin, wrapping around the base of my spine and tightening in my balls. The feeling rises, binds me tighter, when I see Deirdre's nipples hardening right before my very eyes.

She may hate me, but a part of her likes this. Likes being embarrassed, likes being shoved into these situations. Even now, I can see how she's squeezing her thighs together beneath her dress.

I lean forward and suck one of her nipples into my mouth.

The music stops, and she cries out. I release my cock, raise my hand out to the side, then bring it firmly down against her ass. She jerks forward with the force of the motion, gasping. I rub the place I spanked her, tonguing her hot little bud of a nipple through the damp silk before I pull back slightly and meet her wild gaze.

"Now you're at ninety-thousand," I inform her sternly. "*Keep playing.*"

She looks like she wants to drive her bow right through my eye. I drag the silk of the dress to the side, freeing her breast, and tease her nub with my tongue before I tell her that she's about to lose another ten thousand.

Panting, she returns her bow to the strings.

And I return my hand to my cock.

Chapter 22

Deirdre

I saw my way through the melody, barely even aware of what song I'm playing now. I'm completely relying on muscle memory to keep me going as Elio sucks my bare nipple into his mouth, teasing the screaming tip with his tongue. I can't think about what I'm doing. Can't think about any of this. I just have to get through it without falling apart.

Or stopping playing.

My ass cheek stings, sparking tingles emanating outward from where Elio's hand came down on me with a *thwack*. Those sharp, prickly tingles keep fucking spreading, all the way down, down towards my pussy, lighting up my clit. There had been more shock than pain when his hand had connected with my ass, and now any pain there was is morphing into poisonous pleasure, pulsing and burning and making me wonder what it would feel like if he did it again.

But I won't find out. Because I *will not* stop playing. Not now. Not when he's challenged me the way he has. I have to keep going, keep playing by his rules. Keep earning money to chip more and more away at the chains of debt that bind me.

So, I let my arms go, let them do what they know how to do, guiding me through the rhythm of the song when the rest of my body is tumbling headlong towards another disastrous orgasm.

I never knew my nipples were this sensitive. Elio's lips and tongue are firm and wet. Demanding and greedy. Soon, he isn't satisfied with just one breast, and he urges silk away from the other, until both are bared to him. He sucks my other nipple into his mouth, biting it gently, then harder, until I yelp. But I grit my teeth and I don't fucking stop. My notes may be getting clumsy, but I keep going. My bow is my sword and I will fight until the bitter end.

The music is loud in my ears, but even so I can hear the ragged drag of Elio's breath through his nose. The filthy wet sounds his mouth makes against my nipple. The relentless pumping of his cock. A cock that is harder than any human flesh ought to be. I could tell just by looking at it, without even touching, how engorged and unyielding his shaft is. He sucks me harder, and I'm sure that he's testing me. Trying to make me falter. To prove that I can't do this. That I'm not as immune to him as I claimed.

But I keep playing. I keep doing what I know how to do – making music. I keep going until I almost think I might win this time. His mouth is hot, hateful, delicious sin but maybe I can beat him. Maybe I can make it. Just keep going, get to the end of the song, and –

Without warning, his mouth detaches from my nipple, leaving my skin feeling cold and tender. I don't open my eyes, not letting myself get distracted even for a moment.

But because of that, I have absolutely no warning when his tongue returns to me. Not on my breast.

But on my clit.

He's dragged up one side of my skirt, splitting it wide at the slit, and his face is pressed between my legs. I flinch and muffle a moan when he circles my clit in hard, relentless circles with the tip of his tongue. Pleasure and shame shudder through me in equal measure, making my clit swollen and more sensitive than it's ever been. My legs quake, threatening to collapse, as his tongue circles and flicks. When he groans, latches on and sucks, it feels like my entire spine has turned to viscous honey.

I don't realize I've stopped playing until a vicious *thwack!* fills the silence.

"Ah!" I cry. "Fuck!" The burn on my ass cheek is sudden and bright. Just like Elio did last time, he massages me firmly immediately after doing it, dispersing jerky waves of prickling heat over my ass and through my core. It feels like my nerves have been replaced with sparklers. Like everything is darkness until Elio's hand connects and makes white light burst into a million glinting shards.

"Eighty thousand," he rasps into the damp curls between my legs.

Shit. Shit, shit, shit!

My sense of victory is fading fast. I shakily raise my bow and violin, and then moan in complaint when he draws a slick, greedy stripe over my clit with his tongue.

"This isn't fair," I whimper.

"I'm not a fair man, Deirdre."

There's no deep, abiding sense of morality guiding Elio at his core. No good man under the demands and violence. He only speaks the languages of death and sex and money. Languages that, up until this moment, I've never known a word of.

"I... I can't-"

Thwack! Another hot smack. Another long, delirious suck on my clit. Another faltering yet inevitable step closer to climax.

"Seventy thousand."

Why is this happening? Why am I *letting* this happen? Why am I not pushing his head away, kicking and screaming and fighting? No one's ever gone down on me before, and I shouldn't let him be the first.

I shouldn't be panting and clenching, practically vibrating against his tongue. I shouldn't be waiting in wriggling anticipation for his hand to find my ass again.

I shouldn't look down at his dark head at my pussy, because fuck, that's the worst mistake I could have made. Because he looks good, and I don't want to think he looks good, but he *does*. His hair is so black and thick and curling ever so slightly at the ends. It's not cut very short; it's long enough that pieces have tumbled forward over his forehead.

He meets my gaze, looking up through his hair and lashes that are darker and thicker than I'd previously noticed. He lifts his hand, the black leather shape of it in the air like an omen.

Just that, just that simple threat, has my hips rocking forward against his face, nerves in my clit jumping with expectation. But I halt the movement, and furious pride fights against my submission.

I grit my teeth and put my bow to the strings once more.

Only, I truly don't know how long I'll last now. I don't know if Elio is trying to reward me for doing what I'm told, or trying to break me. Because his mouth is suddenly harder, hungrier, his tongue dragging backwards to circle my entrance before moving forward once more to devour my quivering clit. My arms feel like they're full of sand and it's a miracle I can lift them at all at this point. My posture is completely off – I'm hunching further and further forward, like I'm curling towards Elio, curling *around* him, my body seeking contact even though I rebel against it.

I fight to keep my arms in place. Every press and slide of my fingertips is a battle. Every grind of my bow a war.

I don't know if this war is with Elio...

Or with myself.

His tongue dips backwards again, and then jabs inside me, making my toes curl against the smooth hardwood floor. But I won't stop again. I swear I won't. I'll keep going until, until...

Until the firm, leather press of his thumb sends shockwaves through my pulsing clit. He moves his tongue inside me, almost like he's *fucking* me with it, while his thumb grinds on my clit and everything clenches and burns and constricts and I can't, I fucking *can't*.

My violin and bow sag down, and I arch forward, my spine collapsing, until my hands and instruments connect with Elio's broad, muscled back. The pressure of his thumb disappears from my clit, and I know exactly what it fucking means, because I'm trembling and ashamed and so fucking ready for the terrible, electric collision of leather on silk. Hand on flesh.

Elio waits a moment before he does it. Like maybe he's giving me one final chance to finish the song.

Or maybe he just wants the crackling anticipation of the threat to build, build, build alongside the throbbing at my core, the pleasure rising like a dark symphony inside me. I'm right there, *right there*, and I can't stop it. I can't fight it. And the worst part is that maybe I don't even want to, now. Maybe there's something dirty and broken inside me, some part of me that thinks maybe I deserve this, that I need it. That the punishment is an answer to a question I've never dared to ask. The reply to some prayer that's lived, unspoken and unacknowledged, at the very core of my soul for the past ten years.

Elio's hand finally connects, the sound of the slap ripping through the air. A ragged moan tears from my throat. Biting pain and pleasure expand from where his hand grips my flesh, undulating downwards and inwards until my pussy clamps down on his tongue, over and over again.

My hands jerk and then release, my violin and bow sliding down Elio's back until they hit the bed. I fist the back of his jacket so hard I wonder if I'll rip the expensive fabric. The sounds coming out of my mouth are a fucking abomination. I don't recognize my own voice as I moan, so horny and pathetically needy as I come from getting spanked and tongue-fucked by this man who's taken everything from me. I can't even control the grinding motion of my hips now, and I whimper in embarrassment as I ride Elio's tongue, then whimper again, louder, when he pulls it away.

"*Fuck*," he groans. He'd been bent over, hinging at the waist to access my pussy, but now he straightens up in his sitting position. My pussy clenches again at the sight of him. So huge and dangerous and purely masculine, muscled thighs spread, shoulders straining the tight confines of his suit, scarred jaw flexing. Cock standing straight up from a thatch of dark hair at its base, thick and veiny and so engorged his tip is red, almost purple. And, oh God, his *face*. His *eyes*. He's got that look again. The one he had when he watched me lick the cake off my hand at the gala. That expression of murderous darkness. Rage so ravenous I can't tell it apart from desire.

The sight of his dark leather glove curling around his

swollen shaft is so dangerously erotic I can't stand it. My breath rips in and out of my lungs, and my fingers dig in to his shoulders when he strokes a glistening bead of moisture from his tip. Why am I still holding on to him?

"I didn't bring you here for this, you know," he grits out, sliding his fist up and down his cock. "I really did just bring you here to play for me. But you're so fucking disobedient. And so fucking pretty when you do obey."

His words are like a physical caress, and I can't escape them. *So fucking pretty when you obey.*

"My good, bad little Songbird," he groans. "Do you see how fucking hard you make me?"

Of course I do. It would be impossible not to. Something in me shivers with satisfaction that I'm the one who did this to him. I may not have any control over this situation, or even my own body, but at least I have some control over his.

His voice lowers an entire dangerous octave. "You're not supposed to make me so hard I can't see straight."

"Then what am I supposed to do?" I whisper. "Why did you choose me? Is it just about the debt? Because I..." I hesitate, as if I'm not supposed to ask. But it's not like he was hiding them. The CDs were right there on a shelf in the open. "I found the CDs. Recordings of all my performances from the past year and a half."

Elio breathes out, long and hot, a stirring motion over my bared breasts.

The movement of his hand slows.

"Let me tell you a story," he says. "The story of the songbird, the monster, and the man." His hand stops moving altogether. "One hot summer day, the man begged a monster for money. But the monster knew it was a bad deal.

He was just in the process of turning the man down flat when he heard something."

"Heard what?"

"A song. A song that got inside him, a song he couldn't shake. He needed to find out what it was and who the hell could play like that. So, he looked up. And there was the prettiest little songbird he ever did see." His hand isn't moving now, but his hips are, grinding slowly and sensuously up into his leather fist. A new roughness enters his voice as he continues. "In that instant, the monster knew he'd lend the man the money as long as it meant that he could get that songbird for himself. He'd wait, bide his time until the term ran out. But by that point, he was already hopelessly fucking addicted."

His hips buck, fucking his fist faster. I can't tear my gaze away from the way his slick head appears then disappears into the leather.

"So the monster watched the songbird every chance he got. Took her music home, too, to try to get another hit of her, even though it wasn't anywhere near enough."

His words are so rough now, almost slurred.

"And then, one cold winter morning, the first of the new year and the day that songbird turned twenty, time ran out for the man. The monster returned. And this time-" His breath catches, making the words jagged, "the monster took the songbird for himself. And he killed anyone who got in his fucking way."

A creamy jet spurts from Elio's tip, followed by another, and another. Rope after rope of come, raining down on his pants and his glove. Some of it even reaches my naked chest, wet and glistening and staining me. As his come sinks in, so does the story he's just told me. Understanding explodes in my head like a bomb.

He didn't just take me because of my father's debt. He lent my father the money, created that debt in the first fucking place, specifically so that he could have me. I remember something he said before, something I hadn't understood. Until now.

From the very beginning, I didn't consider this a loan, but an investment.

The investment was in me.

Having me wasn't a byproduct of a deal gone bad. It was the *whole fucking point*. The only reason the deal existed in the first place.

"You weren't even going to lend my dad the money until you saw me," I say tightly, my mind spinning. "You engineered this entire situation just so you could have access to me! You created the debt just to trap me with it!"

He drags a finger through the come dripping between my breasts.

"Technically, your father created the debt," Elio says coolly. "He was so deep in the hole by that point that he had no choice but to come begging to Peter in order pay Paul. But otherwise, yes, you are correct. I would never have lent your father that money if I hadn't seen you and heard you play that day." He tucks himself back into his pants and stands, looking down at me with unrepentant eyes. "I lent him that money precisely because I knew I'd never get it back. Because I knew that I'd get you in the end."

It infuriates me how easily he admits it. That he doesn't even care enough about what I think of him to deny what he's done.

"I hate you," I whisper thickly. Tears are building at the backs of my eyes, tightening my throat.

"You're free to do so," Elio says calmly. Almost cavalierly. He swipes his finger through the come on my skin again, dragging it over to my nipple and rubbing it into the agonizingly sensitive peak as he leans down.

"Enjoy it, Deirdre. Enjoy hating me," he whispers against my ear, teasing my nipple into a taut and aching point. "Because it's one of the only freedoms you have left."

I stumble backwards and away from him, reeling.

I spin, seeing the doorless entry into the other bedroom.

There's nowhere to run. And I know the act is hopeless.

But I run anyway.

Chapter 23

Deirdre

When I wake up in the morning, I feel well-rested, and I don't like it. Don't like how incredibly comfortable this bed is. Or how deeply my body fell into slumber after last night. After...

After I came. *Twice.*

I pull the covers up over my head, as if I can hide my shame that way. What is it about Elio, and my body around him, that turns me into someone I don't recognize? Someone I don't know?

My phone buzzes on the bedside table, and I whip off the bedding, reaching for it. Maybe it's my father contacting me. Maybe everything Elio told me about him leaving, about Bridget, was just a lie meant to make me fall further into this trap, this world. To make me trust him.

But there's no word from Dad.

There is, however, a text from Brian, letting me know he's back from Christmas break in Ottawa and wants to see me. I almost laugh, bitterly, about the change in circumstances since December. I spent weeks avoiding Brian, and now I couldn't even see him if I wanted to. Something tells me that meeting up with my ex-boyfriend is absolutely not something Elio would allow. And part of me is pissed about that, not because I want to be anywhere near Brian, but because of the control.

But another part of me, a part low in my belly, tightens strangely. Almost as if I like this. Like the fact that the bars of my cage have both trapped me and protected me.

But I'm not protected, am I? Not from Elio. He's the one I need to focus on, to be most worried about. I wonder what Elio would do if I did somehow meet up with another man. I wonder what he'd do if Brian tried to get to me now.

Probably wouldn't end well for Brian.

And it scares me how that thought brings me a short slice of terrible satisfaction. Fuck, what am I turning into? Elio is not my bodyguard or my boyfriend. He's my abductor. The possessiveness he feels over me is not something to be admired. It's something I need to fight.

Or I will never find my way back to my own life again.

I mentally tally how much was reduced from my debt last night. Twenty thousand from the panties – Jesus Christ, I still can't believe I'm selling my goddamn panties to the mob now – and eighty thousand from last night. Or was it seventy? I remember him getting to eighty-thousand, I remember him saying it directly against me, the words stirring over my aching clit. But I'm pretty sure I stopped then. That's when I... I...

I *came*. For the second time. He spanked me, just hard enough to hurt, just hard enough to let me know exactly how much power he holds and, at the same time, how much he held back, and some buried, dirty part of me had actually liked it.

And the worst thing is, I don't think Elio created that dirty part.

I think it was already there and he just unearthed it. Like he already understands things inside me I don't. Like he knew exactly where to dig.

And then I remember how long he's been watching me. How long he's been wanting me. And I wonder how much he's learned about me while I had no idea he was even there.

My phone buzzes again, and I scowl, assuming it's Brian, but it's not. It's an email to my University of Toronto email address, sent from another U of T address that I don't recognize. It's a student's email address, but I don't know the name. Frowning, I open it.

HEY!!!! It's Willow! I still don't have my phone. I'm at one of the U of T libraries with my neighbour Dylan and I'm using his school email to contact you. Figured that was better than sending a text from his phone because I can log into his email anywhere to check if you've replied, but I don't have a phone for him to forward a text to.

What is happening??? I heard about last night!!! That you showed up at some Titone event at the AGO decked out in diamonds. People are saying that Elio Titone practically fucked you right there in the middle of the floor you two were dancing so close and that he got you a big slice of cake after that. Elio fucking Titone cutting and serving someone cake!!! Absolutely unheard of. Was it birthday cake? Was the party for you??? What the fuck is going on???

I have no idea how to help you right now, but so help me God, if he's hurting you, I will. Fuck Elio and fuck Darragh (who's even more pissed off after last night, just so you know). I will steal a goddamn tank and crash through the side of wherever you're being held to save you if I have to. Just let me know what's happening. Let me know where you are.

Let me know that you're OK.

Willow

My eyes blur with tears, and I clutch my phone to my squeezing chest. It feels like the entire world's forgotten about me. Like my own life has been erased, crushed under the new reality Elio's imposed upon it. But it's not true. Willow's still out there, loving me, fighting for me. Trying to help me.

She can't, of course. And that changes the tears from ones of affectionate gratitude to ones of hopeless rage. She can't help me. It's not even safe for her to be contacting me this way, especially if Darragh's as angry as she says he is. I'm an outcast, my father a traitor, and she absolutely cannot be caught associating with me now.

As much as I want to confide in her, to beg her to help me any way she can, I won't. She wants to protect me, but I need to protect her right now. From her father and from Darragh if he finds out she's trying to help me.

I sniff hard and angrily rub tears from my eyes with the back of my hand before I shakily type a reply. With every letter that appears on the screen, I feel like I'm pulling a door shut between us, inch by inch, until it slams and a lock clicks into place.

Willow,

Thank you so much for finding a way to contact me. It means more than you can know.

That party last night wasn't in my honour, but yes, the cake was a birthday cake for me. It may be hard to believe, but I'm safe. Elio is taking care of me.

I stop typing, chewing on my lip, hating the words I've just written and yet not entirely feeling like they're a lie, either. Elio has trapped me, but he's also showered me in luxury even my father's stolen money couldn't buy. Not that Dad spent much of it on me, I think sourly. Elio's kept me fed, clothed me in finery, ordered me the most amazing birthday cake a bakery could possibly produce, and...

Licked my clit until I came.

He also spanked me, I hiss furiously inside my own head. *He told me he owns every part of me. Is heaping more and more debt on top of me with interest rates he could slash but won't.*

I want to tell Willow everything. To spill my guts to her, let her find a way to fix this. But I can't. Because Willow actually would try to fix it, and I don't want her to be the object of Darragh's ire. Or Elio's. So I grit my teeth and keep on typing.

My dad completely fucked me over. He borrowed millions from Sev Serpico and Elio to cover up what he stole from Darragh and then he didn't pay it back. That's why New Year's went down the way it did (is Mr Byrne OK???)

Elio paid off my father's debt to the Camorra and is letting me work off the money Dad owes him. For some reason he likes the way I play violin. So I'm doing that for him and slowly paying everything back that way. It's going to take a while, so don't expect me to resurface anytime soon.

Not that I can resurface at all if Darragh still wants to get his hands on me. I swallow hard, realizing for the first time that the debt might not be the only thing standing between freedom and me. Even if I pay back every cent, even if Elio lets me go, Darragh will be waiting for me. Unless he finds my father first, but I don't want that, either. Even after everything that's happened and everything he's done, I don't want Dad getting murdered over this. I lost one parent and never truly recovered. I can't handle losing another one.

Though haven't I already lost him in a way?

I might never see my father, my only living parent, again.

I focus on finishing my message to Willow so that I don't completely fall apart.

I'm safe, I type out again. *I'm making this work. You don't need to do anything for me right now. Actually, no – the number one thing you can do for me is to keep yourself safe. Nobody will take kindly to you trying to interact with me now. The last thing I want is you getting hurt over this.*

Stay safe, Willow. I love you so much.

Dee

Just as I send the message, I hear the familiar sound of a cart being pushed into the room. My head snaps up to see Rosa bringing breakfast in – a tray laden with pastries and fresh fruit and...

"Is that a pot of tea?" I ask, almost wondering if all the unshed tears are making me see things.

"*Si, si.* Tea. The boss tell me make, so I make."

The boss...

That has to be Elio.

I stare at the small glass teapot like it's something fantastical, like a unicorn that shouldn't exist but somehow does. *Elio told her to bring me tea. Because that's what I like...*

I'm almost scared to drink it. Scared of what it means. Is this kindness? Some small comfort meant to make me happy? Or is it some kind of trap?

I decide that I don't care. I've been dying for a cup of tea since yesterday, and as soon as Rosa brings the cart to a stop beside the bed, I thank her profusely and pour myself a steaming cup.

The scent hits me, and my eyes flutter shut for a moment as I simply inhale. This must be the best scent in the whole world. It's pure, visceral comfort, and my gratitude towards Elio in this moment is so overwhelming I want to cry all over again. God, this must be Stockholm Syndrome, wanting to thank my captor for a simple cup of tea.

But I can't help it. Tea isn't just tea to me. It's family and blooming warmth and memories. It's quiet, early mornings in the kitchen before school with my mom, pouring each other cups from her beautiful vintage teapot as I filled her in on homework and teachers and boys. It's the drink she made to soothe my tender heart when the boy I adored in grade nine told everyone he'd never date someone with hair the colour of an orange highlighter. It's Christmas and Sunday afternoons and soft murmurs and laughter. I always imagined that, the morning of my wedding, Mom and I wouldn't be drinking champagne as we got ready together, but sweet, strong cups of tea.

Sometimes, when I smell it, I can almost feel her with me. She didn't have a signature perfume, my mom. This – the fragrant waft of Irish breakfast tea – was the scent of her.

If Rosa is wondering why I've pressed the heated cup to my forehead like it's some kind of holy relic to be worshipped instead of something to drink, she doesn't say it aloud. Instead, she goes marching into the bathroom, attacking every surface with spray bottles and polishing rags. Soon, the cup is too hot to keep against my skin, and I lower it, staring into the dark, reflective surface of the drink before I take a sip.

It's good tea, though not as strong as I would have liked. I like tea that's been brewed long enough to really stand up to the milk and sugar I usually add. That's how Mom always made it.

But for now, this is good enough. I add less milk and

sugar than I normally would so I don't overwhelm the flavour, and, throat aching with tears, I chug it like it's water in the desert. It scalds my throat, but the heat of it feels cleansing, and I keep going until I can't anymore, taking a wet and choking breath. I pick away at the food, then scarf it down, realizing that only charcuterie and a bit of birthday cake for the past day wasn't anywhere near enough sustenance.

I pour myself more tea to wash it all down, holding my cup and scooting out of the bed as Rosa approaches, ready to strip the sheets. My face feels hot as she does it. Nothing even happened in this bed, and yet it feels like she'll somehow be able to know, like I've left some kind of stain, some mark of how fucked up I am that I submitted to Elio so easily last night.

No! It wasn't that easy. I tried to fight. I...

I don't even know what happened. All I know is that it can't happen again.

I think about that – submission, and whether that's truly what I did – for most of the day as I sit alone in my room. Elio doesn't come to me, and neither does Valentina. Rosa brings me lunch (the most amazing pesto chicken and mozzarella sandwich on fresh bread) and dinner (equally amazing braised lamb with potatoes and vegetables) but otherwise I see no one. I keep expecting Elio to show up, but it seems that what he said yesterday was true. He won't just be hanging around me all the time waiting for me to pick up my violin and play for him. I'll have to take whatever opportunities I can when they come to try to make a dent in the debt.

And I'll have to play out of his reach next time.

By 9pm the solitude is starting to grate on my nerves. And so is what happened last night. The more I think about it, the more I can't deny how much more I could have done to stop him. If I'd truly wanted to, I could have pulled away. I could have pushed him, kicked him, bit him. I could have told him no.

I go over and over the interaction in Elio's room last night, hoping I've just forgotten the moment I told him to stop. But I didn't forget it. Because I never fucking said it.

And suddenly, I can't sit here like his good little prisoner anymore. I have to prove to him, and maybe even more to myself, that I'm not going to be bent to his will that easily.

I stomp into the bathroom for a shower. I choose the shower this time because I can hang towels precariously from the glass that juts out from the walls and create at least some semblance of privacy. As I toss towels up over the glass with awkward, grunting movements, I wonder if he's watching me even now. I wriggle out of my clothing inside the shower then toss it out, wondering if I should try to sell him this pair of underwear as well.

And then I wonder who the hell I have become to even consider such a thing.

As I scrub myself, I wonder if Elio knows I'm showering. If, right now, his dark eyes are glued to a screen somewhere. I wonder if he's pissed about my towel barriers.

I wonder if his dick is hard. If his leather-encased fist is gripping it, stroking it, running firmly from thick veiny shaft to smooth tip. If he's going to come just knowing that I'm naked and wet in his house.

A resounding pulse between my legs makes me even more angry than I was before. I turn the water to the coldest setting, yelping at the contrast from the warmth. I force myself to wash in that cold water until I'm shivering, then I yank down one of my hanging towels and wrap it around myself, heading for the closet. I pull on a soft cotton T-shirt (there are bras, but none of them are the correct size, so I skip that) then a pair of silk underwear and slouchy pair of sweatpants.

Fully dressed now, my hair soaking the back of my shirt, I head through my bedroom and into Elio's. I don't stop until I'm at the door.

The door the leads into the rest of the house.

I've never heard anyone lock or unlock it. I also haven't been told to stay in here, though it feels like an unspoken rule. But that's exactly why I need to break it. To prove I still have half a goddamn brain in there. To prove that there's still some spirit that will fight back inside me.

My heart careens wildly in my chest, and I'm terrified that I'm going to regret this, but I do it anyway.

I pull on the door handle and open the door.

I tense, holding my breath, half-expecting Elio to be there, just waiting for me to try something like this. But he's not. There's nobody except for a guy at the top of the stairs in a black dress shirt and black trousers. He's alert, watching me closely, but he doesn't tell me to get back inside the room. Emboldened, I hold his gaze and step forward, one foot in the room and one foot out.

He still doesn't say anything, and with a shuddering breath, I step all the way out.

I fight to keep the grin off my face. This feels like a victory, no matter how small. I've stepped out of the room. Now it's time to see just how far I can go.

I turn towards the staircase, and the guard there, and start walking. The closer I get, the more my stomach twists and my nerves jangle. It's like this guy is staying still and quiet to lull me into a false sense of security so that he can grab me and bring Elio down on my head.

But even as I pass by him, my breath strangling in my

throat, he doesn't touch me. I notice that he does follow me down the stairs, but otherwise he makes no move to stop me.

Which must mean...

He's been ordered to let me walk around as I please.

This jolts me into confusion. It almost makes me stop halfway down the stairs. The fact that Elio doesn't mind if I leave the room and wander around his domain. I figured this was, well... not allowed, or something.

I'm about to be grateful to him again, like I was with the tea, but I fiercely tell myself not to be. Elio is not deserving of my gratitude. I shouldn't be thankful I can walk around this house, gorgeous though it is. He's the one who's reduced me to being stuck here in the first place.

The guard from the top of the stairs continues trailing me as I wander. I pass by the front door and cringe when I remember what happened there, what must have been seen on the cameras. When Elio stroked my nipples into aroused hardness after putting in the earrings that are currently on a bedside table upstairs.

I make my way into the kitchen and gape. I'm not a master chef or anything, but I do enjoy cooking, and this is the most insane kitchen I've seen. A massive black granite island floats in the middle, matching the glittering black granite countertops that go along one long end of the open space. Even with all the black, the space doesn't feel cold. The cabinets are a warm natural wood, and there's soft lighting built in everywhere. The fridge is huge – one of those super wide double door stainless steel ones. Most of the other appliances are stainless steel, too, including a very complicated looking espresso machine. Everything is sleek and modern. Except for the stove. I'm sure it's new and seriously expensive, but it has an almost vintage look to it with shiny brass knobs and a gas range top.

I eye the guard who has now stationed himself with his arms crossed at the island I've passed. He doesn't say anything or do anything else to stop me, so I give an internal shrug and head for the fridge. I yank it open, gawking at how much stuff is in this gigantic cooling contraption. Elio did say that there were soldiers stationed all over this house, and I wonder if Rosa cooks for all of them. There's a ton of prepared food in here, containers of meat and pasta and jars of sauces, as well as a small grocery store's worth of raw ingredients – fresh herbs, cheeses, cream. I expect to see tomatoes in here but I don't, and I realize there are tomatoes in a bowl on the countertop. That bowl of beautiful colour lends the spotless kitchen a sense of hominess that feels almost comforting, and I shove it away.

Beyond the kitchen is another jaw-dropping room I hadn't noticed before – a wine cellar. Although, it's above ground, so is it still a cellar? A wine room? I have no idea. I can tell the difference between different kinds of tea at first whiff, but I have absolutely no palette or real knowledge of wine, even though I do like drinking it.

The wine room is separated from the kitchen by a glass wall so clean it's almost invisible, and I nearly walk right into it. I recover just in time, finally finding a section of the glass that opens smoothly with a slight push. It's much cooler in here than in the rest of the house, and goosebumps form along my bare arms. My braless nipples tighten.

Crossing my arms, I head into the cool, large space. It's darker in here than in the kitchen, too, and everything feels hushed. The bottles of wine all float in curved sections of wood along the shelves, reminding me of ships in a harbour.

Right now, a glass of wine sounds absolutely perfect. I have no idea if I'm allowed to do this, but I decide I don't care. The whole point of venturing out here was to prove that I'm not crushed under Elio's thumb and I'm going to go for it. I gaze around the room, having absolutely no idea which bottle to choose, so I take one out at random. It's a red, and it looks fancy and Italian. Before I lose my nerve, I scuttle back into the kitchen with my prize.

The soldier watching me now has a crease between his brows, like I'm doing something unexpected, or maybe something his boss hasn't specifically given him instructions to handle. I smirk, picturing Elio telling the guards to let me wander around the house, but not addressing what to do if the prisoner decides to get wine drunk. Not that I'm going to get drunk. I need to keep my wits about me. But a drink to take the edge off might be just the ticket.

I already feel drunk – drunk on this tiny bit of power. I realize I'm humming as I slam open drawers and cupboards, looking for a corkscrew. I eventually find one and open the wine, leaving the corkscrew with the cork still stuck in its twirly jaws on the counter. I haven't yet discovered where the wineglasses are, but in the cupboard straight ahead of me are little coffee cups for espresso. I grab one and glug the wine into the cup. *Guess I'm doing shots,* I think as I pick up the tiny cup full of wine. I raise it to my lips and am about to take a sip when a voice slices through the quiet air.

"That how you were taught to drink wine?"

The sound of someone – a very male someone – speaking surprises me so much that I slosh some of the wine down my front. I'm pissed, but then I remember that this isn't even my shirt, so why do I care if it's stained? I turn to look at the guard, then jolt into stillness when I see the guard is gone. Elio is watching me, his hip leaning against the island, the black leather on his right hand plastered palm-down against the granite. The rest of his clothing is all black – dress shirt, pants. It matches the coal-black gleam of his thick hair and the intense darkness of his eyes.

His gaze dips to the dark red wetness staining the front of my shirt. Or maybe to my nipples, because I don't have a bra on and now I'm shivering under his gaze. God, I really need that wine after all. It will warm me. Fortify me. I raise the half-empty ceramic cup to my lips.

"Stop."

I inhale sharply at the command uttered in that deadly-soft voice, cup freezing in midair. There's an instinct inside me that wants to obey him, and it's not entirely due to fear. But that's the very same instinct I've been fighting, and I have to overcome it. Now or fucking never.

I hold his gaze and take a sip.

But you're so fucking disobedient.

The sudden crash of his words from last night makes my skin heat, or maybe it's the wine. I take another sip.

Elio doesn't say anything. He moves towards me, and I want to crowd backwards against the counter and away from him, but I force myself to hold my ground. I brace for him to touch me, but he doesn't. Instead, he plants his left hand on the counter behind me with a slight grunt then lifts his other arm to open a cupboard above my head. At the sound he makes, my eyes go to his muscled but injured shoulder, and suddenly I'm in my backyard, the new year bearing down on me with hatred and guns. I'm barefoot and terrified and cold, but he has me, *he has me*, and both our bodies shudder with the impact of the shot.

"Does it hurt?"

I shouldn't be asking. I shouldn't care. I should *want* him to hurt. I'm too tender-hearted for my own good. How many times has Willow told me that? That I need to be harder and sharper, to cut my way through this world like a knife instead of letting myself be led along. Led by people like my father and my teachers and Brian. By the hole that opened up inside me the day tires slid ten years ago.

Elio is a knife. No, he's an axe. He has both the sharp edge and the bludgeoning strength. What would it be like to have power like that? To see obstacles and carve right through them, without fear and without thought? To bend everything and everyone around you to your will?

Not me, I hiss internally as Elio lowers his arm. *I won't be bent.*

I will not be broken.

"Do you care?" Elio asks. There's no sarcastic sneer, no mocking tone in his voice. It's smooth and quiet. Simple and serious. Like he actually wants to hear the answer.

Except I don't even know the answer. The injury – a very serious one at that – that he got protecting me has added yet another layer of complications on top of how I feel about everything that's happened. How I feel about him.

Instead of giving him a straight answer, I ask another question.

"Why did you do it?"

He has a large stemmed wineglass in his hand. He's holding it between us, and he's so fucking close. Still not touching me, but that arm by my hip, that hand on the counter behind me, closes me in. The massive black wall of him looms in front of me, and my head is tipped up, and his tipped down, so we can look at each other.

"No makeup today," he murmurs. A tingle of tension kisses its way up my spine. If both his hands weren't occupied, I'm sure his leathery touch would be brushing against my cheek right now the way his gaze does.

"Do you care?" I shoot back at him, echoing his own

question. I wonder if he prefers me with the mask of makeup. Polished and pretty and presentable.

"I can see your freckles better this way."

My face scorches. God, it's like I'm twelve again. Like when I bought my first foundation to cover my freckles up. Only I had no idea about how to match shades. I didn't have a mom to help me and I ended up wearing foundation as orange as my hair. At least, that's what the girls at school told me between bouts of vicious laughter.

I've come a long, long way from caring about what people think of how I look. I've grown to love my ginger hair, and now freckles are actually in fashion, go freaking figure. Every once in a while, I still catch myself wishing I had blonde hair and skin that tanned instead of burned, but that's only because I miss my mom and want to see more of her gazing back at me from the mirror, not because I necessarily want to look different.

But one sentence from Elio and I'm back there, back to being a desperate, awkward kid. Why the hell do I let him get inside me like this? Why *the fuck* do I care if he doesn't like my freckles? They're part of my face and the only reason he has to look at them in the first place is because *he took me*, because he –

"I like them."

The whirlwind of childhood humiliation and confusion instantly ceases inside me, a storm collapsing in on itself. I shake my head, making wet tendrils of hair slap against my shoulder blades, because I have nothing to say to that.

So I go back to my question. The one he didn't answer.

"Why did you do it? Why did you get shot protecting me?"

Some dark emotion shutters the back of his eyes. He pushes off from the counter, turning towards the island where I left the wine bottle. He pours wine into the wineglass with his back to me and, as casually as someone might mention the state of the weather, says, "This body ain't worth shit, Songbird. I'd put it between you and a bullet any day of the week."

I gape at him, staring at the muscled power of his black-clad back. Scarred though it is, that body is an anatomical marvel. Even someone who hates him has to acknowledge that fact. Acknowledge the power packed into that six-foot-four frame. He's so big that he should be clumsy, but he isn't. Every movement is controlled, dark grace.

This body ain't worth shit.

For the first time, I get a glimpse of something other than the hardened tyrant Elio Titone. I get a glimpse of something I recognize in the most sincerely visceral way. A sense of unworthiness that grows like a thorny, viny weed, watered by guilt and by grief. I recognize it because those same strangling vines grow deep in my belly, too. They've been there ever since my mother died and I didn't.

Something happened to him once. Something I would probably understand all too well if he would ever deign to tell me.

He won't, though. He instantly shuts down that sliver of vulnerability by coolly adding, "Besides, nobody else is allowed to hurt you."

Nobody *else.*

"But you are," I hiss. "You're allowed, is that it? You fucking like it, too. My ass learned that lesson last night."

A new stiffness enters his spine. A moment ago he'd been holding up the wineglass, swirling it, but he sets it down in a tight movement. The crisp sound of the glass hitting the granite rings out like an alarm. This time I actually do step backwards and away from him as he turns and advances on me. The granite edge of the counter digs into my lower back, but the pressure only lasts a second, because Elio's big hands are on my waist and forcefully spinning me around. The movement forces the espresso cup from my hands, and it goes crashing to the floor, sending ceramic shards and the last sips of wine spewing across the stone tile. I gasp, flinching when leather drags at my hips, thumbs hooking into the elastic waistband of the sweatpants and yanking them down. And not just the sweatpants. The panties, too. I'm completely bared to him.

Smooth leather glides across my hip and ass then presses into the place he spanked me. I can't tell if the touch is meant to me soothing or claiming. Maybe both.

"No bruises. No redness," Elio mutters. His fingers dig into my flesh, ever so slightly, and I can feel a terrible, heart-timed pounding drum up between my legs. "I was gentle last night, Songbird. I can go harder. *Much* harder."

I let out a shameful *eep* of protest. Am I protesting his words or my own body's intense reaction to them? Even now, I can feel slick dampness gathering at the apex of my thighs.

"But I didn't go hard," he says, his voice grating slightly, ragged at the edges, "because that wasn't what you needed."

"How the hell do you know what I need?" I grit out, wriggling under the pressure of his hand.

"Because I know you," he says.

It's an absolutely absurd declaration. His ego astounds me. There's not the slightest trace of doubt in his voice. I scoff in disbelief, making an awful, bitter noise at the back of my throat, but he just moves in closer to my back, fabric of his trousers teasing against my bare skin, his breath a hot stir at my ear.

"I know you," he repeats. As if saying it a second time

somehow makes it true. "Under stage lights and sunshine, I've seen you bleed your soul right out of your body."

I still, because no one's ever described my playing in such a painfully beautiful way.

"I know your birthday and your school schedule and the colour of your eyes when you're angry," he continues, and there's something relentless, *merciless*, about the way he speaks now. Like he'll separate out every molecule of my being, unravel my whole entire life.

"I know your freckles are paler now than they will be in the summer. I know your best friend is Willow and your boyfriend was Brian, and that's *was*, not *is*, because if he tried to touch you now he'd have a bullet in his brain before he could fucking blink. I know what kind of panties you're wearing, or rather not wearing, at this very moment. I know how beautiful you look drenched in my blood, that your pussy tastes like paradise, and I know you don't make music only with your violin, because when you come for me, you fucking *sing*."

He knows all of this because he's watched me, watched me even more than I'd thought. This goes beyond my public music performances. This is deeper, deadlier, more obsessive. Thinking about him watching me reminds me of the cameras everywhere, and in as emotionless of a voice as I can muster, I tell him to pull my clothing back up.

I expect him to resist, but he doesn't. He skims his leather touch down the sides of my thighs to grip my sweatpants and underwear. There's something almost worshipful about the way he does it. A reverent slide down my legs, so slow I almost let out a moan. I bite it back and try to revel in the relief of having myself covered. Elio turns back to the island, grabs the wineglass, and hands it to me.

"Here," he says smoothly, as if the previous conversation

hasn't even happened. "This is the kind of glass you need for this wine. It lets the wine breathe. Opens up the flavours." His eyes shift from the drink between us to my mouth. "Try it."

"I don't want it now." I truly don't. My momentary feeling of victory, of freedom, evaporated the moment he entered the room.

One of his dark brows notches up slightly.

"You opened an eighteen-thousand-dollar bottle of wine and now you're not even going to drink it from the proper glass?"

"Eighteen... thousand..." I breathe. I stare down at the drink accusatorily, as if the wine should have somehow warned me about how expensive it was before I took it off the shelf. "Let me guess. It's added onto the sum I owe you."

He gives a shrug of his good shoulder. "That's less than a pair of panties. I could always use a new pocket square."

Is he making another joke? This man is absolutely insane. But he just keeps on going.

"You're wearing a nice shade of blue. Would go well with at least three of my suits." His voice deepens slightly. "Reminds me of your eyes."

I am wearing blue silk underwear, damn him. I can't believe what I'm about to say, but a girl has to work with what she's got. And no matter what, I swear I will survive this and get out of here. If Elio's willing to open his wallet and dump it all out for my used panties like some kind of pervert then so be it.

"Fine. But I want fifty thousand for them," I say, lifting my chin with a defiance I don't quite feel but I'm pretty sure I fake adequately enough. Elio doesn't balk at the thirty-thousand-dollar mark-up. He raises his right hand and draws it along his jaw slowly, fingers rubbing at scar tissue. He narrows his gaze thoughtfully, like he's considering a lucrative business offer. A deal with contracts and figures and complex negotiations. Something glints, then hardens in his gaze. He drops his hand.

"No."

I'm the one balking now, my confidence rattled.

"You're the one who said I should have asked for more last time!" I sputter, feeling like an idiot.

"But you didn't," Elio counters maddeningly. "And now the price has been established. Twenty grand for a pocket square doused in *parfum de Songbird*. I might consider going up to twenty-five because they're the colour of your eyes, but doubling it? They'd have to be extra special. Maybe if..."

He stops, and I'm sure the silence is bait, but I take it anyway.

"Maybe if *what*?" I snap.

"Maybe if you get them extra wet for me first."

My jaw drops.

"You've got to be kidding me."

"I don't kid when it comes to what I want," he says simply, starkly, and they're possibly the truest words he's ever spoken. "Come all over those panties, soak them for me, and you'll get your fifty grand for them."

His gaze dips sardonically to my glass.

"Have a drink if you need to steel yourself first."

I grip the stem of the wineglass so hard I'm surprised it doesn't snap. But maybe I shouldn't be surprised at all. Because I am fucking weak. So weak I take a swig and actually consider doing this.

Fifty grand for an orgasm. Yesterday, getting aroused actually lost me money, but this time it will be the opposite.

It's a good deal.

And then I want to laugh, because apparently I have standards around deals like these now. I have notions of what's a good price and what's a bad one. Fifty thousand dollars for my dignity. Fifty thousand to turn me into the whore he said he didn't even want.

Or maybe I already turned into that last night. First at the gala, then in his room.

But it's *something*. One step closer to getting me out of here. Playing violin for him hasn't turned out to be as straightforward as I was hoping. Maybe this will be easier.

"Fine," I bite out. "I'll be back."

Elio chuckles, and it freezes me.

"Oh, no. You won't be doing it alone. How will I know what I'm buying is the genuine article if I'm not actually there during the process?"

Of course he wants to be involved. I wonder if it will be like last night, with his tongue playing over my clit, but this time through the silk, and my blood simmers, sending a slow, brutal throb of heat into my groin. I take another huge sip of wine and set down the glass.

"Deal," I whisper.

Elio moves towards me. I scrunch my eyes shut and flinch at his proximity. I feel the heat of him, the almost ominous pressure of his presence, before he abruptly draws back. I squeeze open one eye, then the other, to see him at the island, leaning back against it with the wineglass in his hand. He swirls it languorously, watching me.

We stare at each other for so long that awkwardness unfurls. I lick my lips, shifting back and forth on my feet, wondering when he'll touch me. My traitorous body is already anticipating it, my insides coiling, and I think bitterly that if it's wet panties he wants, he won't be disappointed.

"Well?" Elio says, swirling his drink again and taking a sip.

"Well, what?" I huff. "Aren't you... aren't you going to..."

"Help you?" he finally asks. He takes a long, contemplative sip of the wine then says, "No, I don't think I will."

So, he wants a goddamn show then. He wants to stand there, watching me make a mess of myself, completely closed-off and unaffected. Although, maybe not all that unaffected. I risk a glance down to his crotch and see the thickened, swollen outline of his shaft through his pants.

I breathe out harshly. A mixture of relief and disappointment – disappointment that fucking *terrifies* me – floods through me. And with it comes arousal I can't run from or deny. Elio watching me, his eyes dark as the sky between stars, dark with need as toxic as my own, feels like a drug. That gaze is in my bloodstream, demanding and possessive and digging deep inside me. Digging, until he can open me up and find everything, see everything. Know everything.

I know you.

"Pants down. Panties on," he says. The command sounds stern, but I hear the way the words are laced with slight strain. A gruffness he can't keep quiet.

I should stop this. Stop this *now*. But there's fifty grand at stake, a tiny little slice of my future freedom. And there's Elio, his breath coming harder than it should, and fuck, seeing him is what truly makes me want to do this. And I try not to think about what that means, about how screwed up I must be to want this in some strange way, as I hook my thumbs into the pants and I obey.

My glance goes to the camera, like a shiny black orb of an eye on the ceiling, and I wince, wondering if anyone else will see this. If someone else is watching even now. Maybe the guard who trailed me into this room before Elio dismissed him so quietly I didn't even notice. Throat dry, I kick the sweatpants off, letting them skid over the spilled wine on the floor.

"How clear is the image quality from that camera feed?" I ask quietly.

"Crystal," Elio responds, lifting his sparkling glass in the air as if to demonstrate just how clear the image of me falling apart will be for whichever men are watching now.

I'm supposed to be touching myself, I know I am, but my fists curl together in front of my pubic bone, shame spiking through me. This feeling is different from the embarrassment Elio has made me feel, the humiliation he coaxes out of me that's so terribly erotic it takes my breath away. The thought of other men watching me right now just makes me plain anxious, maybe even afraid.

"Songbird."

There's a quietness in the way his voice wraps around the nickname that draws my gaze sharply.

His expression has changed. I've never seen his face like this. It's not... No, it's not soft. But there's *something* there. Like the physical manifestation of an ache. And I can't help but think, for one batshit crazy fraction of a second, that even with the scars, even with the cruelty and the eyes that want to tear me open, when he looks at me like that, like he's *tortured* by something, like he's in *pain*, that he's beautiful.

"I cut off the feed to the main security hub the second I sent Robbie out of this room," he says carefully. "I'm the only one here with you now."

Tears of relief and gratitude burn at the back of my eyes. It's a tiny kindness. Not even a kindness at all, really, but I latch onto it like it's a lifeboat on the stormy sea that's become my life.

"Are you lying?" I whisper.

His eyes are dead serious when he replies.

"I'm not going to let one of my men watch you do this."

Not an act of kindness, then, but one of pure possessiveness. All of me belongs to him, even my pleasure.

"But... the gala..." I can't even say it. Can't even think about how many people must have seen me shuddering so wantonly against his thigh.

"You were fully dressed then. Well, mostly," he says. "And you may not be aware of this, but you were so aroused that you came from barely moving at all. We were dancing close, yes, but that's all anyone would have seen from the outside." He pauses, then bites out, "If you think I'd let anyone else see you undressed, see you truly come undone, then you have no idea who I am."

"Oh, I know who you are, Elio," I say before sliding my fingers over the blue silk between my legs. He physically jolts, and at first I think it's because of what I'm doing with my hand. But then I realize, *no*, it happened a split second before that. *It happened when I said his name.*

It's the first time I've called him by his first name. I'm not sure why I do it, but I say it again, just as my finger circles the tight bud of my swelling clit.

"I know you, *Elio*."

He exhales and puts down the wineglass like he's scared he'll snap the stem. Just like I was, except he's strong enough to actually do it. He doesn't take his eyes from my hand between my legs as he releases the glass onto the sparkling granite of the island.

"You're a tyrant," I breathe, beginning to stroke myself. "A murderer. A monster. Greedy. Selfish. Possessive.

Obsessive." I accentuate every word with a circling movement of my hand until I can't speak anymore. But just because I can't say the words doesn't mean they're not piling up in my brain. *Terrible and cruel and ruinous, but you said you'd put your body between a bullet and me, and you actually fucking did it, and what am I supposed to do with that? Just what am I supposed to do with that?*

He doesn't argue with a single thing I've said. He knows each word is true. Just like I do.

I'm cold and hot at the same time. My nipples are hard, my skin heating like I have a fever. Elio's the point of infection. I know he is. But as I sigh and feel the inevitable rush of pre-climax expanding in my body, I don't know how I'll find the cure.

I can't look at him, can't hold his gaze when I come. I cry out, then try to swallow the sound, my body crunching forward, my chin falling towards my chest. My fingers work faster, faster, then slow as I grow overly sensitive, everything constricting and pulsing inside. When I finally do flutter my eyes open, Elio is there, right in front of me. His thumb and fingers go to my jaw, and he bends slightly. Dizzily, pussy pounding, I wonder if he's about to kiss me.

He gets one breath away from my mouth before he whispers, "Make sure they're good and wet before you take them off."

"I don't need to check," I hiss. I can already tell they're soaked. But Elio isn't satisfied by that, apparently. He grips my waist and lifts me until I'm seated on the counter, then grabs my knees, forcing my legs apart. I let him do it, let him look, if only so that everything is up to par and I don't have to go through this entire insane situation all over again because he didn't get what he wanted the first time around.

Nervously, I glance at him, and my heart practically

stops. The intensity on his face is astounding. It's so focused that at first glance he almost looks expressionless. But on second glance, I can see the tension ticking in his muscles, the fathomless, raging hunger that turns his eyes into burning black holes focused between my legs.

Licking my lips, I glance down, trying to see what he sees, to understand why he looks like that. My pale thighs are spread wide on the counter, my skin in stark contrast to his dark gloves. Pretty blue silk covers my pelvis, and the fabric is dark with slick wetness where it sits snugly over my entrance.

Elio inhales roughly, then draws a single finger up and down that wet area. My body responds instantly, nerves raw and ready for more of what I shouldn't want. He presses firmly, driving some of the soaking fabric ever-so-slightly inside me, and my hips buck in inevitable reaction.

"Just take them off. Just take them," I moan, the muscles of my thighs twitching as Elio strokes shallowly through silk and leather into my core.

"Not yet," he rasps. "Need more."

"But... you said..."

I'm squirming against his touch. Rubbing my clit was one thing, but this, this firm, slow, nowhere-near-deep-enough touch below, is something else entirely. Part of me wants to fling myself off the counter and away from him.

Another part wants to slide the panties to the side so he can put that finger all the way in. Would he leave the glove on while he did it?

"You said I just had to... get them wet," I pant. "I came. I did what you told me to. I-"

"One more," he says, orders, *demands*. "Give me one fucking more." His finger drives the silk a little further in, entering me deeper and tightening the fabric against my clit in the most intoxicating way.

"I... I can't. I-"

"One hundred thousand."

His voice is tight and urgent. My eyes, which had fallen closed, fly open. I find him staring at his hand on my silk-clad pussy, and something like satisfaction flares inside me when I realize he's losing control of this situation and *he knows it*. He's losing control because of his own twisted desire. Desire for me. Desire he can't keep a leash on no matter how hard he tries. He took me for my music, but he can't fight how much he wants the rest of me, too.

And it gives me an idea. A terrible, damning idea. An idea that I could regret for the rest of my god-forsaken life.

The words tumble from my mouth just as I come again, making them breathy and shaky. If it isn't for the way Elio completely turns to stone, I wouldn't even be sure if he hears them.

"How much," I pant and moan, trying not to grind desperately against his finger as I explode, "would you pay for my virginity?"

Chapter 24

Elio

E very muscle in my body seems to shut down when Deirdre's words register. I'm trying to come to terms with them. And come to terms with my own response.

Trying to come to terms with the fact that it turns out I want her any way I can have her. In every way. Even if I have to pay. Even if I have to compromise everything I thought this was, what I thought that this would be.

I want to fucking tell her I'd give her everything, *everything* for that. Money, power, jewels. A thousand and one violins. Buy her a small country. Slit my fucking neck and bleed out if she asked me to, just so I could have my cock inside her when I die.

Well, shit.

I am, without a single shadow of a doubt and in every possible, conceivable, inevitable way, absolutely, categorically, one hundred percent *fucked*.

I will lose my mind, maybe even lose everything, over this girl. I've already started losing control.

And I never, *ever* lose control.

All of this plays out in my head in the space of about half a second. Deirdre is still trembling from her second orgasm, her sweet, wet body practically begging me to do it, to take her right fucking now. My cock is out of control, straining for her, my body answering hers without a goddamn care for what my brain has to say about it.

But there's something she doesn't understand. I'd give her anything. Anything except what she really wants.

"Here's the thing," I say gruffly as she tightens and rocks in tiny movements against my still hand, aftershocks of her pleasure ringing through her like an anthem that goes straight to my dick. "It doesn't matter how much I'd pay, Songbird."

She makes a questioning sound.

"Because," I say through gritted teeth, "If I claim you that way, get your innocent blood on my cock like a brand, then I will absolutely never let you go."

Not like I'm planning to let her go anyway, but still.

"Why not?" she snaps, and there's a new anger in her voice. "It's not like there aren't other beautiful women lining up to sleep with you. You don't need to keep me here."

What the fuck is she talking about?

I mean, she's right. I hadn't lied when I told her I didn't need to pay a whore. There are always women like Natalia around, women turned on by money and violence and what I represent in this world. Women who want just a little bit of that Titone power for themselves, even if it comes in the form of sucking my dick.

Then I remember Nat coming up to me at the gala. And Deirdre's eyes burning a goddamn hole in my head from across the room. No doubt she saw us together.

And no doubt she's relieved by the prospect of me being

focused on someone else. On me wanting other women so that I don't want her.

She doesn't understand.

Reasonable, considering I barely understand myself. Barely understand the hold this young, defiant, brilliant, virginal little Songbird has on me.

How much would you pay for my virginity?

Cristo santo. If I thought I still had a soul I'd fucking sell it.

That has me stepping crisply away from her. I need to create some distance, cool my head, regain some semblance of control, the control I've built my name, our entire empire, on.

"Panties," I say, moving back to our original bargain. Back to a place I feel like I can get a grip on. Something a little colder, more transactional, than contemplating sliding my dick into her tight, pulsing pussy and coming all over her insides.

A flush darkens her cheeks, and she nods, scooting forward and sliding off of the counter. My eyes are glued to her as she slides the wet silk down her pale legs. She bends at the waist, pulling them off of her feet, then uses one hand to stretch the hem of the T-shirt over her bare body as she straightens to hold them out to me.

I move to take them, but she withdraws her hand a little. "One hundred thousand, right?"

I almost want to smile at that. Spine of fucking steel, I swear. Making sure she gets her due, as she well should.

I nod, because though I may be many terrible things, things she listed out for me herself, I am at least a man of my word.

She exhales, the hardness around her mouth soften-ing, finally passing them over. I take them, folding them carefully, methodically, before sticking them into my pocket.

I turn away from her and grab the wine glass, drinking until it's empty, staring blankly out over the kitchen island while my dick throbs. I put down the glass as Deirdre pulls up the sweatpants that had been discarded in a soft grey heap.

A small cry of pain from behind me makes every muscle in my body snap to attention. I spin around, jaw tight, finding Deirdre leaning forward over the counter, gripping it tightly. Her right foot is off the floor, curled around her left ankle, like she's stubbed her toe, or-

I see the spilled wine and the pieces of ceramic on the floor. Sharp white shards scattered like broken teeth.

My breathing feels wrong. So does my heartbeat. It reminds me of the way I felt when I saw Sev's guy aiming his gun at her in the snow that night. Like the entire world was hurled off its axis, everything turning black at the edges.

I propel myself forward without thought. Same way I didn't think, didn't stop, didn't have a fucking care in the world for the bullet that could have gone right through my head and ended everything that night. I grab her and hoist her back up to the counter where she was sitting a moment ago.

"It's fine," she chokes out, wiggling and pulling away from me. I ignore her, finding her right ankle and closing my fingers around it in an iron grip. She bucks and shimmies until she's half lying along the counter, propped on her elbows, ass up in the air, held in place by my hand on her leg.

Keeping one hand wrapped around her ankle, I smooth the other along the inside of the high, slender arch of her foot. There it is. A sharp, nasty chunk of the cup stuck in the ball of her foot. My immediate instinct is to yank it out, but then she'll just start bleeding like crazy and I don't have the shit to deal with that right here.

I hoist her up into my arms and she yelps. It reminds me of our first night, when she told me she'd rather step on broken glass than have me carry her. But she's already stepped on something broken, and I will not be argued with. Maybe she senses that. Because she doesn't even try to fight me now. Doesn't snap at me, or try to stop me. She doesn't fully give in and hold onto me, either, instead crossing her arms in an X over her chest, fists up by her shoulders, like a corpse.

I carry her up the stairs, vaulting two at a time, until I've reached my bedroom. I set Deirdre down on my bed then mutter, "Stay here," as I stalk into the bathroom. I know there's a first aid kit in there somewhere. I find it under the sink after a minute of searching then return to the bedroom.

Only to find Deirdre gone.

"For fuck's sake."

I hear sounds coming from her bathroom, rummaging and clattering. First aid kit in hand, I move quickly to that room. In her bathroom, she's bent over at the waist as she shoves things around under the sink, her injured foot hovering an inch off the ground as she digs for, presumably, the very thing I've got in my hand.

"Looking for this?"

At the sound of my voice her head whips back and she gives me an accusatory look over her shoulder. Her hair, that was damp before, is drying in furious orange waves. It looks like a bonfire, tendrils flashing and flickering as she ignores me and snaps her head forward again, continuing her search in the cupboards under the counter.

I watch her, a muscle pumping in my cheek. I'm not one

to get stressed easily. Usually, I'm cool, collected, weighing every option with the detached precision of a surgeon. I thought I'd be relieved to get Deirdre under my control, like something inside me that appeared one and a half years ago would somehow be satisfied and I could get back to my fucking life. But with her here, all I feel is like I'm on the verge of a goddamn stroke. I watch her, so angry and so small, babying her foot like a wounded deer. If a deer had pride and a temper that was the prettiest and most irritating thing I'd ever seen.

Deirdre's face is mostly hidden, and my gaze goes to her foot. Her *bleeding* foot. In the kitchen, the chunk of ceramic had kept it stoppered well enough, but not anymore. Dark rivulets run down the length of her toes, falling onto the stone floor in slow but steady drips.

"You're bleeding all over the floor," I tell her, striding into the bathroom and standing directly behind her.

Her reply is slightly muffled, her voice bouncing around between the bottles of crap under the sink. "I'll clean it up."

For some reason that reply annoys me.

"Rosa will do it."

She lets out a harsh breath, pulls her head out of the cupboard and straightens. She doesn't turn around to look at me, instead focusing on my reflection in the mirror ahead of us.

"I'm not going to make Rosa clean up my blood!" she snaps at my reflection.

"Why not? She's cleaned mine up plenty of times," I reply.

"Yeah, well, I'm not like you," she practically spits.

I stare at the two of us in the mirror, red and black, beauty and scars, and I am fully fucking aware of that fact. Fully aware that she is on a completely different plane of existence than me, and the fact I've dragged her here at all, dragged her kicking and screaming into my darkness, is a crime against nature and order and all things good in the world.

The worst part is, *I do not fucking care.*

"Sit down," I growl, jerking my chin over at the toilet.

"Just give me the first aid kit and go," she replies irritably.

That's not going to happen. She may think that I just want to hurt her, but the reality is that watching her blood seep out of her body is notching my blood pressure up another level every time my heart beats. I'm not going to let her slap some tiny bandage on there and call it a day.

"Sit down or I will fucking tie you down."

Her eyes flare.

"You already took off my door and now you're threatening to tie me to the toilet? Are you insane?"

"If I am, it's because you've made me that way."

She lets out a sharp, angry laugh at that, and suddenly I have a bone-deep urge to know what her real laughter sounds like.

"You're telling me you were just a normal, psychologically healthy man before I came along? Yeah, I call bullshit on that, buddy."

The casual use of the word *buddy* throws me so off-balance I'm glad she's started hopping over to the toilet all on her own without needing my help. Shaking my head stiffly, I follow her. Buddy. Fucking *buddy*. If a man called me that he'd lose a goddamn finger.

Or five.

"Sit," I reiterate, and she gives me *an are you serious?* sort of look as she hops in a circle to face me in front of the toilet.

"What do you think I'm doing over here if I'm not going to sit down?"

I shrug, forgetting to keep the movement to my good shoulder, and grimace.

"Just checking. You have a perpetual need to disobey."

She slams the toilet seat down and throws her body heavily down on it, then bursts out, "Well maybe that's because I don't want to think about what it means when I do obey!"

I blink slowly at her. She clamps her mouth shut, like she's said something she shouldn't have, redness staining her cheeks.

"Is that why you left the room and went on your little wine raid?" I ask as I kneel before her. "To prove that you haven't submitted to me?"

She doesn't answer and looks away, but I don't need her to respond to know I'm right.

"I never said you couldn't leave the room."

"It was implied!" She crosses her arms over her abdomen and hunches forward, watching me on my knees.

I realize in that moment I've never looked up at a woman like this. I've never been on my knees before anyone.

Only she could get me on my fucking knees without even having to ask.

"Implied how?" I ask, grasping her ankle and examining the wound again. Fuck me, she's a bleeder. I'm going to have to take my gloves off and use the sterile ones in the first aid kit. She may consider me an infection, and maybe I am, but there's no need to make it literal.

"Well, I don't know! I've never been held prisoner before, so forgive me for not knowing all the subtle nuances of the expectations!" she replies.

I can't exactly respond in kind, can't tell her that I've never held a prisoner before either, because that would be a flat-out lie. Although, usually when someone ends up imprisoned by the Titones, it's the final step on their journey before they end up at the bottom of Lake Ontario.

Instead of answering, I grab a bunch of towels and stuff them under her ankle, setting her foot down gently before rising and heading towards the sink. I peel off my leather gloves and suds up my hands before rinsing and drying them. I don't look at my bare skin as I walk back to her and open the first aid kit.

She looks, though. Whatever other remarks she had on the tip of her tongue stay there, her angry eyes sobering.

"Those look bad," she murmurs as I snap one tight white glove on over top of my scars, then another.

"That's because they are," I respond dryly.

"Do they hurt?"

She asked me that before, about the gunshot wound. Why does she wonder if I hurt?

"Not as much as other things," I grunt.

Not as much as the fact I haven't been able to take a full fucking breath into my lungs since I first heard you play.

Almost two years of barely breathing does things to a man. Painful things.

"You mean your shoulder," she says quietly.

Not exactly what I was referring to, but I don't bother to refute her. Because, yeah, that also hurts like a mother-fucker right now.

"I'm sorry."

Now that has me pausing, glancing up at her face. She looks uncomfortable, shifting back and forth on the toilet's closed lid.

"What did you just say?" I ask carefully, not quite sure I heard her right.

Her mouth flattens before her lips part once again to speak.

"I'm sorry. I'm sorry you got shot for me."

I stare at her so long without speaking that it apparently compels her to continue.

"I just feel like... Like, yes, it was your fault you were there in the first place. Because you were coming to take me. It's not like you were at my house to sell Girl Guide cookies. But..." She sighs and runs a fluttery hand through her explosive hair. "But I'm not an idiot. I know I'd probably be dead if you hadn't shown up at that moment." Her hand falls back to her lap, and her fingers worry against each other. "I keep thinking... I keep thinking, what if I hadn't raised that gun?"

"Then your father would probably be dead, or halfway there, instead of on some beach in Bermuda fucking a twenty-four-year-old," I tell her. She flinches at my words, but they're the truth. She distracted Sev's soldier, brought the violence down on her own head, just so her piece of shit papà could get away. O'Malley isn't that old, but he also isn't fast. I doubt he would have made it otherwise.

He has no idea what kind of loyalty Deirdre is capable of. Not a damn clue how much she's worth. What he's lost by leaving her.

But I do. She'll never feel that sort of loyalty towards me, but I can see it in her all the same. Like gold glinting at the bottom of a river. Shining metal holding strong under currents and ice and the thrashing of the seasons.

"Well, fine then. Whatever. You're probably right. I snagged that guy's attention so my dad could get away. And he just went ahead and left, just like he bartered me away, because apparently I'm fucking worthless."

I stiffen.

"If you want to apologize," I say slowly, almost menacingly, "then apologize for the words that just came out of your mouth."

Her brows crash together.

"What-"

"Do not ever, *ever*, say something like that in front of me again."

"Say what?" She pauses, her brows getting even more furrowed.

I grip the broken piece of ceramic and pull it out in a swift, sharp movement that makes Deirdre gasp. I disinfect the wound, knowing it stings but doing it anyway, because this is necessary and I know that she can fucking take it. As anticipated, the blood flows much faster now, and I slam a square of plush gauze against it, holding pressure there the same way I hold Deirdre's gaze.

"I don't pay millions of dollars for things that are worthless," I tell her. "I don't take bullets for things that are worthless." I get out the white medical tape, sticking it tightly to her skin, holding the gauze in place. "What your father did speaks only to his own non-existent value as a person. Not yours."

"What am I to you?" she whispers as I lay her foot back down on the towels.

Music and fire. Heaven and hell. Absolution and ruination, all at once.

I don't say any of that as I rise and snap off the gloves. Her gaze holds the question her mouth just shaped. I look down at her and reply with a single word:

"Mine."

Chapter 25

Deirdre

Elio grabs his leather gloves from beside the sink and leaves me after that, heading into his adjoining bedroom. I stay on the toilet for a long time, staring at my firmly and very precisely wrapped foot, propped up on a cushion of towels. A cushion he put there for me.

I have no idea what is going on between us. No idea why I can't seem to hate him as singularly as before. No idea why his touch sets my blood boiling. No idea why I offered him my fucking virginity when he himself told me it would never get me out of here.

No idea why he bothered to bandage me up when he could have just as easily let me do it all myself. He could have laughed at me, mocked me, left me shaking and angry and bleeding after the humiliation of seeing me come *twice*. But he didn't. Instead, he carried me up here, sank down on his knees before me, with those fathomless eyes and those terribly scarred hands, and took care of me.

Eventually I ease up onto my feet, limping over to the sink to splash my face with water and brush my teeth. I

215

don't see Elio in my bedroom, and I don't hear anything from his. I wonder if he's already asleep, or if he's left altogether. Maybe to go see that beautiful blonde from the gala. Elio is more than six feet of pure, bloodthirsty testosterone. A guy like that probably needs to bend someone over nightly just to stay alive. And he was hard before. With me. The memory goes to my core like a heated blade.

And the thought of him sleeping with that blonde woman twists it.

OK, what the actual hell?

I do not care what other women Elio spends his time with. If anything, the more time he spends with other women, the less he'll spend with me. I should be grateful. Relieved.

Then tell me why I'm not.

Maybe I'm too angry or too traumatized to feel gratitude right now. But then again, I have felt gratitude towards him for other reasons. For telling Rosa to make me tea. For turning off the security camera in the kitchen.

So why am I not grateful for this?

I don't want to think about it. Can't think about it. The same way, just as I told him, I can't think about what it means that I sometimes obey him.

But even though I can't think about it, I suddenly can't stand that I don't know if he's here or not. I dig my fingernails into my palms, willing myself to stay here, in this room. Not to go looking for him because that would be absolutely insane.

But my feet move anyway.

Just one look, I tell myself. *I just want to see if he's still here.*

I feel like I won't be able to sleep until I know for sure. I can't remain in breathless limbo. As I limp slowly to the doorway between his room and mine, I realize I don't truly know what I want to find. If I were sane, if I were normal, I should be happy if I find he's gone. Happy that I can relax a little, that I can breathe.

But...

Shut up, Deirdre.

I don't allow that thought to come to fruition.

His room is dark, but not entirely. Light from my side spills in, illuminating emptiness.

He's gone, then.

I nod jerkily, muttering, "Good," out loud so that the word can blot out any other reaction I might have had. I turn to go back into my room when I hear it.

The sound of a shower running.

I realize that some of the light in here is coming from the doorless entryway into Elio's bathroom. I still can't believe he ripped off all the doors in here, including his own. The man is fucking certifiable.

But maybe I am too. Because now I'm walking towards the bathroom. Towards the sound. Towards him.

I stop when I reach the bathroom. It's very similar to mine, but larger, and I spot Elio immediately. Even in the grand room, his presence is undeniable. A black fucking hole taking over everything.

He hasn't heard me above the streaming of the water. He's in a shower like mine, enclosed by glass. The glass isn't steamed up enough yet to obstruct my view and, Jesus, what a view it is.

You know when you watch nature documentaries and you see some massive predator, a cougar or a python or a bear, just absolutely decimate its prey? And even while you're cringing at the violence and maybe feeling sad for the cute rabbit or soft-skinned doe, a part of you can't help but admire the perfect, savage grace of the destroyer? Can't help but respect the millions of years of evolution that led to this moment, created this monster, as its brutal body strikes again and again and again?

That's what looking at Elio's naked body is like. It's like looking into the open maw of a shark, feeling the terror of the bite to come and simultaneously thinking, *my God, your fangs are beautiful.*

He's so fucking *big.* Colossal. He absolutely fills the large rectangular shower with his bulky frame. Every inch of him is hard and broad and covered in varying quantities and thickness of dark hair. I bite the inside of my cheek when I see the bandages on his shoulder, which I now notice he's keeping out of the water, tipping his head to the side to soak his hair, turning it even blacker than usual. His long legs are splayed slightly, and a tumultuous wave of sensation rocks my insides when I notice the rhythmic contractions in the muscles of his thick thighs and ass.

I can't see his right hand.

Because he's fucking it.

I have no doubt there are countless women who'd leap into his bed if he did no more than crook one of his leather-bound fingers at them. But instead, he chose this.

Maybe all it means is that he's tired, and sore, and doesn't want to go anywhere or deal with anyone else right now. Or maybe he doesn't want to let me out of his sight that easily tonight.

Or maybe it means something else entirely. Something I shouldn't contemplate or care about.

Something that whispers, then yells when I try to shut it up. Something with words that sound a lot like *he won't fuck someone else because all he wants right now is you.*

Something stupid, is what it is. And what's even more

stupid is the small but undeniable flare of sick satisfaction I get from that possibility. The possibility that I'm not the only one affected more than I want to be. I'm not the only one who's been thrown into blood-heating turmoil. I'm not the only one whose entire world seems to have shrunk down into the shape of a single, strange, and solitary person.

What am I to you?

Mine.

I'm rooted to the spot, entranced by the quickening snap of Elio's hips, the tightening of his ass, the tension rippling up and down his back as water beads and rolls. I'll probably hate myself tomorrow for this bizarre urge, but I desperately want to see him come. I want to see him shudder, explode against the wall, fall apart because of how much he wants me.

I didn't see him come last time. I was too wrapped up in the explosion of my own orgasm, the stinging on my ass and the singing in my veins. I was too distracted to notice anything else until his hot spray coated my skin, and then it was basically over.

I want to see it now.

The movement of his hips slows, then stops altogether. His hand picks up the slack, pumping in quick, hard strokes, carving his triceps out of something akin to stone. My breath catches, and it takes everything I have not to reach my hand between my own legs and stroke the place that aches there. I try to tell myself I'm just feeling the aftershocks, lingering sensitivity from the other two orgasms, but I'm not. I'm reacting to this, here, *now*. Elio's nakedness under the hot stream of the water as he strokes the cock I made swell.

He doesn't shake or shudder or tremble when he comes. Instead, everything draws tight, muscles contracting almost like he's in pain. And with his shoulder and scars, maybe he is. Maybe, with the beautiful ruin that is his body, pleasure is always entwined with suffering.

His thighs lurch, driving his hips forward as his head tips back. His hair is much straighter and longer in the water, dripping down the back of his corded neck like ink. A guttural groan rips through the air. It doesn't matter that the sound of it is slightly muted by the water that patters like rain. Because it feels like Elio has put his mouth against my soaked entrance and groaned directly inside me. I feel the sound of it, each brutal vibration tightening in my core until I'm terrified. Terrified that I could come, just from that.

Terrified that he might turn around and see me.

I can't let that happen. I stole this moment, but the second he knows I'm here, all my control will be lost. Elio's head tips forward, his shoulders rounding slightly, before he turns off the water.

The silence crashes down like something catastrophic. A calamity of non-sound after the protective din of the water. I'm sure he can hear me breathing, even from across the room.

He can probably hear my fucking heart beat.

He most certainly hears my stumbling step backwards. I see the sudden alertness in his body as I move away.

If he turns, which I'm sure he does, I don't see him do it. Because so do I.

I run. My foot throbs with every hurried step I take.

And yet, every step hurts far less than it should. And I know it's because of disinfectant and cushiony gauze and a murderously precise tape job.

I hurt less than I should because of *Elio*.

And I have absolutely no idea what to do with that.

Chapter 26

Deirdre

I wake to the now-familiar sound of cart wheels rolling into my room, but what's unusual is the person pushing it. It's not Rosa today, but Valentina.

"Hey," she says, smiling at me as I hurry to sit up in bed. "I brought you the paper and stuff for the letter and saw Rosa with your breakfast. Figured I'd bring it all in together."

"Thank you," I say. I appreciate that she remembered my request. "I'm actually not sure if I'll need it now. Willow found a way to contact me using someone else's email address."

"Oh, nice. OK. You can keep it anyway. Just in case." She nods towards a pile of lined paper and envelopes on the cart beside the breakfast pastries. There's another pot of tea today, thank God, and I mumble another thank you at her as I pour a cup.

"Want any?" I ask, suddenly remembering my manners. I mean, I feel like I can be forgiven for forgetting my manners in a situation like this. But still. I really do appreciate her looking out for me as best she can and wanting to try to connect me with the outside world. Offering her some tea seems like the least I can do.

But she just wrinkles her nose in a slightly less judgmental version of Rosa's reaction.

"No thank you. In order to make tea even remotely palatable, I have to add insane amounts of sugar to it, and my mom is already on my ass about cutting carbs to fit into my wedding dress."

I add milk and sugar, then take a sip.

"Yikes. I'm sorry," is all I manage to mutter in reply to that little tidbit. Valentina is absolutely stunning with her curves, and I shake my head at the idea she needs to trim them down for a wedding she doesn't even seem to want.

"Yeah. You're telling me." She shrugs, then heads towards the bathroom, pulling a lipstick tube out of a large leather bag that bumps her hips with every step. "Be right back," she calls over her shoulder. I drink my tea and eat a croissant while Valentina freshens up, and a few minutes later she returns, her lips freshly painted pink. Her long hair is perfectly straight and shiny, dark golden-blonde at the roots and lighter towards the ends, and she's dressed in a denim romper with incredibly short shorts despite the fact it's January.

"What's with the first aid kit and gloves?" she asks. There's a deceptive lightness in her tone. Like she's just trying to make conversation, but is actually intensely focused on my answer. I think her interest comes from a genuine place of concern, and I force a small smile, sliding my foot out of the blankets and leaning back to heft it up in the air.

"I ran into a situation with a broken cup." My smile turns bitter. "But Elio patched me up."

It doesn't seem like Valentina is easy to shock. She's

small, but I get the sense she's mighty. Not the sort of person to be trifled with or who's prone to being taken by surprise. But her eyebrows snap upwards at my words.

"*Elio* bandaged you up?" She sounds so incredulous I almost feel defensive. It's not like I would make that up. But she seems completely stunned. "And those latex gloves?"

"Yeah, he wore them when he was cleaning the wound and putting on the bandage."

"He... *wore them.*" Everything about her expression says *does not compute.* I kind of wonder if she's just going to echo everything I say with that tone of disbelief.

"Yes," I confirm, letting my foot fall back on to the bed and leaning forward to look at her more closely. "Are you... are you OK?"

She shakes her head slowly, hair swishing with the movement.

"Yes. Damn. Sorry. I just..." She shakes her head again, more quickly this time. "I just have never heard of Elio taking his leather gloves off in front of someone else before. Except for maybe Morelli, I guess, but he's a doctor."

I press my lips together, frowning down at the red duvet and sliding my fingers over its lush surface. For some reason, Valentina's words make me feel weird.

"He must take them off in front of other people sometimes," I say, wrenching my gaze up once more. I don't know why, but I have an instinct that something about this is dangerous. It means something that Elio took his gloves off in front of me, and I don't want to confront whatever that is head-on. So instead, I try to deny it. "He's your cousin. You must have seen it happen at least once. When eating, or cooking..."

Valentina snorts a laugh.

"Cooking? Um, no. That is not what Titone men do."

I swallow, reminding myself that the Titone family isn't a normal one. They're Cosa Nostra, and at the top of the fucking top, I guess Elio can't be expected to roll up his sleeves alongside Rosa and roll out the pasta dough or fill the cannoli.

"But seriously, I've known Elio my entire life," Valentina continues. "He's more like a brother to me than a cousin. And I've never, *ever* seen him take off his gloves or even change them, even though I know he has like a hundred pairs. He even wears them in the summer. Pretty sure he sleeps in them."

I chew the inside of my cheek, processing this.

"So, it's weird that he took them off in front of me?" I say, still not sure what to do with all this information.

She laughs again, more softly this time.

"Weird doesn't even begin to cover it. But then again, everything he's done with you is out of character. He's never brought a woman here before, against her will or otherwise."

Now that surprises me. A tight gold dress, platinum blonde hair, and a manicured hand on Elio's chest flash in the back of my head before I push them away.

"Never? No girlfriends?"

She shrugs.

"He hooks up with women, sure. Never brings them here though. He's actually pretty private. Which makes the fact he put you in the room adjoining his and took off all the doors extremely out of character."

Well, great. Elio's bizarre behaviour isn't just baffling to me, but even to his own family. I truly don't know if that's comforting or alarming.

"Why does he hide those scars? Why does he bother with the gloves?" I ask.

The skin I saw was absolutely ravaged, but Elio doesn't exactly seem like the type to care that much about appearances. Plus, he's helping lead one of the most ruthless crime families in the country. Scars would only serve to show just how strong he is, what he's endured. A badge of brutal honour.

"He doesn't seem to care about hiding his other scars that much," I add. He took his shirt off in front of me the first night here, and I saw the patchwork of violence that was the skin of his chest.

Valentina makes a face.

"I think he has a complex about his hands because of the fire. I kind of can't blame him considering what happened."

My heart speeds up, and I don't understand why. I know about the fire. The one he and his brother survived in Sicily against all odds. But based on Valentina's pained grimace, there must be more to it than what I've heard from the vague local legends that cling to the Titone name like fog.

I hold my breath, wondering if she'll say any more. I want to ask, but don't trust myself to. I shouldn't care about this at all, but for some reason I do, and I'm worried that if I ask too much, or appear too eager, she'll retreat. I can't mistake myself here – she's a Titone. Her loyalty, when it really comes down to it, doesn't lie with me.

She fiddles with the strap of her bag, rolling her pink lips like she's deciding something. Then, she huffs out a breath and nods.

"Look, nobody likes talking about this shit, but I'm going to tell you because you'll never hear it from Elio even though I think you need to know. For some reason, he's attached to you, and you're the one who has to contend with all the shit he's got going on, so I figure the more you understand about him, the better."

"Thank you," I say quietly. I realize how much she's doing for me right now. That she's breaking some sort of family code of silence around this issue simply because she wants to help me navigate the deeply unfamiliar waters that make up Elio Titone. Maybe her loyalties aren't as easy to decipher as I'd first thought.

She drops her bag on the floor then settles herself on the edge of the bed, tucking one leg underneath her bum and facing me.

"So, the whole reason our family came to Canada was because of Elio and Curse's papà, Giuseppe. I don't know all the details about this part, but twenty years ago he did something major to fuck over the ruling *famiglia* in Taormina. So, one night, some soldiers came and torched their house. Giuseppe, Elio, Curse, and my aunt Florencia were all inside."

My hands are starting to shake. I grab my cup of tea and hold it tightly, staring down at the liquid as Valentina goes on.

"It took a while for Elio to wake up. No smoke detectors. By the time he knew what was happening, fire was everywhere. From his room there was a clear shot out of the house, but Curse was stuck in his own bedroom. The fire was spreading between their rooms and licking up Curse's door. The doorknob completely fucked Elio's hand when he tried to open it, and he ended up punching through the burning wood to get to Curse." She stops, and a new thickness enters her voice when she speaks again. "They were only eight and fourteen. Can you fucking imagine that? Sometimes I think I'm tough shit but then I remember this story, remember what happened to them and I just..." She blows out a shaky breath like she's about to cry.

I look up from my tea and try to give her a reassuring look.

"It's alright. You don't need to tell me any more if it's too hard."

I know better than most how much family trauma and childhood loss can break a person down. How hard it is to put those heart-killing moments into words. *Only fourteen years old...*

Valentina inhales deeply and visibly steels herself.

"No. That's only part of it and you should hear the rest."

I steel myself, too. Because this story is getting inside me, it's hurting me, and I don't want to hurt for Elio.

"So, while Elio is fighting his way through literal fire to get to Curse, he sees their dad. Elio and Curse's bedrooms were on the ground floor, and Giuseppe had a workshop down there where he worked on his bike. We think he got drunk and was asleep in there when the fire started, because he wasn't upstairs in the other bedroom with Aunt Florencia. If he'd been upstairs, the piece of shit probably would have died like he goddamn deserved to. But instead, he just watched Elio pounding on that burning door, listened to his wife screaming and his other son crying, and then he *ran.*"

My breath crystallizes and then breaks, every inhale jagged and cutting. My throat contracts as I try to picture what Valentina is telling me. Picture a father watching his children in that kind of situation and choosing to cut and run.

And it almost kills me that I don't even have to imagine it, because I witnessed it myself. I watched my own father sprinting across the snow, away from our house and away from me.

"Anyway, Elio got Curse out. By that time Curse was unconscious from smoke inhalation and Elio wasn't much better off. But as soon as he got Curse out, he went right back in."

"For his mother," I finish for her in a whisper.

Valentina nods.

"At that point, I think she was still alive, just trapped. But she was upstairs and there was just no way to get to her. Elio still would have tried. Except a beam in the entryway collapsed on him, hitting his neck and shoulder and forcing him back outside. I wasn't around yet, but my parents only lived a few houses away and by that time they'd shown up. Elio was physically falling apart, and even so my dad still had to restrain him from running back inside. My dad told me once, when he'd had too much wine, that it was the only time he's ever heard Elio scream."

Her tone turns wistful. "I wish I got to meet my aunt. I don't know a lot about her. Men in this family don't talk much to begin with, but especially about the things that hurt them. But my mom has told me a bit. I do know she was beautiful. She had black hair, like my dad and like Elio and Curse. I know she loved music. Apparently she had a beautiful voice."

My mother had been beautiful, too. And though neither my mother nor I were blessed with good singing voices, we both loved music. I feel the strangest sense of kinship welling up for Florencia. For this faceless woman who'd loved some of the things my own lost mother had loved. This woman who'd created men like Curse and Elio, who'd given them life, and who'd irrevocably shaped them with her death.

"Anyway, Elio has this whole thing about the burn marks on his hands. He'll never say it out loud, but I think they make him feel weak. Remind him of what he couldn't do. Who he couldn't protect."

"He can't blame himself for that. He was only fourteen," I say. I shouldn't feel sorry for present-day Elio. But a fourteen-year-old boy fighting to save his mother when his own father had so badly failed him? Well, that Elio broke my fucking heart.

"Trust me, I know," Valentina replies. Her mouth lifts on one side in a twisting sort of smile. "But I don't think he's exactly rational about that night. Kind of like you."

Her words jar me, and for a second I think she means that I'm also not rational about the night my mother died, and I wonder how the hell she could possibly know that.

"What?" I ask sharply.

"He's not rational when it comes to you."

"Oh," I say. "I mean, yeah." I wave at the doorless doorway into his room. "I could have told you that."

"Yeah, well, it's not something I would have expected," she replies. "Like I said, it's out of character for him. He's usually so focused, so business-like. He does everything for a reason. Every move is calculated and thought-out and he doesn't let anything or anyone fuck up his plans or change his mind or make him lose control. He doesn't have to keep anyone out because he doesn't let anyone in. At least, that's what I thought, until you drop the bomb on me that he took his gloves off in front of you and put a freaking bandage on your foot and now I'm just over here, like, what? Don't get me wrong, I love him, but he can be one cold, mercenary motherfucker."

If that isn't the understatement of the century...

"Anyway, I have to get going. Mamma and I have a

lunch date with the Morellis." She bends to grab her bag, and as she turns to go, she pauses. "Maybe keep this between us. What I told you about Elio."

"Yes. Of course," I reassure her. I appreciate her telling me all this, and I'm not going to go betraying that confidence. Besides, I can't see myself bringing this up with Elio anytime soon, anyway.

But even so, her words stay with me all day long. I can't get them out of my head. Can't get *Elio* out of my head. He morphs and oscillates, swinging wildly between the man I know and what I imagine his fourteen-year-old self to have once been.

After how last night wound up unfolding, I don't venture out of the room today. I hang out in the quiet space, picking away at the lunch and dinner Rosa brings me and staring into the void of my phone. By 9pm, Elio still hasn't come back to his room or mine. I try to be relieved at that and ignore the way his absence niggles at me.

Chapter 27

Deirdre

Elio doesn't come back the next day. Or the next. After four days of not seeing him, I'm starting to get pissed. Is this how it's going to be? Me, alone in this giant, beautiful cage of a house? I can practically feel the interest accumulating on my debt, like a little bit of weight added to my shoulders every day, and I don't even have the chance to work towards paying it off because Elio isn't fucking here.

That's the only reason I want to see him, of course. To keep chipping away at my debt and actually do what I'm supposed to – play violin for him. I don't actually want to see him. Obviously. I'm not insane.

Maybe I'm just lonely. I haven't heard from Willow since that initial email, and I have to think that Paddy's got her under major lock and key right now. I wonder what's happening with Darragh and everybody else. If they're still trying to get their hands on me, or if they've given up after Elio presented me at the gala like his personal, chained-up property.

I wonder about my father sometimes, too, even though I try not to. It's too easy to slip into pity and self-loathing and questions about why I wasn't enough. Enough to protect, enough to stay and fight for.

But maybe I really am worthless, because I apparently no longer even have Elio's interest considering he can't be bothered to show his face.

It's thoughts like these that have me fuming – stewing, literally – in a very hot bath on the fifth day of not seeing Elio. My classes are supposed to resume tomorrow, so I'm in an extra shitty mood because I'm pretty damn sure I'm not going to be allowed out of here to go. All that work to get my Bachelor of Music, down the tubes. I'm halfway through my third year, still have one more to go after this, and I can't see a way around the fact that my education has come to a screeching halt.

I slide down in the hot water until I'm submerged past my shoulders, hoping the scalding heat will burn away my emotions. It would be so much easier to be numb right now. To not feel anything at all. No anger, no disappointment, no grief. No matter what I do, though, I just can't seem to manage it. I can't let go of the hurt and the frustration. But then again, maybe that's not such a bad thing. Maybe the force of that unhappiness, the sense of injustice of it all, is keeping me going. Numbness won't keep you alive. Bone-deep anger will, though. It will keep me standing when nothing else does.

I blow out air through tight lips, sending bubbles from the surface of the bath scattering in a spray of foam. The thick layer of bubbles is the only reason I feel comfortable taking a bath in here instead of doing my usual towel-curtain-shower thing. But then again, considering Elio hasn't even bothered to come check on the prisoner he was so hellbent on keeping, I doubt he's looking at the camera feed, anyway, wherever the hell he is. So maybe the bubbles aren't even necessary.

I glare up at the camera in the ceiling, resenting it and him and everything about this. The resentment grows and grows, pushing out everything else in my chest, even the ability and the desire to breathe. I suck in a huge breath then plunge beneath the water.

My eyes scrunched shut, I let the eerie melody of the water fill my ears and start to count.

One, two, three...

I force my muscles to relax even as the anxious burn I know so well starts to build in my limbs.

Ten, eleven, twelve...

I don't feel desperate for air yet. I love this part, the part before everything gets tingly and twitchy and I really have to fight to stay down here. I love the brutal calm of it. The way my body could be just a leaf or bit of driftwood or maybe even just a part of the water itself, simple and mindless and floating.

Thirty... Thirty-five...

My lungs feel tight. It's hard to stay still.

Sixty... Seventy...

I squeeze my fingers into fists, battling to hold on just a little longer. The longer I can hold it, the more euphoric that first breath when I'm out again. My thighs press together, a needy burn pulsing in my clit. I release one of my fists, strumming back and forth over my clit, fast, fast, *fast*. It has to be fast because I won't last much longer. My spine is winding tight, my legs straightening and bending reflexively.

Eighty...

I'm close. Close to everything. Close to coming, close to

needing the sweet release of breathing. My fingers tingle and twitch as I rub them over my swollen clit. Just a few more seconds... Just a little more... Just-

My orgasm rips through me at the same moment a set of huge hands seizes my shoulders and wrenches me out of the water. I gasp and cough, confusion wrapping around the white-hot, black-edged pleasure that binds my core. I pant heavily, feeling water-logged and weak-limbed, blinking rapidly and scraping hair away from my face as my pussy quakes.

I try to focus my gaze, but I don't have to work too hard to see who's here. His face is a mere inch from mine. *Elio.*

A rush of humiliation makes an aftershock throb in my clit, and I snap my teeth together to keep from moaning. I stare at Elio wordlessly, taking in the absorbing black of his eyes and the furious set of his jaw.

"What the hell are you doing here?" I ask between ragged gasps, trying to get my bearings. Elio hasn't been here for days, and he has to show up *now?*

His eyes darken, though I have no idea how that's even possible. When he speaks, his voice is like ice skating over my heated skin.

"You don't get to ask a single fucking question right now." His hands are still on my shoulders, the leather soaked, and he's bent over the bathtub. The ceramic digs into my spine as he holds me in place. "What the fuck were you thinking?"

"What was I... What? What are you talking about? I was having a bath!" I feel even hotter, and it's not just from the water. It's from his proximity. What he found me doing. His probing interrogation. A quick glance down tells me the bubble layer is still thick and opaque, so at the very least he probably didn't see me masturbating.

"A bath where you stay under the surface and don't fucking breathe?" he asks, deadly quiet. I see now how his own breathing matches mine – quick and ragged. Unsteady. Like maybe he was holding his breath too, though I don't see how that's likely.

"It's none of your business!" Why, why, *why* did he have to come back now? If he's going to leave me alone, why can't he just do it for good?

"Everything about you is my business," he snaps. I get the sense he's trying to maintain a very strained leash of control on himself and his emotions. His words are clipped and tight. "I made you my business six million dollars ago. You've been my business for fucking *years*."

That just makes me even angrier. The reminder that I'm a transaction to him. Something to put on his accounting books. I stiffen and try to yank myself out of his grip, but his fingers tighten on my shoulders. His face gets closer, and something odd flickers in his gaze. A mere moment of emotion, an emotion I don't recognize in him, and then it's gone. He shoves his hands under my arms and straightens, dragging me dripping out of the bath.

He doesn't stop until I'm out of the bath entirely. He pins me naked to the wall, one hand at my shoulder, the other on my jaw, forcing me to look at him.

"Let me go. Let me-"

"Shut up," he grunts. "Shut up and look at me, Deirdre."

The use of my name stuns me. No pet nickname, no Songbird that makes me feel like an animal he owns.

My name.

He takes advantage of the momentary silence, the way I'm caught off-guard.

"This is my house, Deirdre. This is my city. You are in

my fucking world." His eyes practically burn a hole through my head as he hisses out his next words. "And don't you ever, for a single fucking fraction of a second, think that you can take yourself out of it. I will not allow it. Do you hear me? *I will not let you do it.*"

His eyes drop to my mouth, and for a dazed moment I wonder if he's going to crash his lips against mine.

Then the meaning of his words sinks in, piercing through the strange haze of the moment.

"Oh my God," I whisper, shock and fury spinning out inside me. "You think I was trying to *kill myself?* You think I would throw away my own life just to get away from you?" I laugh in his face, the sound bitter and harsh. "The fucking *nerve*. Your ego is absolutely insane. You actually think I'd commit suicide just to escape from you? You think you matter that much?"

The doorless entry to the bathroom is directly behind Elio, catching my attention.

"That's why you took the doors off the rooms, isn't it?"

I remember now that Valentina had found me holding my breath in the bath that first night, and that not five minutes later, Elio had stormed in with a hammer in his hand and barely controlled violence on his face.

He doesn't answer me, but I know I'm right.

I laugh again, and his mouth and gaze tighten at the same time.

"I have news for you, Elio Titone. You may be a bigshot, you may think you're everything to me now, but you're wrong. You are a mere blip on the radar of my life. I will get out of this. I will get away from you. And I promise you that I won't need to die to do it."

I'm half bluffing, half vowing with that statement.

Bluffing because Elio is already far more than a blip, no matter how much I want to deny it.

Vowing because, come hell or high water, I will find a way to regain my life.

And I absolutely *refuse* to die trying.

Chapter 28

Elio

Deirdre looks so pissed off, so offended, that I actually believe her. I try to soothe the side of me that wants to grab the sledgehammer and smash the bathtub to bits, the side of me that wants to fist her hair and tell her, "Only showers from now on." Because even though I believe her now, I don't think I'll ever forget coming home, switching on her room's feed on my phone as I head upstairs, only to see her slip below the water.

And stay there.

"What the hell were you doing?" I ask, my voice softer now. I don't mean for it to be soft. It just happens. A natural response to the relief flowing through me like cool water. I slide my hand up from her shoulder until both hands are cupping her jaw. Fuck, I missed this face.

"I... I was... You don't need to know!" she stammers.

Except I do need to know. I need to know everything. I want to know the thoughts in her head before they even take fucking shape.

I know her. I made that whole damn speech about knowing her. But this Deirdre, this woman who holds

238

herself under hot water and doesn't emerge until she's forcibly pulled, is someone I don't recognize, and I need to know her too.

But she's clamming up. Clamping down. I can see it in the shifting of her gaze, the pursing of her lips.

And I do the only thing I can think to do in that moment. Because apparently I've lost my ever loving mind.

"Five hundred thousand."

Her eyes go wide. Miles and miles of blue under those lashes.

"What?"

"Tell me what you were really doing. Five hundred thousand for the truth."

She stares at me for a beat, the only sound our breathing in tandem.

"Are you serious?"

"One million."

If I weren't cradling her jaw in my hands I'm pretty sure it would have dropped. If past me could see me now, his jaw would be dropping, too. Taking one million off her debt, just like fucking that. Unreal.

"Fine," she says with a stiff nod against my fingers. "I was holding my breath."

I give her a flat look.

"No shit, you were holding your breath. You think I'm going to shave seven figures off your debt for that obvious little announcement?"

She looks indignant now, proud and annoyed, and it makes my dick hard. I want to crowd against her, drag it against her belly, but I hold myself back. For now.

"Tell me," I urge. My mouth is so close to hers that every inhale is her exhale and vice versa. Breathing each other in.

"I just..." Her words brush my lips, and I stiffen. "I really was just holding my breath."

"But why? Why for that long?" I'd been excruciatingly aware of every second it had taken me to get up here. She was under well over a minute. That shit isn't comfortable. Nobody holds their breath that long for no reason.

Her next words come out in a rush. "I just like the way it feels, OK? There! I swear to God, you'd better pay me what you owe because that's the truth. If you don't-"

"You *like the way it feels?*" My dick twitches. "Which part? The not being able to breathe part? Or the part when you come up for air?"

"Both," she whispers, flushing so fiercely that the redness goes down her neck, spreading over her chest, leading my gaze to her tight, round nipples.

And suddenly, I understand what she's saying.

I know exactly why she did it.

"Does it make you come?"

When she tenses, but doesn't reply, I know I have my answer. I drag my right hand down and palm the front of her throat, not exerting pressure. Just the whisper of a promise.

"It's not safe to do that by yourself."

"Safe?" she laughs the word, and I feel the vibration beneath the leather and scars. "Like anything about this situation is safe."

"How many times do I have to say it," I murmur, ever so gently massaging the front of her throat. "You're safer in here than out there."

"And who's going to keep me safe from you?"

She tips her head back slightly, some subconscious part of her wanting to give me more access to her throat. I dig my thumb into the place her heart beats and she swallows a sound.

"I'm not the one sticking your head underwater for more than a minute," I remind her.

"Yeah, well, you haven't even been here for the last five days so how would you even know, anyway?"

This time, I don't hold myself back from thrusting my hard dick against her belly. She's so fucking naked, bare against the wall, and it would be so easy to hike her upwards, settle her thighs around my waist, unzip my pants, and nudge inside.

"Did you miss me?"

"What? No! What are you talking about?" she stammers. Every word, every breath, makes the muscles of her throat contract under my hand and now all I can think about is what that throat would do with my cock hitting the back of it.

I lower my mouth to the pretty shell of her ear and tell her, "Well, I missed you." I give her throat one last, tender squeeze before I finally let her go. Her arm whips to the side, grabbing a towel from a nearby rack and wrapping it around herself so viciously I wonder if she means to tear it in half.

"Yeah, right. Like you don't have women at your beck and call twenty-four seven," she says as she walks past me into her bedroom. It's quiet, under her breath. But since I am attuned to every goddamn atom in her body, because I *own* that breath, I hear it. I follow her into her room.

"Does that bother you?"

I haven't been with another woman since bringing Deirdre here, and does my body ever feel it. But a quick, mindless fuck, which is how it usually goes for me, holds absolutely no appeal right now.

The only things that appeal are angry blue eyes and freckled skin and the face of the girl who hates me.

I almost want to hate her right back for it. For closing my usual methods of release off. For making every other woman but her unpalatable. For making me want her like this when this was supposed to be simpler, supposed to be about the music and money and nothing else.

"Oh, please," she snaps, heading for the closet. "It's a relief. Go spend your time with that blonde woman from the gala. In fact, teach *her* violin. Then maybe you'll leave me alone.

"Deirdre."

"Hell, I'll teach her for you. Subtract my teaching fees from my debt. And then-"

"*Deirdre.*"

In the midst of her rant, she doesn't realize I've followed her into the closet. She whirls and gasps at my proximity. It's a large closet, but still much more confined than the bedroom we've just come from. The lights are off in here, and only a soft glow spills in from the adjacent room. I keep moving forward until her back hits a wall of shelves laden with clothing. It reminds me of New Year's Eve. When I had her spine to the shelves in the pantry of her father's kitchen. Something bittersweet, maybe even nostalgic, pokes in my chest when I remember that night. My shoulder thuds in time with my heart as Deirdre clutches her towel and glares at me.

"I haven't been with anyone else since before your birthday."

It's actually been longer than that, but I don't elaborate.

Something changes in the set of her mouth. I don't get much time to analyze it before she spins around, yanking down some clothing from the shelf. She flinches and drops it when I move in close against her back.

"I truly don't care," she mutters. "I have no idea why you're telling me this."

"Don't you?" I slide the long, wet clump of her hair to the side, baring the back of her neck. I hold back a groan when I see goosebumps rise on her skin. "I think you're jealous but you don't want to admit it."

The thought of Deirdre jealous, sitting at home and wondering where I am, makes something burn low in my belly. I've always found jealousy in women tedious before. An irritation I have absolutely no patience for. But in my Songbird? I fucking love it. It's not the way I should feel about a debtor, someone I've made my prisoner. I should hold all the power, here.

But clearly, I don't. Because imagining Deirdre annoyed and jealous and waiting for me, like a girlfriend, like a *wife*, makes me so hard I can't fucking think. It almost, I think, makes me happy. But I'm not sure, because it's been about twenty years since I felt truly happy, and it's not an emotion I recognize these days.

"I am not jealous. You are delusional," she breathes. Her voice has changed. Some of the anger has ebbed away, replaced with a trembling huskiness.

"Don't lie to me."

I pull the towel and let it fall in a damp heap around Deirdre's ankles. I clamp my hands around her waist before she can try to wriggle away from me. But my leather gloves are soaked, and even though it's driving me nuts, I don't want to create any space between us to go grab another pair.

Without letting myself think too hard about it – because if I do I'll stop and that's the last thing I want right now – I hold her in place with my right hand, biting off my left glove and spitting it down to the floor before repeating the action on the other side.

When my hands, my *bare hands*, settle on her skin, my dick throbs so hard I think I'm going to come in my pants like a teenager. The sound that rips from my throat is guttural, groaning and brutal. I can't remember the last time I touched someone's skin besides my own without gloves. I truly don't even know if I've done it once in the past twenty years. Doctors have examined my hands, but me removing my gloves like this to purposely touch somebody else?

It does not happen.

Sensation sparks under my palms, and I can't stop myself from digging my fingers into Deirdre's sweet little waist. The scarring has numbed a lot of feeling in my hands, and I'm almost grateful, because even this is already overwhelming and I *do not get overwhelmed.*

At least, I didn't. Before.

Back before I saw her, heard her, wanted her. Back when my life was empty and pointless and actually made sense.

None of this makes sense. I was never supposed to take off my gloves. I was never supposed to need her like *this*. Need her beyond anything I've ever known before. This isn't simple lust. I can't even say that it's just obsession, even though I know I am obsessed.

"Fuck. I missed you," I say again. I had to travel up north to Thunder Bay to straighten out some business at our warehouses there, and every day I'd spent away from here, away from her, made pressure build behind my eyes.

She doesn't reply except for making a throaty little sound when my hands come up to cup her breasts. I drop my head forward just as Deirdre tips hers back, my forehead coming to rest against hers.

Her skin against mine is like a drug. It numbs the prickling feeling I get at the base of my skull every time I take off my gloves until all that's left is need. I drag my palms across her breasts, kneading, feeling her nipples rise and press against me.

I want to feel her everywhere. I keep my left hand where it is, gliding the right one down, past the pretty flare of her hip, through the soft brush of her curls. With the state of my skin, it's usually hard for me to tell when things are wet. It's not hard now. She's so slick down there my fingers slide through her folds until the tip of my middle finger is drawn to her entrance. I press, and she practically sucks me in until I'm buried to the second knuckle.

Deirdre's been fairly still and quiet in my hold, almost pliant, until now. She jerks and shudders, her back arching as her pussy clamps down with mind-blowing tightness on my finger.

"What are you doing?" she moans.

I curve my finger, stroking inwards as I grind the hard part of my palm against her clit. Her pussy spasms in response, and I just about lose it when I think of what that pressure would feel like on my dick.

"I'm taking care of your pretty little pussy."

"No." The word is a breathy moan. "I don't mean literally, I mean... *Oh my God...*"

She's close already. I can sense it in the changing of her breathing, the swollen quivering of her cunt.

"I mean," she pants, writhing like a snake, like she's trying to get closer and get away from me all at the same time, "I mean *what are you doing?* What are you doing with me? This wasn't the agreement. This wasn't what you told me when you took me."

I almost want to laugh at myself. Laugh for thinking I

could ever have her here, have her simply play for me, and leave it at that. A beautiful, untouchable performer in a cage. Something so intensely, painfully beautiful it hurts to look at her and hurts even more not to touch her.

I never thought I was a fool. But maybe I am for her. Maybe she's turned me into one.

"Fine," I breathe quietly against her ear. She's seconds away from explosion, but I pull away my hands. She starts to moan in complaint, then slams her mouth shut, tensing. "Get your violin," I tell her, before turning and striding from the room. I head for my bathroom for new gloves and a chance to cool my head. To remind myself why I brought her here. What this is supposed to be.

Even if that feels completely hollow now.

I wash my hands and face in the coldest water possible, revelling in the numbing pain of it. It's not cold enough to distract from the heat pulsing through my veins, though, and after drying my hands and pulling on new gloves I adjust my crotch. I already know I'll be jerking off later and I shake my fucking head, because just what in the teenage hell has my life turned into?

When I emerge, I find Deirdre holding her violin and bow, dressed in a pyjama set. It's probably the frumpiest outfit she could find in there, as if the shapelessness of the pale blue cotton is armour. It's almost obnoxious how she still looks like a haughty, angry queen despite the slouchy garments. I get the sudden, world-tilting sense that I'm in her domain instead of the other way around, and I do not fucking like it.

I need to remind her, remind both of us, what this is.

"Play," I grunt, seating myself on the edge of the bed. She doesn't hesitate this time. She doesn't dither or dawdle or tell me I'm too distracting. She just marches right up to me, lifts her instrument, and starts.

The song is jagged and discordant, a chaotic jumble of notes that somehow threads together into a melody I can latch onto. It's bitter and chaotic, like rage made sound. It's not her usual style, but I soak it up, because it's still her and apparently I can't do anything but drink up every little bit of her I can get.

There's a hard set to her mouth and a bright flush in her cheeks, and I wonder what has pissed her off the most. Me touching her, or me leaving her hanging a moment ago.

I wonder if she finished what I started, all alone in that closet. If she coaxed that soft pussy into coming. My dick pounds.

I close my eyes, letting myself focus on the music instead of how badly I want to see Deirdre rubbing her own clit. The notes practically puncture holes in my brain, they're so sharp and harsh. But even so, even though the song isn't slow or sweet or pretty, I still react to her playing like I always do. Like the song forms a fist around my heart.

She makes me fucking feel.

I'm not used to it. I don't know what the hell to do with it. So, I just sit there with my eyes closed and my chest hurting and I fucking take it. I take it like pain and bullets and blood, because I know what to do with violence and her music, the poetry of her perfect fucking soul, feels like an assault.

Eventually, the song comes to a sudden and silent halt. I keep my eyes closed for a long moment before cracking them open again. The flush in Deirdre's cheeks has ebbed away, leaving her pale under her freckles.

"That's not your usual style," I say.

"Yeah, well, I'm not in my usual sort of mood," she fires

back. Something in her cracks, sorrow bleeding through her anger. "You're going to ruin this for me."

"Ruin what?" I ask in a careful, measured tone.

She lifts her violin up again and gestures to it with the bow.

"This! This was something I shared with my mother. Something special. And now I, I..." She sighs and looks away. "I don't know if I'll ever be able to feel the same way about it again."

Something is ticking inside my head. Like a clock. Or an artery about to pop.

Something I shared with my mother... You're going to ruin this for me.

This wasn't something I had considered before. That by taking and taking and taking from her, I'd be eroding the one thing I was trying so desperately to get a hold of. That by trying so hard to have her, to control her and to cage her, I'd be destroying something precious, something I love.

No.

Need, desire, want.

Not love.

Fuck.

When I first saw Deirdre up on that balcony, it wasn't just the quality of the sound that got its hooks into me. It was the emotion. The pure, inescapable, excruciating joy. Joy, and the way it was balanced against a poignant sort of pain.

I look at my songbird, really look at her, and I don't see a hint of joy inside her now.

"What do you need?" I rasp. "I'll give you whatever you need to perform properly. To play how you want to."

Perform properly. Yeah, sure. Because that's what I care about. That's what nearly drove me out of my fucking mind

248

when I thought she was about to drown in the bathtub. The performance of it all.

I guess Deirdre thinks what I said is just as stupid as I do. She scoffs and shakes her head.

"What I need? What I need is freedom!"

The ticking in my head gets louder, harder, like a heartbeat.

I lift my arms and gesture to the size of the room around us, just one of many in my sprawling structure of a house.

"You can be free inside this cage."

Her eyes narrow.

"Not while you're in here with me."

My hands shoot out without me even meaning for them to. I clasp her waist and haul her into my lap. Her legs are spread, her cunt pressed to my aching shaft. She tenses, and I half wonder if she's about to clock me on the side of the head with her violin. But she and I both know my skull isn't worth damaging the instrument, not to mention the fact that I've got a hard fucking head so it probably wouldn't do any good, anyway. She lays her violin and bow down carefully on the bed just as I tighten my hold on her.

"I'm not going to be on the outside of the bars looking in, Songbird. I've been doing that since you were eighteen and I am fucking done." I pull her closer, dragging her against my hard-on. "Besides, weren't you the one who just complained about the fact I haven't been here for the past five days?"

Her eyes flare.

"That wasn't a complaint! It was... an observation."

"Yeah?" I breathe. Fucking hell, she smells so good. Feels so good. "Well, I have an observation of my own." I meet her gaze steadily. "You are a goddamn liar, Deirdre O'Malley."

Now she's even more pissed, and she starts to fight me. But she's so small.

And I'm not.

Even with my injured shoulder, it's easy to flip her until she's laying across my thighs, ass up. I wrench down the stretchy pyjama pants and panties until she's bare. I don't miss the trembling intake of breath, the anticipation that's already building in her even though she doesn't want to show it.

"Lie to me again and see what happens," I murmur, the leather of my glove and inch away from her creamy skin.

"I hate you," she whispers.

I chuckle darkly in response, but don't spank her yet, because I highly doubt that's a lie.

"You may hate me, but there's a part of you that wants me. Wants this." My fingers twitch, waiting for her to deny it, but she doesn't. "Gone silent on me, Songbird?"

"What am I supposed to say?"

I can't see her face like this, just the damp curtain of her hair.

"I'm not going to just say yes, am I?" she continues. "But if I say no, you'll spank me, and I'll like it for some fucked-up reason, and I'll just prove you right anyway. There's no good answer to that question. I'm trapped and you know it." She lets out a breath and wiggles slightly. "I shouldn't like any of this. You've broken something inside me. Made me as twisted as you."

I laugh out loud at that, because the idea that my beautiful, innocent little Songbird could be as twisted as someone like me is absurd.

"I haven't broken anything," I tell her softly. I lay my hand gently on her skin. She spasms under my touch, expecting more pressure, but I keep the touch soft. "I'm just responding to something that was already there."

"No way. I wasn't like this before," she hisses adamantly.

"You make yourself come by depriving yourself of fucking oxygen. You pleasure yourself and punish yourself at the same time. You gonna tell me you only started doing that after you met me?"

She stills, and then it's like every muscle in her body goes slack. She sags downward onto my lap, deflated by the realization that I'm right. I'm right that she likes desperation and discipline and deep discomfort. And she has for a very long time.

"When did you start doing that?" I ask her. My touch on her is still gentle. So is my voice.

I can't remember the last time I spoke to someone this softly. Maybe to Curse or Valentina when they were kids. It's been years. But I'm glad I manage it now, because maybe it's the quietness that makes her actually respond honestly.

"After my mom died."

It's a choked and tiny whisper. But it explodes in my head like artillery fire. There's smoke all around me, smoke inside me, and suddenly I can't think or feel or see. I grab Deirdre, haul her upwards and against me, clutching her to my chest like I can drag her out of the hole that I know all too well. Because it's a hole that's been hungry and dark inside me for twenty years, swallowing everything that matters. Flames dance at the edge of my vision, and I focus everything I have, everything I am, on holding her.

I can tell my eyes are wide open even though I can barely see anything. I blink, then close them, burying my nose in Deirdre's damp hair.

Her voice filters through the past, through the present, through the smoke and the flames and the pounding in my head.

"Elio? Are you hugging me?"

I don't respond, just hold her tighter. Slowly, the scent of smoke fades, and when I open my eyes, I can see again.

My voice is thick when I speak into her hair.

"When you want to feel that way, when you want to not breathe, you come to me. You don't do that alone. Not anymore."

She doesn't move or speak for a long moment. But she doesn't pull away either. Just lets me hold her even though I should have let go of her by now.

And then, in a movement so tentative and slow I might have missed it if I weren't keyed in to absolutely everything she is and everything she does, she lays her head on my shoulder.

Somehow, through sheer force of will, I remain upright and breathing while that small, simple movement makes my fucking heart stop.

Chapter 29

Deirdre

Elio Titone is hugging me. And not only am I letting him, I'm nuzzling my head against his shoulder as if this is something I want, as if he's someone I care about. As if anything about this makes sense. Something is changing between us, and it scares the hell out of me.

I need to backtrack. To get back to the place where hating him was simple and easy and safe. I need to not think about the things we share, about the things we've both lost, about what he went through when he was fourteen and what I went through when I was ten. We both have pieces missing, and I can't accept that their sharp and broken edges might just match up perfectly.

So, I try to remind myself about who he is, who I am, and what he's done. I need to remind myself that he's a tyrant who doesn't care about my feelings or my freedom. I ask the one thing of him I know he'll refuse me, and that refusal will push me away from him again, back to where I can be angry and safe.

"My classes start tomorrow. I want to go," I say. My

pulse speeds up in anticipation of him saying no. I'm already feeling the thrill of the rage that will flow through me, knowing it will send me right out of his arms. Arms that feel way too warm and solid around me.

"Fine."

I freeze, shocked into stone-stillness. *Did I just hallucinate? There's absolutely no way...*

"What did you just-"

"I said that's fine."

I lift my head from his shoulder so I can stare at him. I must look as confused as I feel, because he shrugs and says, "I told you I'd give you whatever you need to perform to the best of your ability. If that means attending classes, so be it."

I want to push him on this, to question him, but I also don't want to give him a chance to change his mind. I can taste that little bit of freedom already and I won't let it disappear.

"What about my job?" I ask, wondering if he'll give me even more if I request it now. "Teaching at the music school."

Elio quirks a dark brow.

"You already have a job. One that pays infinitely more."

"Yes, but-"

"You aren't returning to that job. All your income will be provided by me. Besides, Maeve's is in the heart of Darragh's territory. Going there isn't safe for you now."

He's right. Maeve literally rents her building from Darragh. There's no way I can go there now. I think about my students and want to cry. I have seven students right now taking private lessons, ranging in ages from six to twelve. I love all of them, even the ones who don't really care about learning violin and are only there because their parents make them go.

I don't want to cry. Not now, not like this. There's something so scarily disarming about Elio holding me like this, and I feel like I'm going to break right open. I finally pull out of his grip, getting to my feet and hiking my panties and pyjama pants back up.

Elio just watches me with those dark predator eyes. As I turn and head for the other bedroom, his voice follows me.

"Get some rest, Songbird. You have school tomorrow."

Chapter 30

Deirdre

When I wake up I still have no reply from Willow. I do, however, have a text and a missed call from Brian. For a split second, I actually consider telling Brian about Elio. Not so Brian can rescue me, but so that he leaves me alone. There's something satisfying about the thought of telling Brian that if he keeps trying to get me back he'll probably end up at the bottom of a lake.

And then my stomach clenches with nausea, because what the hell kind of a thought is that? Having anyone's death on my conscience would destroy me and I know it. And why on earth am I thinking about Elio as my protector in this situation?

I push all of it out of my mind, getting out of bed and heading for the bathroom. Rosa must come in while I'm in the shower, because when I emerge there's a breakfast tray waiting for me and the bed has been stripped and remade. I eat quickly and drink some tea before getting dressed for the day. My hands practically shake as I pull on a pair of jeans and a sweater. I can't believe how excited I am just to go to school. What was once a mundane, everyday occurrence is now a shining beacon of hope and light. It's *something*, something from my old life. Something from the outside world I can hang onto.

After getting dressed I have a second cup of tea, then I start pacing the room. My classes today don't start until 11:30 and it's not even 10am yet. I consider lying about when my classes start just to get out of here now, but then I remember that Elio told me he's memorized my school schedule, so that plan goes out the window.

But I need to do something to pass the time. I have way too much anxious energy to sit around here. My eyes fall on the paper and envelopes Valentina brought me to write to Willow, and suddenly I know what to do. I grab the paper and a pen and start to write letters to each of my students. Saying goodbye, telling them how much I'll miss them, how much potential they have. I have no idea if Valentina will agree to send them, but at least it's something.

By the time I'm finished writing the seven letters, I have to pee desperately. I was on the verge of tears the entire time I was writing, and to stave off a sobbing fit I chugged more and more hot tea. I put down the letters and hurry to the bathroom to do my business, then wash my hands. When I return to the bedroom I nearly jump out of my skin because Elio is standing there.

"Holy... When did you get here?" I ask, gawking at him. Even over the sound of the tap running, I feel like I should have heard him. He's so damn big. He has no right to be as silent as he is.

"You didn't come down, so I came up to get you. Don't want to be late to your first class of the term."

"You... came up to get me?" I echo.

I assumed that maybe Curse, or one of Elio's other men, would drop me off and pick me up. But as I let my gaze drift over Elio, taking in the black leather jacket and the car keys in his hand, I realize I was mistaken.

"Are you my ride or something?" I ask him, trying not to notice that the leather jacket hanging on the bulk of his frame looks way too good.

"Not just your ride," he replies, flipping the keys up and down against the palm of his black glove, the keychain spinning back and forth around his index finger. "Your *chaperone.*"

"My..." The word sinks in. "Oh, no. *No way.* You are not attending classes with me! You're not even a student! They won't let you in."

His mouth twitches, twisting on the scarred side, and I don't know if it's the beginning of a smirk or a frown. His tone when he speaks next gives nothing away besides the kind of cool, implacable confidence that comes from killing and kidnapping whoever you want, whenever you want, with absolute impunity.

"They'll let me in."

I shake my head.

"No way. This isn't happening."

"It isn't happening if you don't have a chaperone," he shoots back blithely. "The St George campus may not be in Darragh's territory but I'm still not sending you there alone." His mouth twitches again, and it's definitely a smirk this time. "Besides, I can't have you making a run for it."

I flush hot and cold, completely unnerved by the fact that I hadn't even considered using this as an opportunity to try to escape. *What the hell does that say about me? That I wouldn't even try to run?* I mean, realistically, I have no money and no allies. I could try to go to the police, but my 9-1-1 call from my first night here can tell me how much good that would do. But still, even knowing all this, I should have at least thought about it. Here I was all morning excited about getting to go to school instead of being excited at the chance to cut and run.

Well, there's clearly no chance of that now. Not if Elio insists on being glued to my side.

"Don't you have things to do?" I ask him. "Like, mafia things? You're basically the head of the Titone empire. How do you have time to go to my classes?"

He stops jangling the keys and walks towards me, not stopping until his chest almost brushes mine.

"I know how to delegate," he murmurs, his voice like warm smoke on my spine. His eyes seem to get even darker. "And prioritize."

There's an immediate, instinctive reaction inside me at those words. An undeniable pleasure that surges at being called his priority. Instantly, embarrassment follows. Because how pathetic am I, how little have I been valued, that I would react in such a way to what he just said?

I lean into the embarrassment, escaping from the thrill he just gave me. I don't need to get any deeper into this Stockholm Syndrome, or whatever it is, than I already am.

I can do this. I can be around Elio and not lose myself. I'll prove it, starting right now.

"Alright, fine," I say, brushing past him like he's nobody important instead of the man who's come to dominate so many aspects of my life. "Let's go."

We head down the stairs together, and I am supremely, uncomfortably aware of Elio's physical presence the entire way. Every time I see him out of the corner of my eye or catch a whiff of his deliriously nice cologne, I remember his hands on me last night.

He took his gloves off again...

And not just for a short time, either. He touched me with those huge, scarred hands and left me branded the same way the fire branded him. His touch on me, skin to skin, was incandescent and ruinous.

Ruinous because I want to feel it again. And what can that mean besides the fact that something inside me really is ruined?

I didn't break you, he told me. *I'm just responding to something that was already there.*

At the bottom of the stairs is a guy I recognize. Robbie. I'm pretty sure that's what Elio called him.

"Good morning," I mutter to him as we pass and head towards the front door. I'm not really sure why I say it. Maybe some kind of ingrained people-pleasing politeness, or a survival instinct that's telling me not to make enemies of anyone here. Robbie's eyes bulge at my greeting, and his gaze shifts to Elio as if he's not sure how he should respond.

"Don't be rude," Elio says. "If she speaks to you, I expect you to respond."

I roll my eyes at that, because I'm pretty sure that kidnapping someone and holding them hostage for their father's debt is way worse on the rudeness scale than not saying good morning.

Robbie jerks his head up and down and clears his throat. "Morning."

Elio is still staring at Robbie. "Where's her coat?"

I try not to admire it, but it really is amazing the way Elio commands. One simple question, and this giant tattooed soldier is hustling over to a nearby closet. He pulls out a long, expensive-looking white parka with a creamy fur-trimmed hood and brings it over. He holds it out to me, but Elio is the one who takes it. He dismisses Robbie with a jerk of his chin then turns to me, holding the jacket open so I can slip it on.

"This is for me to wear?" I ask. I've never had a coat like this, but I instantly recognize the brand. It's the most luxurious winterwear brand in Canada. This coat probably costs as much as a year of tuition at school.

"It's for you, period."

"To keep?" I try to clarify. "Am I paying for it, or..."

Elio moves closer with the coat, a wordless command to put it on. There's no point in fighting him. My own coats are at home, and the weather app on my phone told me it's negative twenty-seven degrees Celsius out there today. I slide my arms into the sleek, puffy sleeves. I go to do up the zipper, but Elio is faster and he's already on it. He slides it all the way up to my chin.

"Consider it part of your uniform. No charge," he says, pulling up the hood until the fur tickles the sides of my face. "Don't want you going hypothermic. Can't play violin if all your fingers fall off from frostbite."

I blink at him.

And then I laugh.

Really, truly laugh. I can't even remember the last time I laughed like this. Maybe with Willow, right before everything fell apart. It's probably a sign of my quickly deteriorating mental state, but man, does it ever feel good to just let go and laugh.

Elio stares at me in astonishment as I shake with laughter. Before I can catch my breath, he does something that completely takes it away.

He grasps the back of my neck beneath the hood and slants his mouth over mine.

I freeze, feeling way too hot in this coat now. My mouth had been open, mid-laugh, giving Elio ample space to slide his tongue inside. He strokes along my teeth and tongue, groaning as his other hand rises to cup my jaw. The leather feels exquisite, combining with the ravenous wet heat of his tongue and lips on mine.

He's kissing me.

The thought feels like it comes from very far away. I know I should be doing something, pushing him away or closing my mouth, but I'm completely stunned into stillness. Elio is *kissing* me. Somehow this is far more intimate than his tongue between my legs.

It doesn't feel how things between us usually feel.

It feels like it did when he hugged me.

What finally breaks the spell is realizing that I'm getting aroused from this. I actually have to fight against the urge to kiss him back, stop myself from meeting the bold movements of his tongue with my own. The warm slide of his mouth, the seeking swipe of his tongue, is making my nipples prick and my clit tingle. I jerk and close my mouth. He makes a rough, raw sound in his throat, and I think he's going to pry my jaws open to get back inside. But instead, he glides the tip of his tongue gently over the seam of my lips in between nipping kisses, probing and prodding until I tremble with the control it takes not to open my mouth with a horny, pathetic moan.

When he finally pauses, I try to piece my braincells back together enough to speak.

"What are you doing?" I croak.

"Don't know," he breathes against my lips. "Your mouth just looks so fucking good when you laugh."

I can't come up with a coherent answer to that, so instead I weakly mutter, "I'll be late."

"No." He kisses me one more time and then lets me go. "You won't."

There's a pair of boots for me, too, and mittens, and after putting them on we head outside. I inhale sharply and blink, shocked by the sunlight and the crackling cold air. This is the first time I've been outside in days.

I don't want to think this property is beautiful, but it really is. The bare trees outside look like crystal sculptures, every branch and twig lined with faceted frost. The spruce trees are still dark with greenish-blue needles, casting stark shadows on the glittering snow.

There's no snow on the huge driveway ahead of us except what's been melted by salt. The pavement gleams like ink.

A car emerges from one of the three garage doors at the far side of the house. It's the black Porsche Elio took me to the gala with. It comes to a stop before us and Curse gets out. Even though it's almost thirty degrees Celsius below freezing, he's not wearing a jacket, just a black dress shirt and pants.

"Enzo's at the campus," Curse says. It's the first time I've ever heard him speak in a full sentence. His voice is a lot like Elio's, and I find that slightly jarring. "So far everything looks good."

"Sorry, who's at the campus?" I ask. I swivel to Elio. "I thought it was just you going with me."

The bright sunshine and the snow make Elio's gaze look even darker.

"Enzo is my head of security. He's scoping things out right now."

I thought attending classes with Elio would be bad

enough, but now there's a made man skulking around the hallways and classrooms?

"Oh, God. He isn't bothering my professors, is he? Or the other students?"

What if he's interrogating people, or intimidating them? Honestly, even the possibility that he's mildly inconveniencing people because of me makes my chest hum with anxiety. I love going to university, but I like blending into the background as much as possible. I don't even usually go to office hours because I don't want to take up my teachers's time. But now I'm the cause of all this weirdness and upheaval.

"Maybe this was a bad idea," I say with a sigh. I glare at the sun-spangled snow to keep tears from forming. I am so stupid. Why did I think I could just go back to class, go back to that part of my life like nothing had ever happened? Like things were normal?

The fact that nothing will ever be normal again almost knocks me over. Even if I somehow pay my debt to Elio and gain my freedom, my life is beyond shattered. My dad is gone, and I'll still be enemy number one for Darragh if he can't find my dad. Even with the warmth of the parka cocooning me, I shiver. The only reason I'm alive right now, the reason I'm warm and wrapped up in this gorgeous coat, is because of Elio. The man who took me, caged me, lords himself over me like I'm his possession. Fury and fear go to war inside me when I consider the fact that I would be completely lost without him. I have no money to run away and start a new life. I have no close friends except Willow who can't fraternize with me for her own safety.

The sound of the passenger car door opening draws my attention. I swallow hard and look at Elio, holding it open for me like he's guiding me into a dark, enclosed future. A future he created.

And I walk straight to him. Enter through that door and let him close it behind me.

Because as much as I hate to admit it, Elio Titone is all I have left.

Chapter 31

Elio

"Seatbelt," I grunt at Deirdre as I slide into the driver's seat.

"I always wear my seatbelt," she says crisply, sounding annoyed by my command.

"Then why aren't you?"

She looks down at herself, confused, as if she doesn't understand what's happening.

"Oh. I thought I already did it. Lost in thought, I guess."

I watch her buckle up, making sure she does it properly, before starting the engine.

"Penny for your thoughts?" I say, putting the car into drive and heading down the long driveway. The soldier at the gatehouse nods at me through the bulletproof glass and opens the gate the leads out onto the street.

"Only a penny," Deidre says with an ironic sort of laugh. It's nothing like the real, beautiful laugh I heard inside the house. The laugh that turned me sideways and had me kissing her when I haven't kissed anyone like that in years.

"Typical man. You'll pay a fortune for my wet underwear, but only a single coin for what I actually think."

"It's just a saying," I mutter. I keep my left hand on the wheel and use my other to grab a pair of dark sunglasses I keep in the car, sliding them onto my face. I love winter here, love the lung-constricting cold of it, but I cannot fucking stand the flame-like dance of bright sun reflecting on snow.

"Just a saying. So you won't even pay a penny, then?" she replies tartly. Something's got her more pissed off than usual, and I wonder what it is. She didn't seem angry when I was kissing her just moments ago. She seemed disarmed and pliant and quivery in a way that made me want to say *fuck school so you can fuck me instead.*

"One hundred thousand and one. Dollars," I clarify when I feel her questioning frown turn to me. *Merda*, she's cute in that coat with the fluffy hood framing her face. Like some kind of Irish ice princess. "Tell me what you're thinking."

She sighs, turning away to look out the window. I think she's going to reject my offer, but my Songbird is smart and she knows she can't afford to.

"I was thinking about what happens when I pay off my debt. What I'm going to do without..."

She doesn't finish that sentence. Something lurches inside me.

"Without me, you mean."

Her silence is all the confirmation I need.

"Are you worried about that?" I ask.

"I'm worried about the fact I don't have a single friend in the world who can help me when I'm out of here!" she bursts out. "I can't even rely on my own family!" She tips her head back against the headrest. All I can see of her profile from the corner of my eye is her cute freckly nose.

"You don't need friends or family. You have me." *Until the end of fucking time.*

"But what about after? After the debt is paid and you let me go."

"Not gonna happen."

Her voice hardens. "I told you I would pay my debt and get out of here no matter what it takes."

We're getting close to downtown now, the buildings crowding together.

"The interest is mounting faster than you're paying it off," I counter. I mean, that's by design. That was the whole fucking point of the deal I made with O'Malley.

"We'll see about that," she whispers. Her voice remains quiet when she suddenly asks, "But what happens if you don't want to deal with me anymore? If I do something to make you angry, or you just want to be done with me?"

"Also not gonna happen." I want to wring her father's neck even more than usual at this moment. He's made her feel like something dispensable, something to abandon.

"You never know. You could get bored with me."

My jaw tightens as I manoeuvre through Toronto's downtown.

"I have watched you and waited for you since you were eighteen years old. You have turned me into a bleeding goddamn heart, or at least a bleeding wallet. I just paid six figures to find out what is going on in that head of yours because I can't stand not knowing a single thing about you. Getting bored is not even in the realm of possibility."

We're outside the building for her first class of the term, a lecture for her *Musical Developments from the Middle Ages to the Renaissance* course. There's nowhere to pull over, so I stop the car in the middle of traffic. Honking bleats from behind me, but I ignore it, focused solely on Deirdre.

"I just need to know where I stand," she says, unbuckling her seatbelt.

I take off my sunglasses and put them down, then grab the bag I arranged for her.

"You will stand where I tell you to," I reply. I get out of the car and walk around it. After opening the passenger door, I grab her hand and pull her to her feet. I hold her hand a second longer than is necessary while traffic piles up behind us, our covered palms sealed together. "You stand right beside me."

Chapter 32

Deirdre

Elio's gaze is so absorbing, dark and expansive, that the sound of angry Toronto drivers behind us is completely wiped out. The sun is bright on the buildings, wet with winter, creating a sparkling, steely backdrop. One of Elio's wayward curls has fallen forward again, and I both want to brush it back into place and tug it further forward to make him look more mussed, more human.

"All clear, Boss."

A voice from directly beside us pulls me out of Elio's void. Elio lets go of my hand, but quickly loops an arm around my waist, drawing me into his side as we turn to face a tall man with short hair and hazel eyes.

Elio hands the keys to him.

"Good. Go park, then keep your eye on things, Enzo."

Enzo nods and gets into the car, putting it into drive and taking off down the street.

"Ready?" Elio asks me. I glance from him to the building behind him. Students are streaming through the doors, carrying normal, everyday things like coffees and laptops and books.

"Not really," I say. "I don't even have my school stuff." I'll just have to pay really close attention since I can't take any notes. *Yeah, pay attention with the most dangerous man in the city breathing down my neck. Sure.*

Elio hoists a bag, holding it up in front of me. I hadn't seen it before, and now that the car is gone it's like he's pulled a rabbit out of a hat. Like the bag came from thin, cold air.

It's a gorgeous bag – a creamy leather backpack the same colour as the fur on the hood of my new coat. I take it from him, opening it to find a brand-new rose gold laptop, along with the books I'll need for the two classes I'm attending today.

"I already have a school laptop," I say with dismay, imagining more money piling on top of my debt. I picture it like a leaning tower of Piza of bills in my head. Like it's about to topple and bury me. I close the bag. "I feel like there should be a rule where if you buy me something I already have, don't need, and didn't ask for, then I shouldn't have to pay for it."

"I highly doubt you still have a laptop," Elio says. "It's pretty likely that Sev's guys took anything of value after your dad left. Or Darragh ransacked the place. Maybe both."

My stomach lurches. I don't know why I assumed the house and my possessions would still be waiting for me after this whole ordeal is over, but I did. *Stupid. I am so stupid.*

"How come you didn't do that? How come you haven't started repossessing all our stuff?"

Elio doesn't speak for a moment. Instead, he takes one of my hands, then the other, lifting each arm and sliding the straps of the backpack up until it hangs on my back. He tightens the straps at the front of my shoulders.

"There was only one single thing of any value to me in that house. Worth more than everything else put together," he finally says. His eyes flick to mine. "And I already got her."

"*Got her.*" I snort. "You mean *took.*"

Elio grins lazily at me, the expression made crooked by his scars.

"Tom-*ay*-to, tom-*ah*-to."

He still hasn't explicitly told me if this bag and laptop is a gift or not, and I give up on trying to figure it out, at least for now. Rather cynically, I wonder, *what's a few thousand more on top of everything now?*

We walk together into the building. It's hard to feel through the coat, but even so it's unmistakeable – the firm, possessive press of Elio's hand on my lower back. The pressure there reignites the curling burn of pleasure from his kiss, and I try to focus on each step I take over the tiled floors instead of his touch and the stupid response my body makes to it.

Luckily, my first class is a lecture of about a hundred people, so Elio's presence doesn't cause any sort of problem. There are too many students in this lecture hall to recognize everyone, so no one really stands out as a stranger, but even so, countless eyes are drawn to Elio as he guides me into the room. He's just so *big,* plus he's older than about 95% of the people here. And he's so commanding. Walking through the aisles and seats like he owns them.

I wonder how he does it. Even though people are looking at him more than me, my cheeks are on fire. This level of attention, just from walking through the room, makes me want to internally combust. But he doesn't seem to feel it at all. There's something magnetic about confidence like that. To go anywhere, be anywhere, and not care what anyone thinks. And it's not like he belongs here – a filthy rich mafia murderer hanging out in a university lecture hall. He is *extremely* out of place. But it just doesn't fucking matter. Because just by being here, he creates his own place. He slices his way through the skin of the world by doing nothing more than walking into a room that shouldn't want him.

The heat bubbling in my veins gets even hotter when I realize that Elio is leading me to a seat in the middle of the front row. The green plastic seat is attached to the desk, but it swivels to allow people in and out. He grabs the back of it and turns it towards me.

"Sit."

"I never sit in the front row," I say, shifting back and forth on my feet. I need to get this freaking coat off. There will probably be steam erupting from me when I do.

"You do now," Elio says. "I won't have you slacking off in the back row."

"Slacking off!" I whisper-hiss at him, all too aware of the fact I'm standing front and centre in the room. "If anything keeps me from giving the prof all my attention it is going to be *you*!"

"Glad to know I'm such a distraction."

"No, not like that. I-"

"Seats, everyone!" calls out a voice from the doorway. Doctor Heaney, a musical historian, tosses her grey hair behind her shoulders as she enters the room. Elio doesn't budge, still holding the chair in its open position for me. Biting my tongue, I plop myself into it, because at this point sitting in the front is preferable to marching to a whole new row after the prof has asked us to sit. Elio crams himself into the seat beside me, and it looks like he's sitting on furniture meant for children.

Luckily, the lecture passes without incident. Somehow, I manage to cobble together a decent set of notes, even with Elio's heavy arm slung across the back of my chair, his eyes endlessly gliding back and forth between what I'm typing and my face in profile.

I'm both relieved and disappointed when the lecture ends. Disappointed because, even with the weirdness of Elio beside me, I can't deny how nice it is to be out of the house and in class again. And relieved because one and a half hours of him doing nothing but sitting quietly beside me with his arm around me watching me take notes made me feel like my spine was melting into my pelvis. Like everything inside me was molten and oozing. I'm almost surprised my legs are still solid and holding my weight when I stand up

There's still one more class to go today, in a room just down the hall from my lecture. This one is a small seminar, and it's the one that's got me stressed. Unlike my morning lecture, this is a very small group of about fifteen students, and it's the same group of students I had a seminar with last term. We all know each other, and the prof knows all our names. Walking in with Elio won't be nearly as unobtrusive as it was last time.

When we get to the room, our professor, a short, grey-haired man with glasses named Doctor Frank is standing in the doorway, handing out the term syllabus to students walking in. I pretty much want to die every time I have to participate in class, but I do it in his seminar because he's such a warm, kind, mentoring sort of person. He smiles when he sees me approach, and I can't help but smile back.

"Deirdre! Hello, hello. Here's your syllabus. Ah." His bushy grey eyebrows furrow when he sees Elio trying to enter the room with me. "I'm sorry. Only students inside."

Doctor Frank isn't a tall guy, and he has to crane his neck back to look at Elio.

"Where she goes, I go," Elio says smoothly. "I'm her emotional support monster."

Doctor Frank's brows furrow further. Which is understandable, considering how fucking insane Elio sounds.

"I don't really know what's going on here," my prof says with a small shake of his head, "but I can't let anyone in here who isn't registered for the course."

By now the students who got here ahead of me are staring from their seats, and I silently beg the floor to swallow me up.

"Let's just go," I whisper to Elio. Maybe I can switch my schedule around to only include lectures this term.

Or maybe I shouldn't have bothered coming here at all.

But Elio acts like he doesn't even hear me. In a quick, controlled movement, he swipes the papers from Doctor Frank's hands.

"Excuse me, Sir!" Doctor Frank blusters, his cheeks turning red. Derek, one of the bigger guys in the class stands, apparently ready to step in even though he wouldn't stand a fucking chance.

Elio ignores everyone, thumbing through the syllabus papers until he gets to a different paper at the end. He pulls it to the front, and I recognize the names there. It's the class's attendance list with the names of the registered students in this seminar. Elio grabs a pen from his jacket, then holds the paper against the wall, scrawling a new name at the bottom of the list. *Elio Titone.*

When Doctor Frank sees the name, he clamps his mouth shut, the red instantly sucked from his cheeks.

"There," Elio says, thrusting the pile of papers back to

the prof with the attendance list on top. "Now I'm on the list."

"So you are, Mr. Titone," Doctor Frank says in a mangled rush. "My apologies."

"Feel free to let the rest of the department know," Elio responds. "Since I will be attending every one of Deirdre's classes from here on out."

Doctor Frank nods so rapidly I think his glasses might fly off of his face. God, I don't know what's worse. The scene we've just caused, or the fact that my prof looks like he knows exactly who I'm with. Doctor Frank watches me closely with a pinched look as Elio pulls out a chair for me, no doubt wondering how the hell the quiet violinist in his class has gotten herself mixed up with someone like Elio. If I could talk to him alone, I wonder if he'd try to help me somehow. He cares about his students, and I know instantly he probably would. But that would likely just put him in danger, so the thought wilts before I even let it take root.

Because this class is a seminar, we're all sitting at desks arranged in a circle instead of rows, and I try not to make eye contact with anyone when I sit down. I watch Elio take his seat from the corner of my eye as I open up the laptop. In the lecture hall, Elio had typed in the password for me, as the laptop was already set up with an account for me. But it's locked me out since I closed it up, and I quietly ask him for the password as the last few students filter in.

Instead of saying the password, he spells it out for me, letter by letter, and it's only when I get to the last part that I realize I've just typed in *iloveelio*.

Jesus Christ.

Since it's such a small group, and we all already know each other, Elio's presence is a lot more disruptive than in my previous class. He's like an invasive species, upsetting the balance of the ecosystem. Doctor Frank chooses not to introduce him or acknowledge him when he settles into a nervous, jittery version of his *welcome to the new term* spiel. While I normally try to participate in this class, today I don't say a word. The other students are quieter than normal, too, and I don't need to think too hard about why that might be.

Getting through that seminar is like pulling teeth, and the bit of excitement and relief I felt at attending my earlier lecture is totally gone now. I practically bolt out of there when class is done, barely registering Doctor Frank's comments about next week's assignment.

"Damn, you're fast. You here on a track scholarship?" Elio asks from behind me as I weave through students in the hallway.

"Wouldn't matter if I was," I shoot back. "I'm dropping out."

I shove open the doors and hurl myself out into the bright winter day. In my haste to get out of there, I haven't zipped up my jacket. The bitter cold knifes right through the front of my sweater, but I welcome it. It feels so painfully good that I take the jacket off entirely, breathing in the January air. I know Elio is right behind me before he even speaks.

"You're not dropping out."

"Yes, I am," I snap, whirling on him. He's standing there with the bag, carrying my books like my fucking boyfriend or something. "I can't do this anymore."

"Can't do what? Attend class?"

"Not anymore. Not with you," I tell him.

"Why not? I was quiet, wasn't I? Just sat there like a good boy."

"Oh, *yes*, a very good boy," I huff, clutching the jacket against my front. "You're practically a *saint*."

"Elio, Patron Saint of Songbirds," he drawls. "Has a nice ring to it."

"I can't with you today. We are done here."

The crackle of dark humour in his gaze goes cold, glinting like onyx.

"I decide when things begin and I decide when they end," he growls. "You told me you wanted to go to school. That it's important to you, and to your craft. So, you will go to fucking school. And if I have to get you up and dressed and drag you here myself, I fucking will."

"But I don't belong here anymore!" I stammer, off-balance from the sudden shift in his tone. "And neither do you! When we entered that room, *God*, it was like we poisoned it or something. Everyone was staring at us! My teacher looked like he was on the verge of passing out!"

"My sweet little Songbird, the only one you're capable of poisoning is me. You're in my fucking blood, and I'm pretty sure you've passed the blood-brain barrier, because these days I can barely think around the space you take up inside my head." He raises the arm that's not busy holding the bag, gesturing his thumb backwards over his shoulder towards the doors we just came out of. "And those other dopey fucks in there? They're lucky to even breathe the same air as you. Why do you care what they think? Why would them staring at you keep you from something you want?"

"I don't even know what I want anymore."

"But I do," he says, every word stony with conviction. "And your pretty little ass better be ready for school tomorrow morning, or you'll have to stand at the back of the class because it's going to be too sore to sit on those shitty plastic seats."

A bolt of confused pleasure goes straight to my clit at his clipped commands.

"Well, we'll just see about that," I say with a shiver.

"Yes," Elio says darkly. "We will."

Chapter 33

Deirdre

The next morning I get up and shower, but after that I waffle back and forth about what to do. Should I get ready for class or not? Am I dropping out or staying? I absolutely do not want to repeat yesterday – that was mortifying – but if I go to class there's no way around it. Elio's coming with me. A twisted part of me almost wants to bait Elio. To sit here in my wet towel until he has to come and get me. To see if he really will drag me there. Imagining him storming in here and ripping away my towel makes my insides curl and my thighs squeeze, and it's the rebellion against that arousal that finally has me hurrying to get ready.

I'll go to class, at least today. Going there and suffering humiliation in public is better than submitting to the private humiliation in here. The humiliation that makes me wet. I blow dry my hair, not bothering to style it, and it dries in a frizzy tumble that I tie up in a knot on the top of my head.

The only problem is that I spent so long dithering about what to do that I really might actually be late at this point. My first class is at ten today, and I'm going to be cutting it close. I'm running from the bathroom to the closet, clutching my towel, when Elio strides into the room. He looks the same way he did yesterday – tall and broad in all black, leather jacket and gloves on, keys in hand. He stops short when he sees me.

"You're not ready."

"I am. Almost," I say hurriedly, continuing my way into the closet. He follows me, and my heart starts banging a chaotic rhythm against my ribs.

And my clit.

"I told you what would happen if you weren't ready," he says from behind my back, so softly that it belies the bite of the threat in the words.

"And I told you I'm almost ready," I shoot back.

"Doesn't look that way to me."

I yelp as the towel gets tugged away from me. Before I can cross my arms or try to hide myself, Elio grabs the back of my neck from behind me and shoves my head forward.

"Grab the shelves."

"No," I pant. The feeling of his leather glove on the back of my neck is so fucking hot I can't stand it. I can't let this go any further. Can't let him see what he's doing to me. That's how he wins. Every single time.

Elio keeps his hold on my neck and steps forward, bumping my ass with his thighs until I lose my balance and I'm forced to grasp the edge of the shelf ahead of me. Now I'm doing exactly what he told me to. I'm bent over and bare for him. Even if I tried to stand up, I couldn't, because the weight of his hand on the back of my neck is like an anchor. He isn't even pushing me down, and that's the worst part. The anchor only exists in my head because of how far he's dug his way inside me.

"I told you that you are going to school today and I told

you what would happen to this ass if you weren't ready," Elio says from above and behind me. "You know what time your classes are. You know what time you needed to be ready. And you know I don't break my promises." His left hand grazes my hip, and I start, my pussy throbbing. "Don't try to act all innocent and affronted on me now. You're baiting me, waiting for me in only a towel when you're supposed to be dressed and ready."

His hand lifts from my hip, and I tense, waiting in angry, defensive, delirious anticipation of what's to come.

"I told you at the gala that taunting me is not a good idea."

His hand comes down with a tight, sharp movement, searing my flesh. I hold my breath, an instinctive reaction, so that I don't give him the satisfaction of hearing my cry of deranged pleasure. But Elio slides his right hand around the front of my throat, massaging there, until I'm forced to open my mouth and take a breath. With his left hand, he spanks me again, and this time I can't hold back my mangled moan.

"No holding your breath," he orders me huskily. "No shutting down. No silence. I want to hear that pretty fucking song of yours."

It doesn't sound like a song to me. It sounds like panting, pathetic mewling. A reedy, throaty chorus punctured by the staccato beat of Elio's leather glove against my skin. My back is arching, my fingers tight against the shelf, and I can't fucking stop it, because for some reason I need this and I need *more*. After every slap, my ass shoves backward, upward, begging him to keep going.

"I told you, Songbird," Elio rasps. "I told you I could go harder. And look how fucking good you're being. Look how fucking well you take it." He groans, long and low, pausing the spanking to grip my ass cheek and spread it to the side. "Look how fucking well you wear my marks. It's like your skin was made for this."

The unexpected praise mixed with the pain and heat and degradation has me close to coming. I hold onto the shelf for dear life, my thighs trembling, my clit screaming. I can't even feel my own heartbeat now. It's been replaced by the rhythm Elio has created. The stinging slaps that echo through my body even when both of us are still.

Elio's hand eases from my neck, and I hear the unmistakable jingle of a belt being undone and pants hitting the floor. Dread and desire bloom inside me, and I can't move, *I cannot move*, as Elio guides the head of his cock against my pussy.

"Fuck, you're soaked," he groans. "*Cristo santo*, your dripping pussy nestled below that bright red ass is a work of fucking art."

My muscles jump, and I'm at war with myself. My body is frozen under the weight of competing instincts. The instinct to wiggle backwards, to soothe the pulsing emptiness by taking Elio inside me.

And the instinct to run for my life.

"Touch yourself."

When I don't answer or move, another slap makes my nerves spark and sing.

"*Touch yourself.*"

My right arm practically falls from the shelf, like it's dead weight. My fingers find their way between my legs, and I almost fall to my knees at how incredibly sensitive my clit is. I start grinding my clit, already on that breathless edge, as Elio watches and breathes unevenly behind me.

"Good, Songbird," he murmurs, petting the place he's

spanked me. That gentle scrape of leather over my burning skin is sensation overload, and I can't get enough. I wonder if Elio's going to press inside me.

I wonder if I'd even be capable of putting together enough coherent sounds to tell him not to if he tried.

His fat tip is right at my slick entrance. I quiver and clench around nothing. One tiny movement, one concise and brutal thrust, and he'd be buried inside me.

His cock jerks, his head nudging slightly harder against my folds, and I strum my clit harder, faster, focusing on my building orgasm so I can't focus on the fact that if he fucks me, I can never come back from it.

With a ragged grunt, his cock pulls away, and I want to strangle the sudden dismay I feel. It's good we're not going that far. I should be relieved. And I am, I swear, I-

"I am going to come all over your ass," Elio growls. He spreads my ass cheek further, opening me. His cock makes contact again, this time thrusting up towards my lower back, the underside of his shaft grinding against me. "And then I am going to rub my come into that skin I've made so pretty and red. And after that, I am going to take you to class so you can sit on it and think about exactly what you've done."

My eyes fly open, and I try to say *no* because I am absolutely not going to class now, not without showering again, at least. But I can't say it, because my throat constricts and all that comes out is a strangled cry. My whole body shakes and then tightens until I'm shattering, *shattered*, completely broken open, the pieces scattered on a dark and undulating sea of molten pleasure. Through the shameful sounds I'm making, I can hear Elio stroking himself, hard and fast and feral, leather sliding over engorged flesh. He grips my hip, holding me still, then lets out a tight, hissed breath. A second later, warmth erupts over my stinging skin, and that sudden sensation makes me shudder and clench and moan all over again.

As promised, Elio rubs the come into my skin, the touch soothing and burning all at once. The evaporating wetness makes my heated skin feel slightly cooler, and I suddenly can't stand that this actually feels good. This smooth, massaging motion, so gentle, almost reverent, when a moment ago that hand was so hard, might even be better than the orgasm. If I ignore the circumstances, it almost feels loving, like he's taking care of me.

But the circumstances blare all around me, like neon signs trying to guide me back to sanity. He's not taking loving care of me. He's rubbing his fucking come into skin he just spanked nearly raw.

"Get dressed," he says, drawing his hand away and pulling up his pants. "I'm going to get new gloves, and then we're leaving."

"No," I whisper. "I'm having another shower."

"Absolutely not," he says. "At this rate you'll only be fifteen minutes late for class. If you have another shower, you'll miss the entire lecture."

I unclench my left hand from the shelf, straightening up shakily and turning around.

"My shower won't take that long. I won't even get my hair wet." I narrow my gaze at him. "I only need to wash something off of *one* part of my body."

"You go in that shower and just see what fucking happens."

I chew on my lip, seething. There's a slight darkness to Elio's cheeks that I've never seen on him before, and I realize with a treacherous flutter in my belly that that flush is there because of me. His breathing hasn't returned to normal yet, either.

"Get dressed," he says again.

And then he turns and walks away.

Chapter 34

Elio

It only takes me about thirty seconds to get new gloves from my room. When I come back into Deirdre's bedroom, I don't hear the shower running, and I'm both satisfied and annoyed that she obeyed. If she'd gone into the shower now, I would have followed her. And then I would have had her up against the shower wall because there's no way I would have been able to stop myself. I barely held myself back from shoving inside her and claiming her when she made that little virgin pussy come so sweetly for me.

Fuck. I'm already going to get hard again. I take my keys out of my pocket and clench them in my fist, focusing on the feeling of blunted metal pressing through my glove.

I can hear fabric rustling in the closet. While I wait for Deirdre to finish getting dressed, I pace the room, pausing in front of her violin and bow. I run a single, gentle finger down the flexible part of the bow that connects with the violin's strings. It's called the bow hair, and it's made from horse hair, one of the many odd, endless facts I've committed to memory in preparation for Deirdre's arrival here.

Something else catches my eye, and I turn my attention to a small stack of envelopes. I pick them up and shuffle through them, wondering who the hell Deirdre might be trying to contact through the mail.

There are seven envelopes, and the mailing address is the same on every one – the address for Maeve's Music School. But the names are all different. Hannah Jankowski, Mingming Li, Hazel Martin, Sam Ford, Leshawn Andrews, Eun-Ji Park, Noah Barber. I use my car key to slide under the seal of the envelope addressed to Noah, open it, and take out the letter.

Dear Noah,

I have had so much fun being your violin teacher! I never want you to forget that. The fact that I'm not your teacher anymore has nothing to do with you, and if I could be there with you right now, I would.

Even though I'm sad I won't get to teach you any longer, I just want you to know how happy I am that I got a chance to get to know you and help you along your music journey, even if just for a little while. You are funny, expressive, and so, so talented.

I know you sometimes get frustrated when the notes don't come out the way you want them to, or when you think the song doesn't sound quite right, but just keep going. Keep trying. Keep practising. Don't ever get discouraged. Remember that the song already exists inside you. The instrument is just our way of letting it out. The violin simply gives voice to what already exists, and Noah, it doesn't just exist in you, it shines. No matter who your teacher is, you have everything you'll ever need to excel.

Thank you so much for being my student. Don't ever forget how special your song is,

Love, Miss Dee

"That's private."

Deirdre's voice makes me look up from the paper. I gesture the stack of letters towards the lack of door between her room and mine.

"Right," she says, rolling her eyes. "Nothing's private here."

"You don't have stamps. What is this, some writing exercise?" I fold Noah's letter back up and slide it into the envelope.

She stares at me, and I stare back, because fuck she looks good after she comes. Her skin is flushed and glowing. Tiny baby hairs are escaping from her hairstyle, creating an electric orange halo of frizz. My beautiful hellfire angel.

"I was going to see if Valentina would put stamps on them and send them."

"I'm in charge of what comes in and out of this house, not Valentina."

Something unhappy crashes in the blue of her eyes.

"Fine, then," she snaps. "May as well throw them in the fire now because I know you won't let me send them."

Her own reaction to what she just said is almost comical to watch. Like a cartoon character giving life to the phrase "biting my tongue." She tenses, her mouth snapping shut so hard and fast that I think it's probably a good thing I haven't put my dick in there, because that's a hell of a lot of jaw power. I wait without speaking, because I've never been one to find silence awkward, boring a hole into her head with my gaze while hers traces grooves along the wood floorboards.

"Sorry," she finally says, so fucking softly. She uncrosses

her arms and starts twining her fingers together in front of her. "That was the wrong choice of words."

She knows.

Not just about the fire, because everybody knows about the fire. My fucking face tells people about the fire.

But she knows it was more than just a fire. She knows what I lost. She knows exactly how I failed.

Fucking Valentina.

The ticking in my head is back, an incessant, uneven thrum that sounds like flames crackling over wood. My hands start tensing, and I have to fight the urge to pulverize the stack of letters in my fist.

"Just throw them away already," Deirdre says.

"I'm not going to throw them away," I say evenly.

"What, going to read them all out loud and then rip them up in front of me?"

"Nope."

She lets out an exasperated breath.

"What, then?"

"I'm going to reseal this one and add it back with the others. Then, I'm going to put stamps on them. And then I am going to send them."

Her ginger eyebrows practically crawl all the way up to her hairline. It seems like she can't stop the question of "Why?" from escaping her mouth. It comes out as a gasp, because what other reaction would an act of humanity in me elicit than pure fucking shock?

I don't have an answer for her. At least not one I want to say out loud. It's something to do with the fact that I know what it's like to lose a woman you love and look up to with no closure and no goodbye when you're a kid.

And it's something to do with the way the image of

Deirdre bent over the desk writing such kind, devoted letters makes my chest feel tight.

It isn't just that she's not from this world, like Valentina said. It's that she's too fucking good for it. And if I were a better man, she'd never have ended up here at all.

But then again, if I were a better man, I wouldn't have done the things I've done to have the money I have. I wouldn't have been able to pay her papà and help keep her head above water from the dark and shadowy sidelines. And I wouldn't have been there to take a fucking bullet for her seconds into her twentieth birthday.

"Doesn't matter. Come on," is all I say in reply.

Chapter 35

Deirdre

Other than the fact that we walk into my lecture late and make everyone turn and stare, today goes a lot smoother than yesterday. I'm actually able to somewhat focus, and when Elio notices me squirming to keep weight off tender places, he folds up his leather jacket and shoves it under me like a cushion while giving me a dark look that tells me not to argue or refuse him.

Which is pretty much the last thing I expect him to do. Wasn't he the one who told me if I didn't listen, if I wasn't ready for school, that I'd be too sore to sit on the seats? I assumed that would be part of the punishment, but now here he is turning his own jacket into a pillow for me. Between this and the fact that he sent the letters to my students (I watched him put them in the mailbox myself as we left the property this morning) I can't get my head around who or what he is these days.

A monster. A man. Some scarred, mangled mixture of the two.

And the fact that I seem to crave his touch more and

more, the fact that I stayed bent over for him this morning, that I didn't even wash his claim off my skin, means I don't even know who I am, either. From the very first night he took me, there's been this slow, steady, toxic pulse of desire even inside my rage against him. And it only seems to be getting stronger. Faster.

I almost lost my virginity to him this morning. It was only his decision to pull his cock away, and not anything I did, that kept that from happening.

Why didn't he do it?

Did I want him to?

I can't answer that question definitively, which only makes me even more confused. When Brian tried to push himself on me, that fumbling, drunken night in his apartment, I hadn't wanted any part of it. I'd liked him well enough on our dates, but at that moment he became completely repulsive to me, and I couldn't even stomach his beer-scented breath wafting over my skin. My whole body was filled with dread and nausea.

Why don't I feel repulsed by Elio? Elio is ten times worse than an idiot like Brian. He's literally killed people. He's trapped me and punished me and coerced me. But I can't even make myself as afraid of him as I was when Brian was against me, panting, his crotch tented stiffly at the front.

I wonder if my own thoughts somehow conjure him, because when we exit the building after my last lecture of the day, I hear that familiar voice calling my name.

"Deirdre? Deirdre! Hey, Red!"

Elio hears it, too, and his arm descends fast and hard around my shoulders, like the possessive downward sweep of a guillotine. He doesn't stop walking, and neither do I, swept along by his long strides and the other people moving the same direction. God, I hate it, but it actually feels good.

It feels good to be with Elio right now. To have his arm so tight around me. Brian's showed up a bunch of times begging for me back, and I'd always been alone.

Not this time.

I don't bother looking back. Elio's got me too tightly pinned against his side. The crowd thins out as we head away from the school building until it's just Elio and me on the sidewalk and a guy running a small poutine cart in the near vicinity.

At least, I thought it was just us. But then I hear the call of "Red!" again, along with the sound of boots hitting the slushy sidewalk in a jog. "Would you just stop and fucking talk to me?"

I'm fully prepared to ignore Brian like I've being doing up until now. I keep on walking, momentum pulling me forward, so that it takes me a second to realize Elio is no longer holding me, no longer walking beside me. I stop and spin just in time to see the black fingers of Elio's right hand close around Brian's throat as he backs him up against the brick wall of a building.

"How about I talk, you listen?" Elio murmurs so softly that goosebumps rise on my skin under my clothes and coat. Once again, Elio's carrying my backpack, and it looks fucking insane, this hulking six-foot-four giant with a woman's book bag on his shoulder and his fist around another man's throat. I have to quell a horrible surge of something that feels icky and dark and wonderful at the sight of Elio towering over Brian the way he does. Brian's not a small guy. He's about six feet tall and I know he works out, but compared to Elio he looks like a gangly kid. And seeing Elio so totally subdue him does something to me. Something bad and wrong that I need to hide from, need to heal from.

If Brian wants to say anything now, he can't. His eyes are wide, and his face is an alarming shade of crimson.

"You will not contact Deirdre. You will not touch her. If you ever see her again, you turn around and walk the other fucking away."

Brian makes a gurgling sound that makes me think Elio has tightened his grip. His boots slip in the slush and he claws at Elio's arm, but it has absolutely no effect. Elio's only holding him with one fucking hand, his other one secured around the strap of the small backpack slung over his injured shoulder. Like he's worried about my books falling into the salt-melted snow. And once again I feel that dark, wrong, lovely feeling. The feeling of being cared for, being protected when my own father couldn't even have been bothered to do it before.

No. This is not a good thing. He's not a good man.

And that not good man is about to murder someone right in front of me.

"Elio," I whisper in alarm. "Please stop. Don't kill him."

I can't witness a murder. I can't watch Brian suffocate like this. I *can't.*

A car pulls up beside us, and how fucked-up am I, how far-gone have I become, that my first instinct is fear that whoever's in the car will get Elio in trouble? My reaction isn't to turn to them for help, to save Brian and maybe even get myself out of Elio's grip entirely. It's alarm on Elio's behalf.

The car is Elio's, though, and Enzo pops out of it, hustling around the hood of the vehicle, his hand inside his jacket in a way that makes my stomach drop and the word *gun* repeat inside my head on an endless loop.

"No, Enzo, wait-"

He ignores me and stops at Elio's side.

"Boss?"

Brian is still conscious, but his movements are getting weaker. Slower.

"Don't kill him!" I whisper-cry in reply to Enzo, even though I know he didn't ask me for direction on what to do next.

Elio doesn't answer Enzo or me. He's still speaking to Brian in that silky-smooth, deceptively calm voice.

"You're lucky my Songbird has such a tender heart, or you'd be nothing but a stain on the sidewalk right about now."

I swallow hard and wonder if Elio knows. If he somehow knows why I ended things with Brian. If he knows what Brian tried to do that night. This reaction seems over the top, even for Elio.

"Make sure he's never on campus at the same time as Deirdre," he mutters to Enzo, finally letting Brian go. Brian sags back against the wall, gasping and clutching his neck before sliding down to sit in the slush.

"Got it," Enzo says instantly. He pulls his hand out of his jacket, sans gun, thank God. My eyes dart up and down the small street. The poutine guy is staring at us. He pulls his tuque further down over his ears. *Hear no evil.*

"Didn't see nothin', Ma'am. Nothin' at all. Hey, you or your man want some poutine? On the house."

I shake my head weakly at him.

My man.

He's not my man. He's my disaster.

Enzo passes Elio the keys and Elio puts his arm around me once again, steering me towards the car.

He doesn't say anything, and neither do I.

But Brian does, because he really is the biggest fucking

fool in the world right about now. His voice is weak and croaky, but the words are unmistakeable.

"What the hell, Red? You didn't want to be with me and now you're fucking some forty-year-old psycho?"

Uh oh.

Enzo grabs Brian and instantly hauls him upwards, pinning Brian's back against his front by locking his elbows under Brian's arms.

Elio turns slowly back to Brian, who's now fighting fiercely to get out of Enzo's hold to no avail.

"I'm thirty-four, actually," Elio says. "And her nickname isn't Red, it's Songbird."

When Elio's fist connects with Brian's face, I know his nose breaks, because I *hear* it. A crackling, crunching sound. Like a boot going through too-thin ice.

This time, Brian doesn't say a word as Elio trundles me into the car.

Chapter 36

Elio

I'm still annoyed that all I did was break that fucker's nose as we drive home. I stew on it, replaying the entire interaction, almost wishing Deirdre hadn't been there so I could have ripped that idiot's tongue out the way I'd wanted to. Red? What the hell kind of nickname is that? Reducing her down to something as basic and obvious as her hair colour. No fucking imagination, no art, no homage to the trilling melody of her soul. *Red. Red Red Red Red. Cristo Santo*, I hate it even more than usual now. The only good thing that word's got going for it is that it rhymes with dead which is what that spineless little law student should be right about now. But Deirdre's terrified voice is still there in the back of my head. *Please don't kill him!*

She's too sweet. Too soft. She probably would have blamed his death on herself, and I don't want her wasting a single second of emotion, guilt or grief, on him.

We're nearing the gate to the house when she finally lets out a shaky breath and says, "So, that was a lot."

Not nearly enough.

When I don't reply, she says, "You broke his nose."

"He needed it broken. His face was too symmetrical. Now it'll have some character," I mutter as the gate slides open.

"Is that all?"

"What do you mean?" I ask.

"I just thought... I just wondered, because you were watching me, if you knew. Somehow. If... Never mind."

My fingers tighten involuntarily on the wheel as we pull up the drive to the house. She takes off her seatbelt.

"If I knew what?" I put the car in park and grab Deirdre's wrist, holding her in place so she can't run from my questions. She avoids my gaze while I drill mine into her. "What happened?" I pull her closer and cup her face with my other hand, running my thumb back and forth across her flushed, freckled cheek.

"It's nothing. We broke up, OK?"

"I know that."

She knows I've been watching her. She knows that I know she stopped seeing him weeks ago.

"But why?" I press. "Other than the fact that he's a snivelling, snot-nosed prat who isn't fit to lick your fucking boots. What happened?"

She's doing that thing where she rolls her lips inward between her teeth. She's shutting down. Shutting me out.

"Deirdre," I growl. "If you don't talk, I'll have to go track him down and make *him* talk. And a lot more will be broken than his nose."

"Nothing happened," she cries suddenly, a burst of sound. She says it so firmly, almost fervently, that it sounds like she's trying to convince herself as well as me. "He just... He wanted to, but I didn't want to. He tried to, but... Nothing happened. I got away. I got out of his apartment and ghosted him after that."

I've taken quite a few hits to the head in my time, but I'm able to piece together what she says just fucking fine.

That pulsing tick is back in my brain, but this time it sounds like Brian's voice saying *Red Red Red Red Red Red* over and over again. It's all I hear. All I see. The car, the streets, the whole city red with the blood of the man I am about to obliterate.

Maybe my eyes have gone completely red even from the outside. Deirdre must see something change in me, because she puts her smooth, cool hands on either side of my jaw. It's the first time she's ever touched me like this. It's both soothing and infuriating, because that one tender, possessive touch makes me want to get down in the slush and the salt and the snow, press my forehead to the ground, and bow. Her hands on my face, on my skin and my scars, solid and unflinching like this, makes me want to fucking beg. Beg her for something but I don't know what. It's both nostalgic and foreign to me, because I haven't begged anyone for anything in decades. Not since I begged God that night in the fire.

"Elio," she says, just a whisper.

And then, for the first time, she kisses me.

It's timid at first. Tentative. Like she's afraid she might be breaking a rule of some kind but she's going to do it anyway. Her lips are so fucking soft, fluttering over mine in timid, exploratory pecks. Last time we kissed, it was all me. I grabbed her and I did it and she stood there and took it like a good fucking girl.

But this time, it's her. *She* is coming to *me*. Before I know it, my eyes are closed. Other than my dick swelling, I don't move a goddamn muscle. I don't want to shatter the spell. I don't want to forget how good it feels to have her hands on my face and her mouth on mine because she's the one who chose to put them there. And maybe it's pure manipulation on her part. Just meant to distract me. But I decide that I don't care. Because right now, I'd crawl over broken glass for her. Walk shoeless through snow and ice for her.

Run back into a burning house for her.

And that kind of devotion is terrible. Terrifying. I haven't prayed at the altar of anything besides death and wrath and money for a long, long time. I want to stay the man I've been for twenty years. The kind of man who doesn't let himself feel anything besides anger and greed and desire.

The kind of man who'd steal a songbird simply because he decided that he wanted her. So that he could trap her, bind her, *own* her.

Not so that he could fucking love her.

When Deirdre's tongue touches my lips, I can't stay still anymore. With a muted groan, I grab her ass and haul her into my lap. Remembering what I did to her ass this morning, the way my come is on her skin right now, makes my cock leap under my jeans. Deirdre gasps against my mouth when she feels that hardening movement against her crotch.

I grind myself up against her, left arm locked around her back while my shoulder pounds, right hand cradling the back of her skull so she can't back up, can't lean away, can't escape. My tongue shoves inside her mouth.

Fuck, kissing her is incredible. It's like an accelerant and an antidote all at once. I'm devouring her, taking everything I can, tasting everywhere.

When she pulls back and whispers, "Don't kill him," all I can do is say, "I won't."

I don't add the next part. She doesn't need to know.

I won't kill him.

I'll just make him wish he was dead.

———————

One hour and forty-eight minutes after getting Deirdre home after her classes, Curse and I have Brian tied up in the trunk of Curse's SUV. We're heading north, back up to one of our warehouses on the outskirts of Thunder Bay. Usually, I'd fly there. But the fifteen-hour drive is good. Gives me all the time in the world to think about exactly what I'm going to do to him. Normally, I don't go this far from Toronto just to make some asshole regret everything he's ever done, but I can't stomach the idea of him in the same city as my Songbird for one second longer.

Curse and I take turns driving. The drive takes longer than fifteen hours because of the snow on the roads. We don't pull up to the desolate, snow-covered warehouse until 7am. It's still pitch black out – no sun. No light at all except for one streetlight illuminating the snowy parking lot we pull into. Besides our vehicle, there's only one other – an old pickup truck. Its owner, Aleksej, is waiting for us, just like I told him to be when we set out from Toronto. Aleksej is one of the only guys working this closely with me who's not a made man. He's not Sicilian, but Serbian, and he's as solid as they fucking come. Works like a dog and, most importantly, he keeps his mouth shut. He and his father ran into problems with the Serbian mafia and relocated here years ago, and Aleksej's worked for me ever since.

Curse and I get out of the vehicle as Aleksej approaches. I head for the back of the car, opening the trunk and hauling Brian out. Curse sedated him, and he's still too out of it to stand or walk. I let him drop to the cold hard ground, then grab the back of his jacket and start dragging him. Aleksej walks ahead and unlocks the metal door of the warehouse, holding it open, his grey eyes looking back out towards the parking lot to make sure no one's followed. Once we're all inside, the metal door closes behind us with a final, brutal clang.

"Strip him down and get him in the chair."

Curse and Aleksej do it, peeling off Brian's jacket and everything else until he's slouched over naked in a plastic chair in the centre of the darkened warehouse. His wrists are tied to the arms of the chair, his ankles tied at the bottom, and at the last moment Curse ties his shoulders to the back of the chair, too. He's barely conscious, and without being tied upright he'd keep flopping over.

Once he's done tying Brian up, Curse cracks his knuckles. I know he's ready to get started, because he always is. He lives for this shit.

"I want him all the way awake before we start," I tell my brother.

"I could break a couple of his fingers. That might wake him up," Curse replies casually.

Aleksej stations himself by the door with his arms crossed, completely unphased by the conversation we're having. He silently watches with his icy grey gaze, the single bulb overhead casting light down on his ash-blond hair tied back in a ponytail and his closely-cropped beard.

"We wait," I say firmly.

It takes a long time. Hours before the piece of shit in the chair can even lift his head with his weak, wobbly neck. Another thirty minutes after that before he can talk, and the fucker's first words are to beg for water. He's clearly seen a doctor since our earlier run in, because his nose is packed and there's a temporary splint taped on. I walk towards him as his eyes try to focus. I can tell when they do because he balks at the sight of me.

"What the fuck. You again? God, what do you want?"

Just his stupid fucking voice makes me want to slit his throat. *Should have never told her I wouldn't kill him.*

I crouch down before him and slowly, gently, remove the splint from his nose. Then I press my thumb against the smashed bridge and press down. *Hard.*

He's definitely awake now. Pressing on his broken nose lights up a live wire inside him. He snaps his head backwards, but Curse is there, gripping the sides of his skull to keep him in place. So, he starts trying to move other parts. His arms and legs that are bound to the chair, squirming and grunting and hissing in pain.

"The more you fight, the harder I will press," I mutter.

His eyes are wild, and despite the cold and his lack of clothing, he's drenched in sweat. His chest heaves, but he stops moving, hoping I'll let up the pressure. I do, just for a moment, and he lets out a watery breath.

"What do you want?" he asks again, his voice sounding choked-off from his destroyed nasal passages. "Money? I have money, man. I-"

I nod at Curse. My brother releases Brian's head.

Then grasps both his thumbs and twists them from their sockets.

The sweating, quivering man in the chair howls. Curse closes his eyes and breathes out, like he's just taken a hit of his favourite drug.

"Look at me," I say to Brian. He doesn't listen. His face is screwed up with agony and his eyes stay closed. "For fuck's sake. Make him look at me."

Curse returns to his place behind Brian, grabbing his head roughly once more.

"If you wanna keep your eyes in your head, you will open them right now," Curse murmurs. With what looks like a colossal effort, Brian opens them. Tears stream down his face.

"This is about earlier? Shit, I'm sorry!" he babbles, he's blinking hard against the tears, but I can tell he's trying not to. He's trying to look at me like he's supposed to. Pretty fucking wise move, considering Curse really would cut out the guy's eyes if I let him. "I don't know what's going on with you and Deirdre, but it's fine. It's fine! I won't talk to her again."

"No, you won't," I agree. "But this isn't about what you will or won't do. It's about what you've done."

"What I've... What? What are you talking about?"

I stand, and Curse wrenches Brian's head back at the same time, so he's forced to look up at me.

I stare down at his swollen, blotchy face, and pure, unadulterated hatred spews through my body. Hatred and repulsion for this pathetic, stupid, pretty boy with the big straight white horse teeth in a weak jaw that just scream expensive orthodontics. The fact he thought he could even exist in the same room as Deirdre, let alone touch her, is an affront to the natural fucking order of things and I will not stand for it.

"Here's what's going to happen," I tell him, pulling my gun from my jacket.

Every muscle in his chest tightens as he strains against his ties when he sees the weapon. He starts blabbering, like I knew he fucking would, because preppy little rich kids like this can act tough but that's all it ever is – an act.

"No, no, please, wait. I have money. No. God, *no*, please, please, please-"

I give Curse a look, and my brother smashes Brian in the temple with his fist, stunning him into silence.

"As I was saying," I continue, "here is what is going to happen. For some reason my Songbird doesn't want you to die, and for some reason I find I can't refuse her. So, when we are done here, Aleksej is going to take you to a very good, very discreet doctor under my employ who's going to make sure that you don't bleed out."

"Bleed... out..." Brian echoes dazedly.

"After that, you will disappear. You will leave the country. You will not come back. If I hear one fucking whisper about you setting foot back here, my Songbird's misguided mercy won't be enough to save you."

His eyes fixate on my gun as mine roam over his body, deciding where to put the bullets. Kneecaps might be good... Or blow a couple holes through his hands...

"This is insane! You can't do this to me," Brian finally stammers. "Don't you know who I am? Who my father is? I'm on track to make partner at one of the best law firms in Toronto by the time I'm thirty!"

I let out a mirthless bark of a laugh.

"So fucking sue me then."

I put my gun against his dick and pull the trigger.

Chapter 37

Deirdre

After the incident with Brian at school I don't see Elio for three days. I still go to class, accompanied by Enzo now, and I have to admit it's a hell of a lot easier to concentrate without Elio's menacing bulk beside me. I'm still with a gangster, but Enzo keeps his mouth mostly shut. That and the fact he doesn't make me attend class with my tender ass covered in his dry come means going to school with him is practically mundane.

I don't see or hear from Brian either, which is a relief. Getting his nose smashed in must have finally gotten it through his thick head that we're done. Sometimes, at night, when Elio hasn't come back, I replay that punch over and over again. The swift, decisive arc of Elio's fist. The crunching of bone. I want to hate the violence of it. But something in that violence calls to me more than it repels me. It feels good to be stood up for, to be protected, even if the person doing the protecting is the most dangerous one of all.

On the morning of the fourth day, I still haven't seen Elio. There's no class today either, so I have nothing to distract me and nothing to focus on. And I need distraction, today of all days. I've been avoiding thinking about it, avoiding confronting this date the way I do every year. And every year, it still manages to sneak up on me and get its hands around my throat.

The anniversary of Mom's death. The anniversary of the night we crashed.

I do some homework, tapping away on the keyboard of the laptop Elio bought me, as if I can escape into academia. But as the minutes turn to hours, and evening approaches, a sorrow-soaked dread starts closing in on me. Every few words I type get blurred with choking tears, until I'm rising from the small desk and almost blindly stumbling out of the room.

I ignore Robbie, who dutifully follows me from his place at the top of the stairs as I descend. Getting out of the room was good, I decide. I don't feel quite so claustrophobic. Normally, on this day, Willow would come get me out of the house. We'd go see a movie or something. But I still haven't heard from her since that first email she sent, and there's basically zero chance she'll be breaking me out of here tonight.

I swipe at my eyes and wander into the living room that leads into the kitchen. There's floor to ceiling windows here, and heavy, beautiful snowflakes drift down onto the towering pine and spruce trees all around the property. The ground is velvet white, the sky darkening like a bruise.

He still hasn't come back.

I get it. I get that I'm a prisoner here and that he can walk in and out of this house anytime he likes while I cannot. But something about this – about him not being here on this night of all nights – feels worse than usual. I can't hide from the fact that if anyone would understand how I feel right now, it would be Elio. He may never tell me what happened with his mom in his own words, but his wound matches mine in the deepest and most painful of ways.

And right now, it hurts that he's not here. It's terrible and shameful and maybe I'm just insane with grief, but I want him. I fucking miss him, God help me. *God help me.*

I watch the snow falling. As the sky steeps itself in darkness, the snowfall gets heavier, thicker, until I can barely see the trees outside. I probably would stand there all night, numbing myself with the sight of the snow, if the sound of the front door opening and closing didn't make me spin so fast I almost fall over.

Elio.

But it's not Elio. And the resulting disappointment shatters any illusion of numbness. Tears choke me, and I try to swallow and blink them back as Valentina takes off a pair of boots and heads for me.

"Hey! My mom sent me over here to grab something from the kitchen. We're out of the good balsamic, but Rosa has some. Have you heard from Elio, by the way?" Valentina stops in front of me. Her red parka is dusted with rapidly melting snow, as are her long, fluttery lashes. "Are you OK?"

"I'm fine." How many times have I said that?

How many times has it been a lie?

Valentina squints at me for a long moment, and I muster a tight smile. Then she sighs.

"Papà doesn't like when Elio and Curse drop off the map like this. Neither of them are answering our texts or calls. Although..." Her eyes brighten, like she's just gotten a wicked idea. "Maybe if you texted Elio, he'd actually deign to answer."

"Yeah, right. He didn't even tell me he was leaving in the first place. And I don't even have his number," I say, and the words come out much more bitter than anticipated. I wonder if Valentina notices that. If she does, she mercifully doesn't comment on it.

"I can give you his number. I bet if you texted or called him right now, he really would reply."

Honestly, screw that. Yes, I want to see him, but I'm also more and more pissed that he just waltzed out of here and away from me. I'm not pathetic enough to call him after that.

Before I can stop her, Valentina's grabbed my phone out of my back pocket.

"Hey!" I say, stretching my hand for it. But she hustles out of reach.

"Relax. I just want to add Elio's number to your contacts. What's the passcode?"

I clench and unclench my fists, deciding if I should unlock my phone for her or not. I don't need Elio's number in my phone. It's not like I'll ever use it.

But... maybe...

Maybe it might be nice just to know it's there.

"I'll unlock it."

She holds up the phone for me, and I draw the pattern to unlock it. Valentina goes to my contacts and starts typing. Once she's typed in Elio's number, she hands it back, leaving the name field blank. Still annoyed with this whole situation, I name the contact *Monster*.

At the last moment, without even knowing why I do it, I add *My* in front of it.

"I added my number in there as well," Valentina tells me.

I look, and see her number and name, along with a glittery heart and kissing lips emoji at the end.

"Look, I'm not gonna make you call or text Elio, but if you do, and he responds, would you let me know?"

I have absolutely no intention of calling or texting him, but I nod anyway.

"Thanks," she says with a smile.

For a second, I almost ask her to stay. To hang out with me, distract me. But before I know it, she's gotten her bottle of balsamic and has disappeared back out into the snowy night.

I stay in the living room a while longer. There's a massive TV down here, and I turn it on and stare at it blindly. I think it's a cooking show. Or maybe a travel show. I'm so disconnected I don't even know. The entire time, Robbie watches me, and when I can't stand his eyes on me anymore I trudge back up the stairs, heading through Elio's room into mine. My laptop has long since gone to sleep, and the lights are off, making the room dark and still. And empty.

Coming back up here alone was a mistake. Because it's dark just like that night was dark. Dark until headlights shone through our windshield, forcing my mom to crank the wheel and send us careening off the road. I can still hear her yelp of terrified shock, the rapid turning of the steering wheel. I don't remember the impact of the crash itself. Just the breathless moments before. The pure terror of sliding and sliding and not being able to stop. The tires didn't squeal. They made this wet grinding sound across the snow and slush, and it fills my head until I'm desperate to hear anything, anything besides that sound.

I don't even know what the hell I'm doing when I fish

my phone shakily out of my pocket. I don't call Valentina. I don't try calling Willow.

I call my monster.

And he answers on the very first ring.

"Songbird," he drawls silkily.

I don't even realize I'm crying until I hear the thick tears in my voice when I reply.

"Elio."

The smooth satisfaction of his voice vanishes. His next words come out sharp and strained.

"What is it?"

What am I supposed to say? *My mom died and I'm sad and lonely and the only fucking person on the planet I'm reaching out to, the only one I want right now, is the monster who locked me up and walked the fuck away.*

Absolutely not. Instead, I retreat into anger.

"Where the hell have you been?" I practically spit.

I expect him to make some joke, to say *Miss me?* in that cruel and knowing tone like he did last time. But maybe it's the tears he hears in my voice. Or maybe things have started to change between us since then. Because he seems serious and sincere when he replies.

"I had to straighten something out up north. Weather's been too bad to fly or drive back the past couple days."

"You... you could have told me that," I whisper, feeling like a fucking idiot. Why did I call him? What did I hope to gain from this?

"Are you telling me you wanted to hear from me while I was gone?"

I want more than to hear from him, and that's what pisses me off the most.

"No," I snap. "Take as long as you need up north. In fact, don't even come back at all if you don't need to."

"But I do need to," he counters instantly, and it sounds weird. Too loud. Like it's coming from behind me, all around me, rather than from my phone. "Because this is where my Songbird is."

I gasp, and my phone falls from my hand as I turn and find him there. My emotions form a cacophony inside me, a chaotic, jumbled song of fear and sorrow and anger and relief.

"You're here," I whisper, taking in the sight of him, wondering if my grief has conjured some kind of hallucination.

"You're crying," he replies softly. He steps into the room, further and further into the darkness with me, like some onyx angel, no, some demon who's not afraid of the shadows. Who's not afraid to go as far or as deep as it takes to reach me. His leather gloves are cold when they graze my neck. He must have just come in from outside and sprinted up the stairs.

His mouth is warm though, warm when it finds the tracks of my tears, kissing the salted liquid from my skin. That warmth seeps into me, turning molten, turning to something that burns all the way down my spine. Scorching need obliterates everything else inside me. Bludgeons the sadness, a cauterizing plug to a bleeding fucking wound. My mouth opens and searches for Elio's blindly as my hands grip the front of his shirt and pull him harder to me.

He claims my mouth and walks, backing me up until the backs of my legs collide with the bed. My stomach flip-flops, because even after everything we've done in these rooms, we've never been in a bed together and I know what it means. I know what it will lead to, and I don't care and can't stop it. Not now, not tonight. Not when this need has eclipsed everything I thought I ever knew.

Elio's hands find the hem of my sweater, tugging it upwards. I stop kissing him (if you can even call it that, because my movements are desperate and messy) and let him pull it off. I didn't bother with a bra beneath the sweater today, and every muscle and nerve jumps to attention when Elio's gloves skim over my nipples.

"You're still crying," Elio murmurs before lowering his head and sucking my right nipple into the demanding heat of his mouth. I cry out, my back arching, and bury my fingers in his hair. He's right. I can feel the warm liquid coursing down my cheeks.

"That's because... tonight..." I breathe, my words halting as pleasurable pangs echo outward from my breast. Elio gives one last, long suck before letting go and pinning me with a dark gaze.

"I know what tonight is." And just like that, he has me. He's got me in his grip, because he knows what tonight is and he knows what I'm feeling and I don't need to say a single word. I don't need to speak or explain because he already knows.

"It's why I drove like a bat out of fucking hell all day to get here when we couldn't fly back," he continues softly, undoing the button and zipper of my pants and sliding them downwards.

He came for me. He came for me because he knew I would be hurting.

He knows what I need, just like he told me. He knows what I need and what I fucking need right now is *him*.

His jacket comes off, then his shirt, then his pants, and then I'm flat on my back beneath him, marvelling at the brutal planes of his body, the heaving of his chest, the frenetic, consuming gleam of his eyes. Some of his hair falls forward into his eyes, and for the first time I don't stop myself from brushing the unruly strands back from his fore-head. It's an undeniably tender motion, and I stroke down to his jaw.

"You came for me."

A flicker of agony passes over Elio's face, and he presses his face against my hands. His voice splits the darkness.

"I will always fucking come back for you. Even when you don't want me to. Even when you scream and beg and cry for me to leave, even when you push me away, I won't go. I will come back *every single time*, do you hear me? I will *fucking* be here. *Always*."

The *always* part should alarm me, because always was never part of the plan. I'm not staying here, not with him, not forever.

But right now, I don't want to think about that. I just want to lose myself in the drugging reality that there's some-body who would never abandon me, never lose me, never let me go. He's solid and so fucking warm and God, he's taken his gloves off, his scarred hands running up and down my body, taking possession. One hand settles between my legs, sliding through wetness until I pant and tremble.

The other settles around my throat.

"Right now," Elio whispers against my temple as he works my clit in expert, erotic circles, "you need to feel something other than what you were feeling earlier tonight. You need pleasure. You need oblivion."

I nod, even though it's hard with his fingers closed around my throat, because he's right. He's ripped me open with a few well-placed words and now he's the only one who can put me back together. He gently presses on my throat, and I choke out a moan, my eyes rolling back in my head as my pussy clenches.

"You need *this*, don't you, Deirdre?"

I can't even nod now, let alone speak, because of his grip. But I don't need to, because he knows the answer just like I do. I need this. I need to let go of some control. Let him take away my breath and take away my pain.

He slides a finger inside me, and I try to gasp, but barely get half a breath in my lungs.

"I've strangled men with my bare hands," Elio suddenly rasps, and I must be perverted because my pussy clenches again. "I know how much pressure to exert. I know when to stop." His hand tightens around my throat, and my breathing becomes the barest whistle. "But even so..." He crooks his finger inside me, stroking firmly until I'm shaking, the blood roaring through my body as it searches for oxygen. "Tap my shoulder twice to make me stop."

I'm already on the cusp of coming, about to fall the fuck apart, but Elio stops the movement of his finger.

"Tap my shoulder once, now, to show me that you understand."

My hands feel like they're made of lead, but I raise my right one and tap his shoulder.

He groans. "Good little Songbird."

He starts working his finger again, firm and fast and filling me, adding another while clamping down on my throat until all I can feel is the desperate, breathless writhing inside me. That panicky pleasure that narrows my focus of feeling to my chest and the place between my legs. I don't even know if my eyes are open or closed – everything is black. The oblivion he promised me is rising, constricting all around me, a pulsing, living darkness that expands inside me until I come.

Just as my insides clamp down on Elio's fingers, he pulls them out. At the same moment, he releases my throat. Instinctively, I suck in a huge, raw breath, the explosion of oxygen only adding to the intensity of the moment. I'm flying and falling at the same time, and only Elio can anchor me. I reach quivering arms around his neck, pull him down to me just as I feel pressure, pressure right *there*. A searching nudge, and then the violent forward motion of a thrust inside.

Pain surges up alongside the pleasure. My mouth falls open in a soundless scream as Elio completely fills me, stretching me, breaking into me. Breaking down the last of the barriers between us. I'm crying again – I can hear the sobs more than I can feel them. Because all I can feel right now is him. The pain of him inside me. The searing juncture of our bodies.

Elio lets out a ragged sound, then thrusts again. My arms are still around him, and I'm squeezing, holding onto him. I could tap his shoulder twice. See if that would make him stop. When he thrusts a third time, harder, I almost do it because it hurts too fucking much.

"Does it hurt, Songbird? Fuck, I can feel you opening for me. Feel you bleeding for me."

Two little taps. That's all it would take.

Elio's moving faster now, and something in the angle has changed, because even though it still hurts there's something new undulating behind that pain. The wetness of my orgasm and the blood of my lost virginity eases the way ever so slightly for Elio's girth until he's grinding even deeper than before, hitting a screaming, shuddering place inside me that makes me feel like everything is loosening and tightening all at once. I'm going to come again. I'm going to come, even while I'm hurting. He's going to make me. It's building so intensely I almost feel like I'm going to pee myself. One of his thumbs starts rubbing hard against my clit, and I know I'm nearly gone now.

"Every time I pull out I can see your blood on me," Elio groans. "You're claiming my cock with your blood the same way I've already stained you with mine. That first night, Songbird, do you remember? When I got shot and bled all over you." He seems to lose his rhythm, his hips snapping chaotically as he breathes. "I would have fucking died for you that night."

The bandages on his shoulder scrape against my wrist as I cling to him. Cling to the man who I should be doing everything I can to run from. But I can't run – not now. Not while my body is reacting like this to his. I moan through the tears as my pussy convulses.

"*Yes*," Elio hisses between clenched teeth. "My sweet little Songbird. My good fucking girl. Come on my fucking cock *just like that*."

And once again, like so many times before, I cannot help but obey. I scream, muscles clamping down on his so hard I can tell it's affecting his movements. He jams himself further inside as white-hot stars spin out in my pelvis, scattering and shattering. I'm so tight around him, so fused to him, that I feel it happen. Feel the throb of him deep inside as he shunts his hips forward for the final time.

He's coming, shuddering and tensing and coming, coming, coming so hard inside me. As his desire spills into me and mixes with my blood, he lowers his mouth to mine and says directly against my lips. "We are fucking bound together, you and me."

As aftershocks of my orgasm wrack my body, my pussy squeezing him like I can't bear to let him go, I know that he's right.

There's no way to come back from this now. Not for him.

And not for me.

Chapter 38

Elio

I f I could stay inside of Deirdre forever, I would. It's like I was fucking made for this, made for her, like my entire body was designed to have her arms and legs and cunt wrapped around me. It's the closest thing to peace I've felt since childhood.

"I need to go clean up," Deirdre whispers.

"No, you don't," I reply instantly. I want her drenched and staying that way. Stained with my fluids and her own. I don't want to already feel her pulling away from me, which I'm sure she will. Starting with washing this night off of her skin.

Before she can say anything else, a grumbling sound distracts us both. She unwraps her arms from around my neck and places her hands over her face, like she's embarrassed.

"When was the last time you ate?" I ask, pulling one of her hands away. She can't hide herself from me. Not now.

"I ate some breakfast... I think. Rosa brought me lunch and dinner. I just couldn't force myself to eat it."

I understand that. For years, the entire month of August

was a fucking shit show for me. Every August from the age of fourteen to well into my twenties, I lost weight no matter what I did.

"Stay here," I say quietly. Slowly, I pull out, and the little mewling sound she emits in return makes me want to plunge right back inside. I force myself not to do it, then get out of the bed, pulling on my pants and gloves. I glance back at her to find her splayed and limp. She's quiet. Not crying now.

"I'll be right back." I say, though she doesn't seem to hear me.

I head for the kitchen, pulling open cupboards and drawers, piling bread and pastries and cookies onto a plate. When that's taken care of, I slide my phone from my back pocket and use voice-to-text in a search engine.

"How do you make tea?"

I've never done it before, and fuck if I know how. In fact, I don't think I've literally ever made anything in the kitchen for anyone. A quick scroll of the results, and I feel like I have my legs under me. I boil water in the kettle, then pour it over a couple of Irish breakfast tea bags in a teapot to let it steep. Grabbing a cup, a pitcher of milk, and a bowl of sugar, I plonk them on the plate and then carry it all up alongside the teapot.

When I return to Deirdre's room, a lamp by the side of the bed is on. It illuminates an empty bed. A flush of the toilet, then running water, tells me where she is. She emerges from the bathroom a moment later in sweatpants and a hoodie. Her hair is tied up in a messy bun on the top of her head. Her eyes are swollen, her nose is wet and red, and I don't think I've ever seen her look more goddamn beautiful.

She sniffs, then sees me with the snacks.

"Sit and eat," I tell her, placing the stuff on a bedside table. For a second, I think she's going to disobey me. My voice hardens, because I'm not going to stand by and watch her pass out. "Eat this yourself or I will feed it to you."

She gives a small nod then climbs up on the bed. I notice how gingerly she sits when she settles herself.

"Are you still bleeding?" I ask.

"Yeah. I'm wearing a pad."

I want to see. Want to strip off her clothes, see the white material marked by the innocent blood I've drawn.

But that's not what she needs right now. So instead, I pour her a cup of tea.

"What do you put in this shit?" I ask her while eyeing the brown liquid with distaste, and holy fucking heavens above, she actually laughs. It's teary, but real, and I stare at her without blinking, memorizing the sound of it and the sight of her in this moment.

"I'll do it," she says, still smiling. She adds milk and sugar. I watch her closely as she takes a sip. She closes her eyes and sighs, and a pinched area of tension between my shoulder blades I didn't even know was there relaxes.

"This is good. Thank you," she says softly before taking another sip. "Never thought I'd see the day when Elio Titone is making me tea."

"Neither did I," I say, sitting beside her on the bed. "Don't tell anyone, alright? Would ruin my reputation in this town."

There it is again. The beautiful laugh that cuts straight through me, just like her music does. Because the laugh, just like the music, is an expression of what's in there, what's inside her. How did Deirdre word it in that letter? *The violin simply gives voice to what already exists.* It's the same with her laughter, her tears, her voice. Everything she does.

It's not just her music I've been drawn to, that I've been trying to understand, it's *her*. The essence of her that spills out like goddamn sunshine, bathing me in light when I've spent half my life in the darkness.

She munches on a few of the sweets I've brought, and slowly some colour returns to her cheeks.

"I used to drink this kind of tea with my mom," she says. She reaches over and pours a little more into her cup. "God, she had the most beautiful teapot. A vintage one with the most exquisite rosebud pattern."

The teapot she's holding now is stainless steel. It looks cold and sterile compared to what she's just described.

"Where is it now?"

She sighs, takes another sip, then puts down her cup.

"I broke it. Can you believe that?" She shakes her head. "It was right after her funeral. I was out of my mind with grief. I was alone in the kitchen where we'd always drink tea together and I was so desperate to be close to her again. She would always fill the teapot with warm water while the kettle was boiling, so I did that, too. I tried to, anyway. But I dropped it in the sink and it completely smashed." She stops speaking for a moment, staring at a place on the floor before she continues. "I kept all the pieces in a box in my closet, but it was too far gone for me to try to fix. I've looked for a replacement, but they're really hard to find. Plus, it wouldn't be the same, anyway. It wouldn't be the same teapot. The same one she held, you know?"

I do know. I know because all our mamma's things burned and that fact has fucking haunted me.

"I don't even know why I'm telling you this. I haven't been able to tell anyone about that teapot. Not Willow or *anybody*. I didn't even tell my dad. Can you believe he didn't even notice it was gone?" She wipes her eyes. "But then again, he never wanted to go to her grave with me, either, so maybe I shouldn't be all that surprised."

I slide off the bed, turn, grab her by the waist, and set her on her feet on the floor.

"Get your coat and boots," I tell her, reaching for my shirt and pulling it back on.

Her eyebrows pucker. "Why? Where are we going?"

"We're going to visit your mamma."

Chapter 39

Deirdre

I'm still not entirely sure how I've ended up in Elio's car, heading towards my mother's grave, within an hour of losing my virginity. The place between my legs feels tender and wet and strange. I hunker down in my coat, wrapping my arms around myself. Elio flicks at a button on the dash, and soon I feel gorgeous heat rising from the seat and seeping through my coat and pants. The heat soothes the ache between my legs and eases the muscles in my back. Another uncanny reminder that maybe Elio really does know what I need before I do.

As we pass through the gate and then turn onto the street, Elio calls someone on his phone. It takes a few rings for the other person to answer, and when he does, I can hear a sleepy gruffness to the "Hello?"

"Tony, get out of bed and get down to the store," Elio says without greeting or preamble. I hear the muted response of acquiescence before Elio hangs up. I have no idea who Tony is, or why we need to go to a store right now when it's past midnight, but I don't bother asking. I'm sure I'll find out soon enough.

And I do when we pull up in front of a small shop called *Rosetti's Blooms*. A short, balding man is hunched down in a leather bomber-style jacket. When he sees us pull up he nods deferentially and unlocks the front door. Elio opens my car door for me and helps me out, murmuring to watch the ice as he guides me up onto the curb. Lights come on in the shop just as we pass through the door.

It's a flower shop. I stand there, basically dressed in pyjamas under this four-figure-price-tag coat, my face and hair a mess, and I blink like a mole against the bright light. Elio clearly doesn't feel any of my hesitation or confusion. Instead, he sweeps through the shop, taking bunches of flowers from different tables and fridges and peppering Tony with orders. I stand there, still and slow and watching him. He moves with such merciless competence, such dangerous grace, that I can't look anywhere but him. Soon enough, Tony's got a whole array of blooms before him on the counter – red roses and white lilies and delicate little snowdrops – and he gets to work arranging them. When he's finished, he ties the stunning bouquet together with a white silk ribbon.

I don't know why I expect Elio to pay, but of course, he doesn't. He probably owns this shop, or at least controls a good part of it. Even though we've dragged him out of bed, raided his flowers, and haven't paid him, Tony's the one who says, "Thank you," as we leave.

We get back in the car, and I hold tightly to the bouquet as Elio drives us out of downtown. Frankly, I'm shocked that Elio even thought to do this. That he cares about things like flowers for the dead.

"Why'd you do this? The flowers," I ask him as the cemetery comes into sight.

"There's no way I'm going to your mamma's grave

empty-handed," he says firmly, keeping his eyes ahead as he pulls up and stops. He pauses, like he's not going to say the next part, but then does it anyway. "Never got the chance to lay flowers at my own mamma's grave."

I shunt the flowers over to one side, then reach out with a free hand, capturing his gloved fingers in mine just as he takes them from the steering wheel. He stares at me in silence for a long moment, then raises my hand, brushing his lips over my knuckles before letting go.

He doesn't let me go for long. Once he opens the door for me he grabs my hand and holds it all the way to Mom's grave.

I know where it is even though I haven't been here in a few years. It's always been hard for me to come here alone, and Dad always got all weird and flighty when I asked him to come with me, so eventually I just kind of stopped. I tried to tell myself that she wasn't here, anyway. She was in other places. The sky, the sunshine, the music she'd once shared with me. And yet, it feels good and bad and right that I'm here now. It hurts, but in a satisfying way. Like I'm doing something I'm supposed to do.

And I'm supposed to do it with him.

It's the strangest feeling. The feeling that I'm where I should be, even though it's Elio beside me. I look down at our interlocked hands, then the striking profile of his face, his expression sombre, and I'm glad he's with me.

The snowfall stopped at some earlier point in the evening, and the sky is clear, a bright moon illuminating the carpet of white between the gravestones. I see Mom's, and my heart lurches in my chest. It's a feeling of pained remembrance. Of homecoming and knowing that my home will never exist again.

We come to a stop before her grave. I clench my teeth

and try not to cry, because crying outside in the winter is horrible, and I've already shed enough tears tonight. But I can't hold them back when Elio lets go of my hand, gets down on his knees in the snow, and starts clearing off her grave. I sniff hard, over and over again, watching him meticulously clean snow from every surface, every angle, every letter of the stone slab. When he's done, I assume he'll get up, but he doesn't. Instead, he lays his dark glove against the stone beside my mother's name, Fiona Kathleen O'Malley. Finally, he rises, turns to me, and nods.

I nod back at him, stepping forward with the flowers.

"Hey, Mom," I whisper. It's all I can manage at the moment, and I know she'd probably think that was good enough. I was always good enough for her, even when I didn't feel like it. I bend and lower the bouquet, admiring the silver sheen of moonlight on the blooms, turning them from fresh flowers into what look like crystal carvings.

And then there's a sound. A sound that makes me think of birthdays and blood. The bouquet explodes in my hands, petals ripped and falling like snow.

"Get the fuck down!"

Something solid collides with my back. It's Elio. He crowds over me, shoving me down against the gravestone, before spinning with his gun in his hands. He's so fucking fast I don't even see who he shoots before they fall.

"Elio! What-"

I can't finish my sentence because Elio has turned and aimed somewhere over my head.

He fires, then fires again. A man I can't see screams.

Then hits the ground.

Chapter 40

Elio

Fucking Mad Darragh. These don't look like Sev's guys. They're Irish. At least three of them. I crouch down beside Deirdre, keeping my gun ready in one hand while I pass my other hand over her. They shot the bouquet right out of her hands, and I frantically count every slender finger before I let myself take a breath when I get to ten.

"Are you hurt?" I ask her. She shakes her head, her eyes as big as dinner plates. "Good. Stay here."

I rise, breathing hard, scanning the graveyard.

But I don't see anyone else. At least, not yet. I call Curse, telling him to get Enzo and Robbie down here. Just as I hang up, I hear a groan from behind the grave.

Motherfucker ain't dead yet.

After making sure Deirdre isn't going anywhere and that nobody else is coming for her, I vault over the gravestone. The guy is writhing and choking on his own blood, his gun out of reach. He tries to get it anyway. I press my boot down on his fingers and don't let up until I hear bones crack.

328

"Did Darragh send you?"

"We weren't gonna kill her," the man wheezes. "Darragh wants her alive. Fuck!"

I press down harder on his hand.

"Just give her up. She's not one of yours. She's Irish. *Ours*."

The ticking in my head is so loud I swear it makes the gravestones move.

"She is not fucking yours," I hiss, cocking my gun and aiming it at his head. "She is mine in every conceivable way. And if Darragh wants to take her, then he will be starting a fucking war, because he won't be coming after one of his own, he'll be coming after a *Titone*."

It's all become so clear. What I need to do. I don't know how I didn't see it before. Parading Deirdre around at the gala and at school wasn't enough.

But this will be. This will make her completely fucking untouchable, unless Darragh wants to bathe this entire city in blood.

Even though the guy at my feet won't live to pass this message on to his boss, I tell him anyway, because it just feels so fucking good to say it.

"Her name won't be Deirdre O'Malley for long," I say quietly, crouching down. "Because I will fucking *marry* her. And just fucking see what happens when you come after *my wife*. Just see what happens when you try to hurt *Deirdre fucking Titone*."

The man's eyes bulge. He understood me, I have no doubt. He's the first one to hear my glad tidings, the lucky bastard.

I put a bullet in his head just to fully sanctify that honour.

Chapter 41

Deirdre

I stay huddled in the snow in front of my mother's grave, clutching the ruined flowers. My ears ring, and every breath I take sounds far too loud inside my own head. I think Elio's talking but I can't make out any of the words. Another shot, and then the speaking stops.

Dead.

Once again, Elio's shot someone. Someone who threatened me. He and I are caught in an endless, terrible loop. No matter what I do, I can't claw my way out to something normal. Not while Elio's with me. And not while my father hides from what he's done.

I'm not even afraid now. Just numbed to it all. Emptied out by all the violence, the death, and the destruction. I barely register when Elio scoops me up into his arms and jogs back to the car. Just as he's hauling the door open and helping me inside, another dark vehicle swerves towards us. Curse and Enzo jump out, and Elio bites out orders at them. I only catch some of the words. *Irish. Make sure... No others... Bodies...*

Elio slides into the driver's seat. He starts the car with

quick, sharp movements, but doesn't drive until he's fastened my seatbelt. Thank God he does it, because I'm not sure I have the strength to. My arms, no, my whole body is shaking. Torn and crushed rose petals fall from my hands as the car finally gets into motion.

"We shouldn't have come here," I whisper.

"Yes, we should have. They shouldn't have," Elio bites out.

"They're never going to stop. They're never going to leave me alone," I say dully. I thought being trapped with Elio was bad enough. But knowing that even if I ever get away from him, I'll never be safe, makes me feel like my entire life is getting snuffed out before my very eyes.

"No, they probably won't. Not unless I drag your papà back here and dump him on Darragh's doorstep."

"No," I say instantly.

Muscles go stone-hard in Elio's jaw.

"Even after everything he put you through, you still want to protect him?"

"I just can't have another person around me die!" I cry out. "I can't! I can't handle all this guilt. It's like I'm being buried alive!"

"Darragh's men keep coming for you because they consider you one of theirs," Elio says. "You're Irish. In their minds, you belong to them, not me." He takes a sharp turn, and I flinch at the swerving motion of it. "There's one way to put that thought out of their minds. One way to prove that you're irrevocably mine. Mine in a way that they'd never dare to touch you."

"What? What way?" I thought that was the whole point of me going to the gala on his arm. Clearly, that didn't work.

"You take my ring. You take my name."

"I... What?"

He doesn't look at me as he takes another fast turn, making my insides lurch.

"You marry me."

No. There's no way. I'm sure I've heard him wrong. My blood sloshes in my head. I lean forward and grip my knees, trying to breathe slowly between clenched teeth.

But he says it again. And this time, there's no mistaking the words. There's no mistaking the threat of them. The way they bind me to him more than any debt ever could.

"You marry me, Songbird. Marry me, or I'll tell Darragh exactly where your fucking father is."

Want part two? Elio and Deirdre's story continues in A Vow So Soulless.

I've taken everything from my Songbird. Her freedom. Her innocence.

Even her name. She'll no longer be known as Deirdre O'Malley, but Deirdre Titone. ***My wife.*** *Whether she wants to be or not.*

It's the only real way to show this city who she belongs to. The only way to tell the world that she's as protected as she is possessed. I'll keep her safe, even if there's no one left to keep her safe from me.

My Songbird made me believe in souls again. And maybe I don't have one. Maybe I never did.

But she does. And I won't stop until I've taken it along with everything else.

Get a free exclusive bonus story/deleted scene of Elio going to Deirdre's first violin performance after he sees her on the balcony by subscribing to my newsletter at www.veroheath.com/contact-and-newsletter

---

TITANS AND TYRANTS
A Debt So Ruthless (Deirdre and Elio part 1)
A Vow So Soulless (Deirdre and Elio part 2)

Made in the USA
Coppell, TX
30 July 2025

52529400R00198